DEATH
in the
Dark

ALSO BY KITTY MURPHY

Death in Heels

DEATH
in the
Dark

KITTY MURPHY

THOMAS & MERCER

Text copyright © 2023 by Kitty Murphy

Published by Thomas & Mercer, Seattle

www.apub.com

Amazon, the Amazon logo, and Thomas & Mercer are trademarks of Amazon.com, Inc., or its affiliates.

ISBN-13: 9781542037242
ISBN-10: 1542037247

Cover design by Whitefox, Andrew Davis

Printed in the United States of America

DEATH
in the
Dark

The room smelled dank. The only light came from a small window at the top of the wall, and the bars over the murky glass grew from the concrete like talons, dividing the faint early morning haze.

Niall blinked as shapes formed in the fog – stairs, cardboard boxes, a fridge or freezer plugged in and whirring, a bare light bulb hanging from the middle of the ceiling. A thin, sequined cloth had been stretched between a bent nail by the fridge and a hook jammed into the underside of the stairs, making a curtain behind him, strange against the grey concrete. As his vision cleared, he realised that the opposite wall was covered – every spare inch plastered with the same repeated posters, over and over again, the same words and the same face staring down at him.

Niall gaped in horror as his own face stared back.

March 12 – SPARKLE McCAVITY stars at TRASH

November 6 – DRAG AND DINE – WITH PERFORMANCES FROM SPARKLE McCAVITY

January 24 – ONE NIGHT ONLY, AN AUDIENCE WITH GLORIA De BACLE AND SPARKLE McCAVITY

The posters watched him, their corners torn, pin-marks ripped, edges crumpled and creased. His giant drag head: the bigger the hair, the bigger the make-up, the more powerful the stare.

In the corner by the stairs was his very first poster, the one Niall had framed and hung by his mirror at home. In his own bedroom, the plain sheet had pride of place; here it was tucked away, the words below – *INTRODUCING SPARKLE McCAVITY* – almost faded to nothing on the damp wall.

Where the hell was he?

Niall pushed himself up. He had been lying on a plastic-covered foam mattress. As he moved, his head throbbed and a pain rang behind his eyes. The dim light was too bright, the silence too loud. The posters swam and his face laughed at him.

He rubbed his eyes. He had lashes on . . .

He looked down at his body, his head pounding with every turn. He was naked, covered only in a soft pink blanket that smelled vaguely of lily of the valley and of a musty cupboard or drawer. Niall wrapped his arms around his body. He pressed his nails into his skin—

He still had nails on. Bright red nails, long and pointed. He touched his face and felt the smooth crack of old make-up.

He tried to piece together what had happened. It was such a blur. He remembered being on stage, and then they'd had a few drinks.

He had gone outside for a smoke. There had been people there that he knew . . .

A blinding pain shot through his head.

It had been a fairly run of the mill Thursday, the usual faces in the crowd, some cute guys, and he'd been talking to someone . . .

He forced his mind back through the stabbing pain. He'd been chatting to a few of the young lads there, just having a laugh, like, and—

And his drink had tasted funny. He'd noticed it right away. There was a guy across the room who was really cute, but one of the lads beside him wouldn't stop talking.

Niall put his fingers to his lips.

He'd even said how his drink tasted weird, and the man agreed that his did too. They'd laughed about something silly. He'd seen the guy around . . . one of the fans . . . he knew him, Niall was sure, but he couldn't think . . .

But then it was getting cold, and Niall said how he was about to go in . . .

Niall pulled the blanket closer and edged his back against the wall. He remembered the cold, the way his body crawled with shivers . . .

The picture rippled and faded.

Then . . . nothing.

Niall looked around the room. Four walls. What looked like a small toilet in the far corner. The only exit at the top of the stairs.

He had to get out of there. Slowly, inch by inch, he tried to stand up, one hand holding the blanket around him, and the other flat against the wall, gripping at the rough plaster under the sequin-covered sheet. Sweat rolled from his body as he pushed on his weak legs to find his balance. His feet felt heavy. They felt really weird. He ground his teeth and pushed again, forcing his head up as he tried to stand . . .

He was almost there when he heard a key in the lock of the solid wooden door at the top of the stairs.

Panic rushed through his blood. He had to get free. He looked around for something to take hold of, to defend himself with, but as he moved his feet he found a metal band fixed around his ankle, attached to a thick chain. Bolted to the wall.

The door opened wide. The face was in shadow against the light behind it, the body a silhouette.

'Hello,' said the man. 'I'm so glad you're awake.'

Chapter One

The night was nearly, nearly done, and so was I.

TRASH – Dublin's third most popular drag venue, and my home from home since my best friend, Robyn, became the drag queen Mae B – was finally winding down for the night.

Holding my drink high, I threaded my way through the crowds, up the spiral staircase to the little balcony. A door to the side led to the office and the dressing room. Two young men stood in the space, waiting to be noticed by their heroes. At the back of the balcony, the DJ was arguing with Mark, the manager. On the side seats two men were deep in conversation, pressing their mouths to the other's ear in turn, oblivious to the world. I crept past the fans to my favourite spot – the far end of the front bench, where I could look down over the sea of people on the dance floor below.

An old-fashioned stage light – a big, heavy thing that used to live behind the curtains – had been moved just under the balcony in the way of the dancing throng. Its open bulb pointed at the stage, the square flaps sticking out around the sides and the central pole thick and mean. It was interesting. It looked nothing like the rigs over the stage. I wondered if they'd let me use it for some portrait photography.

I could dress the stage to suit, I thought. Del had some fabulous 1930s drag tucked away in the back of his wardrobe that I knew he hadn't worn in ages. And Mae B looked great in flapper dresses, especially when she wore the long gloves and little heeled shoes. Mae had the frame for it; her shoulders were gorgeous.

Del Peen and Mae B . . .

I could pose them both together. A black and white photograph. Concentrate on the details, and maybe use the old fans from the office and borrow some huge potted plants from somewhere – fancy ferns and things.

My mind spun happily. I loved shooting the queens. They knew their light.

I leaned against the wall. A little chipped, a little rough around the edges, there was something comfortable about the weariness of TRASH. Not bothered about being the most popular or even the most successful of Dublin's gay clubs, TRASH did what it did best: good quality drag on budget queens, as Del would say.

As if conjuring himself from my mind, my friend's face appeared around the side of the door to the dressing room.

'Fi?'

I grinned. As he moved, his gold wig sprung out in a halo of corkscrew curls and snakes, like ten glittering slinkies on his head. His make-up was beautiful, high drag brows and shades of pink and silver over his eyes. His grin was set with sparkling pink lips. He squeezed past the two fans, picked up his skirts and stepped over the bench.

'Hey.' I stood up to kiss him.

'Are you waiting to come through?' he said. 'Mae B is stuck in her dress again. It's all hands on deck.'

I chuckled. 'I told her it was too tight.'

'Honey, we all told her it was too tight. The new boobs aren't helping.'

'I'll come now,' I said.

'Finish your drink, Mae can wait.' He glanced back to the door, then tugged me down to my seat. 'Actually, I needed to warn you – Merkin wants a word.'

'With me?' I said.

Del shrugged. 'It can't be that important or she would tell me what it's about, but she's in a vile mood. I'd avoid her unless you want to spend an hour in the office discussing the finer points of piping on a boned corset and exactly why she is right and the rest of the world is all wrong about pretty much everything else.'

'But—' I started.

He held up his hand. 'Fi, for goodness' sake, honey, when someone warns you not to go into the dragon's lair . . .'

'If she needs me . . .'

'Well, she says she does. But trust me,' said Del, 'she'll keep until tomorrow. She probably just wants you to take some more photos. It didn't sound urgent and I'm not giving her your number because whatever it is, it can wait until morning. Give me five minutes, I'll pop her in a taxi and then give you a wave, and you can help us peel PVC from your flatmate's sticky body.'

He started back across the bench. The fans launched themselves at him like excited spaniel puppies.

I turned back around to watch the dancers. My drink was full, the ice bobbing, the glass cold. I set it down on the bench. He was right. In a few minutes, the room would settle, and we could relax.

I loved watching the drag shows, of course, and the TRASH performers were incredible, especially my friends, but it was the last hour that was my favourite time of the night. When most people had gone, the dance floor was nearly empty, the bar was packing up, and it was just us and the ghosts in the quiet halls of the old club.

There was something magical about watching the transformation of the queens back to their boy selves, as they took off their drag, removed the wigs and the make-up and the lashes, and became just Del, Daniel and Robyn.

Not that I'd often seen Miss Merkin out of drag.

I frowned, wondering what it was the older queen wanted.

Behind me, the DJ stopped arguing with Mark long enough to croon into her microphone. The music changed, the beat easing into the last track of the night. Slowly, the bar gentled and smoothed below me. The lights dulled. The bar twinkled with the clinking of glasses going into the dishwasher trays.

I put my thumbs to my temples, trying to ease a throbbing behind my eyes.

'Fi?' Mark leaned down to touch my shoulder.

'Hi! How are you?' I spun around. 'I, umm . . .'

'Merkin wants a word,' he said. 'She was looking for you. Can you call her?'

'Right, sure. Do you know wh—'

He turned, walked away without answering. The fans gleamed and shone as Mark came toward them, then spun back and glared at me as he walked straight through the door without stopping.

A squeal of laughter rang from the dressing room. The two young men gave up on being noticed and trotted back down the stairs. Del leaned out again, checking on me. He had been watching over me all night, and Mae was just as bad. From the bar, Sam waved to me, lifting a glass. I shook my head and they blew me a kiss.

Everyone was being Overly Nice.

As Del had said, it was one thing being attacked by Robyn's homicidal maniac of a sister – that was nothing special, Karen hated all of us and Robyn the most – but it was entirely another thing losing the man you love.

Thanks to Karen, Del's husband was dead. I had nothing to complain about. My *lost man* was only on the other side of the world. And it was my fault he had been lost to me.

I leaned back against the wall again, staring at the emptying dance floor.

The night before he told me he was leaving, Patrick came with me to watch the queens. He'd roared and clapped as Del and Mae B ruled the stage, and he cheered louder than ever when Miss Merkin did her Cher routine. Seeing him with my friends was everything, it was . . .

I closed my eyes.

It was like family.

That night, when the show was over and the queens were getting changed, Sam had left two drinks on the bar. The main door was closed. The only people there were TRASH people. Jazz played softly on the sound system, deep and low. Patrick and I were standing on the dance floor. Not dancing, just messing about, chatting. The lights changed. I looked up and saw Robyn at the board. He winked, and then the house dimmed. With a flick of his finger, the giant glitter ball bathed us in hundreds of tiny lights, like snowflakes. I started to laugh. Patrick pushed his glasses into place. I thought he'd say something flippant or silly, but then he kissed me.

'Nothing in the world so powerful as a kiss,' Sam teased me after, as I was getting my coat.

I'd told everyone not to be daft. Patrick and I were early days, we were barely a couple. I'd grinned. It was nothing serious, I said.

And then two days later Patrick had gone away to the other side of the world and I was back to sitting on the TRASH balcony on my own, waiting for my friends to finish getting changed. It had been a moment, that was all. And now, in October, the moment was as distant and forgotten as the summer sun.

I picked up my drink, set it down again.

I didn't tell them it was the most romantic moment of my life, because who actually said stuff like that out loud?

With a whoop and a cheer, Robyn burst from the dressing room, waking me from my self-indulgent sulk. With sequins flying from him as he ran, he scuttled past me in his cincher and knickers. The last trace of his make-up was smeared over his eyes, his short hair sticking up, his body pink with heat. Del came running after him, a long scarf in his hands.

Giggling, Robyn leaned back against the rail as he shied away. 'Save me,' he shrieked.

I grabbed him. 'Fall over there and there's none of us who can save you, you idiot!'

'Hiding behind Fi is pathetic,' said Del. He flicked the scarf.

'Fi's tough, she'll defend me,' said Robyn.

'Oh yeah, how?' Del rolled his eyes. 'She'll take a photograph of you and post it on her blog?'

'Watch it,' I told him. 'I have a shot of you from last Thursday, after the tequila came out.'

'You wouldn't! You don't even know what he's done.'

'I'm innocent,' Robyn told me.

'That I doubt,' I said.

'But I never touched his phone!'

I grabbed my drink before it was spilled. Leaving them to fight out who was messing with the other's phone, or who stole whose purple lipstick, or whatever it was this time, I made my way back down to the bar. I drifted between the tables, gathering up empty glasses.

I was reaching for a spilled martini glass when my phone rang, an unknown caller.

'Fi,' said Merkin. 'Del gave me your number.'

And there solved the question of who had been using Del's phone, I thought.

'Hi,' I said. Merkin had never rung me before. She barely looked at me if I was in a room.

'I'm calling from the taxi. I need to talk to you,' said Merkin.

'Of course. I—'

'Shall we say tomorrow? Ten thirty, at my shop?'

'Ten thirty in the morning?'

'When else?'

'Of course,' I said. 'Only I have work, you see, and . . .'

Merkin sighed, the deep breath lasting longer than the middle eight from a Spice Girls number.

'I can be there straight after work?' I said. 'Five fifteen? Five twenty?'

I waited for some kind of cutting remark, something bitter and mean, but when she spoke, Merkin's voice broke.

'I'm very grateful,' she said. 'I'll be honest, Fi, I'm scared.'

The line went dead.

Chapter Two

The alarm clock bleeped at me from across the room. I've never been brilliant at early mornings. As far as I'm concerned, anything before eight is too early.

I stumbled around the flat. After a few minutes, Robyn's alarm buzzed through the walls. I checked for Gavin's coat on the peg and got out three mugs instead of two.

'Coffee's made,' I called quietly.

Robyn mumbled something as he emerged in his jogging bottoms. His chest still carried the pink rash he got from the silicone breastplate.

I handed him a full mug of creamy coffee and he kissed my cheek.

'Remind me why we get up this early?' he said.

'Because we need our jobs to pay the rent.'

'Then why am I not a world-famous drag queen yet?' he grumbled. 'I didn't get in until nearly four and my feet are still hurting. I should be lying in bed all warm and snuggly.'

'It's only a matter of time,' I told him. 'And at least Thora pays you now.'

He grumbled as he staggered into the bathroom.

Yawning, I stared into my wardrobe. I pulled on some underwear. I was just weighing up which sleeveless pullover to wear when the door opened a crack.

'Are you decent?' said Robyn.

I tugged my knickers to cover both cheeks. 'Mostly,' I said.

He frowned at the comfy pullover in my hands, took it from me and hung it back in the wardrobe.

'I think I worked out why Merkin wants to see you.' He plucked a dark green shirt from its hanger, held it up against me.

'Do you have the green bra?' I pulled out my choices.

'Do you think sharing bras is weird?'

'We're not sharing. I bought the green bra and you borrowed it before I had a chance to wear it.'

He wandered out, returning with the bra. 'I think I stretched it,' he said. 'But I gave you the gold one last week, so . . .'

'I'm not wearing gold,' I said, wriggling into my jeans. 'I'd feel like a *Heat* magazine cover. Call it a swap for the black sweater that I'm not giving up.'

'That's Del's. Anyway, I'm trying to tell you something, honey. Merkin has been throwing a hissy fit all week and now even Del says it sounds a bit strange, but then Gavin said—'

'What's strange? Merkin throwing a hissy fit? That's not news.'

I gulped back my coffee. I was nearly late. I grabbed my phone and my keys. I had to remember to pick up some cash, and take the cushions I'd bought to change at Dunnes . . .

'Sparkle!' said Robyn.

'What?'

'Fi, are you even listening to me?'

I turned around, falling over my boots.

'I'm trying to tell you about Sparkle McCavity,' he said. 'The new queen that Stan knows? Niall?'

I scrubbed my hands over my face. It was too early. 'Who's Stan?' I said. 'And what about a Niall?'

With a gesture of exasperation, Robyn gently pushed me to sit on the bed.

'Sparkle is the drag queen Merkin booked for the club. Sparkle McCavity. She's . . .' Robyn rolled his eyes as he tried to think of the right word. '. . . fresh, or something. Anyway, his boy name is Niall. He's disappeared,' he said. 'He was meant to be on stage last night. Mark was furious. Niall didn't even call to cancel and he didn't answer his phone at all. And worse than that, he works in the day at Merkin's shop but he hasn't shown up there for a week either.'

'Maybe he's gone away?' I said.

'That's what I thought,' said Robyn. 'But then Gavin said that *Mark* said that *Merkin* said it was weird. And you're our resident expert in weird.'

I shrugged. 'There's probably a simple explanation.'

'So you'll do it?' he said.

'Go over to Merkin's? Well, yes, of course. Can you hand me my hairbrush?'

'No, I mean you'll look into Niall's disappearance?' he said. 'You'll investigate it for her?'

I laughed. 'Honey, I'm not Columbo,' I told him. 'And I don't even know this Niall bloke.'

Robyn flicked away my protest. 'Pah! A missing person? A drag queen disappeared into thin air? No note, no phone call even? This is right up your alley, Fi. And you know Merkin. And anyway,' he said, looking slightly embarrassed. 'I kind of already texted her and told her you would.'

I shook my head. 'Oh no,' I told him firmly. 'After last time, I'm not getting involved with anything like th—'

His face greyed. He looked away. 'Last time was my sister,' he said. 'And I've said I'm sorry a hundred times.'

'Not your fault,' I told him quickly. I patted his arm. 'You know what Thora said: we are not responsible for our homicidal sisters. So don't you be apologising for what Karen did.'

'But you'll look for Niall? If Merkin asks, that is?'

'No,' I said.

'Then I'm asking you now, as your best friend . . .'

'You already used that this week to have the last of the ice-cream,' I said.

He grinned, and I rolled my eyes.

'Just talk to her,' said Robyn. 'Please? I know she's kind of hard work, but she's genuinely upset about this.'

I glanced outside at the gloomy sky, the wet Dublin streets. In fairness, I thought, I could really use a long beige macintosh.

◆ ◆ ◆

The day dragged, each ping on the conveyor belt pinching at the inside of my brain. I tried to smile at the customers, as Mr Jenkins commanded.

Smile. Ask a question. Be nice, Fi.

Not that my boss was a jerk. Or no more than Robyn's boss at the phone shop anyway. But recently, the hypnotic, eternal pinging of the tills and the meaningless conversations with the customers left too much space in my brain to think about the things I would rather forget.

Loss.

Murder.

The way Robyn took everything as his fault.

Seeing him sitting in court, day after day with his mum, Edna, at Karen's trial. Watching him being there for his sister in the only way he could, even while he was grieving his friends who she'd killed.

And the other stuff. The way Patrick had met me at court every evening. He'd picked up flowers on the last day – not for me but for Robyn, because he knew my friend's heart was broken.

I shook my head. Think of something else, that was the answer. *Think of now*, as Robyn's therapist would say.

I wondered if Merkin really had called me about the missing drag queen.

I mulled over the little I knew so far about Sparkle McCavity, most of it gleaned from Instagram on my break and a hurried call with Del when Jenkins stepped out on an errand.

With impeccable make-up and skilled use of Instagram filters, it was impossible to age Sparkle from her drag persona. Younger than Del, but older than Robyn. Around thirty, I figured, looking at her hands.

His boy name was Niall Ash, and he worked as Miss Merkin's assistant in her exclusive bridal gown shop. As Sparkle McCavity, exquisitely dressed and presented, she was one of Dublin's successful new drag queens. Her look was high-end couture and dramatic custom pieces. A stark comparison to Robyn's original collection of second-hand dresses and hand-me-down wigs that he'd used when he first became Mae B.

I fiddled with the till pen. The end was Sellotaped to a long piece of string so I couldn't walk away with it. It caught against my sleeve when I slid in the customers' fifty-euro notes.

A movement distracted me from behind the organic muesli. Mr Jenkins had positioned himself so he could see me. I arranged my face into my most convincing welcoming smile. I asked a customer if she had tried our new blend of coffee. The following one I told to have a nice day, and then the next I gave a beaming grin, frightening him a little with my enthusiastic display of teeth, and asked him if he'd like a cinnamon whirl with that.

It was a job. And without it, as Jenkins kept reminding me, I'd be sleeping in the park.

As the last few minutes ticked away, I tidied my till station. I'd go to Merkin's shop, but I couldn't see how I could help her. So,

I'd have the quick chat with her as requested, she would say three snarky things about how women shouldn't be in drag venues unless they're performing, and then send me on my way. With any luck I'd be home by seven with takeaway noodles from the Mongolian Barbeque place, and while Del and Robyn hit the TRASH stage in all their finery, I'd be in my pyjamas watching *Poirot*.

It was a good plan, I told myself.

The air hung damp in the thin streets, the murky atmosphere enhanced by the Halloween decorations strung in the shop windows.

Some of the smaller, classier places on Exchequer Street had shied away from the plastic pumpkins and tissue-paper ghosts and instead embraced the autumn with pretty bronze and gold leaves and stacks of very clean branches. The jeweller's window was decorated with willow sticks hung on silver wire, dripping with sparkling necklaces, and engagement rings displayed on round pebbles taken from a beach. The rings were pretty, if you liked that kind of thing.

I turned away, forcing myself to count nail bars until my dull self pity eased. It wasn't like Patrick and I had been anywhere near that stage. We had barely been a couple.

I really had to get it together and stop pining for ghosts. Even good-looking ghosts in nice glasses. It happened. It was just a break-up, I told myself. People had them. I liked a guy and I thought he liked me, and then he took a job in South America and didn't call me. Perfectly normal.

I checked the address and turned for the thin, cobbled street just after the French café.

Bride of Life had a quiet elegance. A tall, slender, terraced building, it had one window to the street, dressed in white. A stunning wedding dress was displayed on a headless Grecian mannequin. The neckline was dotted with pearls., the fabric fell like perfectly sculpted water. The price tag, I imagined, was more terrifying than all the witches back on the main street.

On the door, gold letters declared Miss M as the owner, and Niall Ash as the manager.

Robyn was right. It was a bit weird for Niall to just walk away from everything, but there was probably a reason. People usually had a reason, even if it wasn't good.

Either way, I really wasn't going to get involved this time. I was done running around after the dead, or running into situations that were clearly none of my business.

I stood at the window, stamping my feet in the cold.

It could be anything. Niall could be ill with the flu, or visiting family, or he might have fallen in love with a handsome suitor at some wedding fair . . .

I'd have a quick chat with Merkin and then it was home for pyjamas and *Poirot*.

I rang the bell.

I looked into the shop. My reflection in the window set my head on the mannequin's body. I turned away. I was a strong, independent woman and I didn't need a ridiculous dress or overpriced jewellery to prove anything. I had been single before Patrick for many years. It was fine.

I'd never been one of the girls who read bridal magazines. I didn't believe in fairy-tale princes who could only see a bride if she were wearing a huge sparkling dress and uncomfortable glass slippers. I preferred the godmothers – their dresses were better, and they looked gorgeous, wigs and all. Much more fun than some wanky prince with a bad haircut.

Finally, the door inched open. Miss Merkin looked me up and down.

'Fi.'

'Hi,' I said.

She held open the door. 'Wipe your feet and don't touch anything until we're upstairs.' She stopped, considered herself. 'And thank you for coming.'

I wiped my feet thoroughly, knocking over an umbrella stand as I moved through the hall. 'Oh, of course,' I said. 'Happy to help.'

The first room was as clean and expensive-looking as the window display. White silks, white satins, white lace, white carpet, white paintwork, white flowers in a tall glass vase, a white table and white chairs.

I followed Merkin through a doorway into the next room to a place where all colour had been imprisoned – every shade and every kind of dress from short to long to ridiculous, all jammed in together, away from the strict whites of the wedding gowns. I blinked.

'Bridesmaids,' said Merkin, with disdain. 'Keep walking. I made coffee. I gather from Del that you cannot function without it.'

We traipsed past more rooms and up more stairs. In the next gallery, I gasped. The entire room shone with drag.

I'd seen Del's spare room and I lived with a drag queen, but never in my life had I seen so much drag in one place. Dresses, playsuits, tops; corsets, bra-tops; huge ball gowns and slinky, skin-tight tubes; golds and silvers and bright electric pinks; capes and cinchers and sashes and bows; every colour of every fabric, from leopard print to emerald green to bright pink to black and gold, and all shades between.

'Straight through here to—'

'Wow,' I said.

Merkin looked back. She chuckled. 'Welcome to the real Spark of Life,' she said.

She cast a long sweep of her hand over the outfits. She was proud, and rightfully so. I knew she made outfits for the drag family but I had no idea how big a business this had become. Merkin lifted a long black lace train and let it run through her fingers.

'This is . . . mine.'

'This is incredible,' I breathed.

'It's something.'

'It's stunning,' I told her.

She patted her hair. 'Funny thing,' she said. 'When I first started my little shop here it was the brides who paid the mortgage and the drag that bought the drinks. Now I'm selling two drags to every one of the bridal gowns downstairs.'

I reached out to touch a blue feather trim on a long dress.

'Come on,' she said. 'The fire's lit in my office. And, Fi, I am warning you now, if I read one single thing on your blog about all this messy business I will come after you.'

Messy . . . A strange word to use in such a place of extreme cleanliness and order.

'Fi?' she warned.

'No, of course not,' I said quickly.

Beside the blue feather trim was a gold headdress glittering with jewels. Behind that was a floor-length rainbow cloak with extendable wings. I couldn't stop staring.

'Along here,' said Merkin. 'Mind the step into the kitchen there. You know, I wouldn't have called you at all, only . . .'

She stopped at a thin door and turned the handle.

'It's ridiculous,' she said. 'Young men are exhausting. You're very sensible having nothing to do with them.'

'That wasn't a conscious decision on my part,' I said.

She looked at me with the same critical stare she might give a dress made from grey fleece and old, faded denim.

'Come in,' she told me. 'We may as well get this done.'

The office was a small room at the back of the building. The window looked down into a cobbled yard, four or five floors below.

The room was cosy and yet strange. The walls were lined with shelves crammed full of books, every space taken. A standing desk in one corner held a stack of hard-backed sketchbooks and a pot of pens. On the other side of the room was an open fire with the smallest fireplace I'd ever seen. Two chairs rested either side: one a ribbon-back Chippendale, worn and comfortable, its feet well ground into the rug on the floor, and the other a simple wooden chair clearly brought in for my behind. A coffee pot stood on the hearth.

A sketchpad was open on the desk. A line drawing of a dress.

'You like it?' she said.

It was huge, dramatic and very bridal. 'It's not really my style,' I said, turning away.

She pursed her lips. My skin itched under my clothes.

'It's very nice though,' I added. 'It looks . . . shiny?'

'Sit,' she said, clearly unsurprised at my inability to fawn over a frock.

Merkin poured the coffee into ornate gold-rimmed coffee cups. She perched on the Chippendale, leaving me the spare chair.

The room felt small. The fire crackled and spat in the hearth. Slowly, I began to notice the other things around us. The worn Persian rug underneath us. The porcelain figures on the mantelpiece, the books on the shelf, and two white ribbons tied together, framed, held behind glass.

I wondered what Patrick was doing while I was up here in the sewing house. If he had nice things around him when he'd finished his day's work. If he thought of me . . .

Merkin settled herself.

'Now,' she said. 'Tell me about him.'

'Right,' I said. I pushed myself back to the matter in hand, mentally grabbing at my pencil and notepad. I was there to talk about Niall. 'I mean, I don't know much,' I started. 'I gather that Niall has been missing for—'

'Not Niall,' said Merkin. 'We can get to that one. Tell me about the gorgeous streak of a man, that nerdy hunk you were attached to back in June with the glasses on him that make a girl want to play dirty librarian all night long.'

'Oh, umm . . .'

'What did he do?' said Merkin. 'Did he cheat on you? The dirty wee bastard. You want me to have him killed?' she said. 'Wouldn't that be the kicker if he was found face down in the Liffey, and it was you and me that did it?'

'No!' I laughed. 'Really, it's fine,' I said. It so, so wasn't fine. 'Patrick and I were just hanging out . . . and anyway, it was nothing.' It was everything. 'We were hardly together much more than a few silly kisses.'

Just long enough for me to mess everything up.

An alarm beeped from her phone. Merkin reached into a messenger bag behind the chair and took out a small pill bottle, slipped a tablet into her mouth. She rustled back in the bag, sorting through three or four more pill pots and took another two tablets. She met my glance and took the pills dry.

'I'm blessed with the ability to swallow anything,' she said. 'It's a skill. So, you want to spill the tea, as the young people say?'

I looked down at the coffee slurps in my lap.

The tea. The truth.

The truth was simple. He got a job. He asked me what I thought and I said it sounded great and he should definitely go for it, sure why wouldn't he? So he left. I cried. The end. I screwed up.

I was an idiot. Same reason I got myself so twisted in my head, I didn't reply to his texts from the airport, even though I really wanted to.

No, I didn't want to talk about the truth at all, because the truth sucked.

I tugged my hair behind my ears.

'So, Niall,' I said. 'Robyn says you wanted to talk to me about him?'

Merkin held her coffee cup in both hands. She bowed her head. A tiny watch ticked on her left wrist, the tick-tick of the little second hand sounding sweet against the crackle of the fire. Outside, a scooter rumbled. Somewhere deep in the warren-like building, a door closed and another one opened.

I took out my notebook. It was beige mac time.

'Did Niall work with you for long?' I asked.

'Two years full time, another two part time before that. A few weekends.'

'And do you have any other staff working here?'

'You think I can do all this myself?' She snapped a laugh. 'Of course. Three full-time stitchers, one embroiderer. A second for piecework, if I need him – darling young man from Wexford, learned to use a needle when he was in Limerick prison. And a beading lady for the lacework, she's incredible. Comes in once a month. I send out nothing. That's why I'm so expensive. If I can't do something then it can't be done. And I have Niall for everything I can't manage. I try not to complicate things, Fi.'

Lie number one, I thought. Even her coffee was complicated, in a fancy pot.

'Weddings are big business,' she said, waving away my ignorance. 'My brides want the best. They pay for it. Women come to me from all over the world to make sure they look fabulous. I would never let one of my brides walk down the aisle looking anything other than her best. That's why I don't sell off the peg – every body is different. You, for instance . . . you'd look ridiculous in a mermaid.'

'Gee, thanks,' I laughed.

'That frock up there.' She gestured to her sketchbook. 'It's all shades of wrong for you. You have a great figure underneath the layers of loose jersey and well-washed denim, but you wouldn't be comfortable with your tits pushed up and your arse laced into a Pippa Middleton. You'd feel exposed. You wouldn't look your best.'

'I'll keep that in mind,' I said, resisting the urge to roll my eyes.

'The reason all my ladies look so good is simple: they feel good. You make someone feel good and they shine,' she said. 'And that's the secret. Every bride wants to shine, honey.'

Look at the lights, I thought. *Look at the shine and not at the price tag.*

'So, how did Niall shine?' I asked her.

Merkin smiled. 'He became Sparkle McCavity.'

◆　◆　◆

We talked for over an hour.

Outside of his drag persona, Niall was a quiet young man, intensely serious about his apprenticeship and clearly focussed on his career in bridal fashion. He lived alone with no pets. He liked to travel, regularly flying to Paris or New York for Merkin's business. He worked long hours for her, often including weekends, and when he closed up the shop at the end of the day he'd then spend three hours making up his face and getting ready to go out as Sparkle, working all over the country at events, parties and the occasional red-carpet premiere event to which the likes of Thora and Del had never been invited.

Merkin talked softly.

He had simply disappeared. He hadn't been seen for a week, she told me. He was meant to open the shop for an early customer. They accommodate all hours, she said, as some of their brides had come a long way to find the right dress, but by the time she reached the shop herself that day, the bride was fuming on the doorstep, the shop was still closed, and Niall was nowhere to be seen. He hadn't answered his phone, or his email, or any social media. He didn't answer his doorbell when she went to his apartment building and rang it.

'Thing is—' she said.

She stopped.

The sky was dark outside the window; all around us, in the terrace of houses, people were moving and working and talking and creating.

'He sent me this,' she said.

She pulled out her phone from the bag. The message was there on her screen.

Stop calling. I'm not coming back. I have a new friend now. from Sparkle.

'That's a bit rude,' I said.

I thought she'd agree. I looked up.

Merkin ran her finger along her jawline. Gone were the shop talk and the glamour. She was old, fragile.

'I don't think he sent it,' she said quietly. 'He's a beautiful boy, Niall is. Even when he's mad at me.' She smiled, far away. 'He handles all the calls, he manages my whole life. I sort of forgot what it was to be without him.' She touched the backs of her fingers to her eyes.

'Maybe he did meet someone else?' I said. 'Maybe he fell in love?'

Merkin shook her head. 'He wasn't that kind of man,' she said. 'He didn't date much. We'd get gifts for him here. Flowers, sometimes. Chocolates. But the young queens get attention like that.

25

He wasn't bothered about any of them. He was doing well on stage too. He had four nights booked at TRASH and I was so excited to be working with him! But it's not even that.' She lifted her phone again. 'He never signs his messages *from*. Who signs *from*?' She sniffed. 'He signed them with a kiss,' she said.

The fire hissed and spat. Merkin leaned forward, disturbing the embers with a long poker, sending fresh flames dancing over the logs.

'I can see this is really upsetting,' I said. 'The thing is, umm . . . I'm not really sure what you want me to do?'

'I need you to find out what's going on, of course,' she said. 'I can't ask the others. Thora's at her aunts' with her ankle in a cast. Del is broken, missing Ben. Mark is scary and terrifies anyone he's trying to ask a question, and Robyn is in love, which is nearly as hopeless as grief, when it comes to getting anything done. Usually, I'd ask Niall . . .'

She turned to me, and smiled.

'So it seems I am stuck with you,' she said.

Marvellous, I thought.

We talked a little more about Niall's job, but she was tired.

I muttered about taking a quick look around. With no idea what I was looking for, I checked his locker in the kitchen and cast a vague eye over the rest of the building, but it was a waste of both our time. Merkin clearly had a huge crush on the young man; chances were he'd become fed up with her demanding ways, and found somewhere else to work.

Still, she'd asked me, and somehow I hadn't said no.

In an attempt to mollify her, I took a picture of the message on her phone, but in my mind I was already ordering my noodles.

It wasn't that strange, I thought. People walk in and out of one another's lives all the time. In my case, they travelled several thousand miles to the other side of the world. What *was* weird about

Niall, though, I thought, was that the rest of the TRASH family couldn't get through on his phone either. Even Del, and everyone loves Del. But there was probably a good reason for the line block thing, too. Maybe his phone was dead.

Sometimes, a mystery really isn't a mystery at all. Especially if you leave it alone to fix itself.

'I'll get my coat,' Merkin said, as I finished up explaining there was really nothing I could do. 'We can walk down to TRASH together.'

'Oh, I—'

Noodles . . . *Poirot* . . .

'I thought you wanted to see his place of work?' she said.

'Well, yes, but I've been to TRASH,' I said. 'I mean—'

'It's funny,' said Merkin, 'Robyn told me I could trust you. He was right. They call you Hagatha for good reason.' She smiled, and her eyes softened as she looked at me. 'I feel better already. Who'd have thought?'

◆ ◆ ◆

She led the way through the dark streets. She walked fast, still talking.

'Young Niall is a nice boy. That's what bothers me – mind that puddle, dear, your boots don't need any further damage, poor little mites – he tells me everything, Fi. I'm his mama. He wasn't even seeing anyone. I'd love it if he was seeing someone, I'd be happy for him.'

Lie number two.

We walked down the alley to TRASH.

'Hang on . . .' She took a bunch of keys from her pocket and unlocked the door to the club. A single earring glittered from the mat. In a dip Robyn might have been proud of, Merkin plucked it from the floor.

'These girls,' she said.

She went to type in the code to the alarm, but then froze.

'What?' I said.

Merkin put out her finger, warning. In a breath, she whispered, 'The alarm is already switched off.' Her face paled. 'There's someone here,' she said.

'Maybe it's Thora?' I said.

She shook her head. 'She's stuck with her ankle. I talked to Mark a few minutes before you arrived. He's not due in for another hour or so, and Chris is in Galway today with their dad.'

The interior door was closed. The stairs were still.

'No. There's something wrong,' she said. 'I can feel it.'

The hairs on my arms stood up. I opened the front door wide to the street and clipped it on the latch. *Always make sure there's an exit* . . . In the dark, the scarce drops of rain were lit up by the single streetlight.

I took out my phone, held it in my left hand. My keys in my right. Merkin reached into a cupboard behind the interior door and slid out a long steel pole with a bend at the end. She held it with both hands.

The building was silent.

There was a smell . . .

Merkin nodded.

We both turned together. I put my hand on the interior door and pushed. It swung with a loud, screamingly obvious creak.

The bar lights were on.

We moved slowly. There was something on the dance floor, under the balcony, something tall and weirdly bulky. I started toward it. Merkin came in beside me. I took another step, and another. Merkin put her hand in front of me. She held the metal bar like a hurley.

I saw the blood on the floor before I saw the corpse.

'Shit,' I muttered.

The old stage light beneath the balcony was bent and twisted under the weight of a body. A young woman, prone, stuck, the metal pole pierced through her belly – right through her – the box light knocked from its position, twisted to the side.

Blood pooled over the floor. The smell . . . It seemed to coat the back of my throat.

I gagged.

Merkin inched away, the steel bar shaking in her grip. I stabbed at my phone but she pulled me away in jolts, then faster and faster, almost running alongside me as we fell into the street. She slammed the heavy front door behind us.

I gulped at the night air.

There was a dead woman in the club.

I stared at nothing. I couldn't think.

She was dead. Really, really dead. Dead, in the club – dead, on the pole – dead – dead – dead – dead – DEAD!

I couldn't breathe.

'Dial the number,' said Merkin, her voice catching. 'Call the guards, Fi.'

I pressed the buttons. The line connected but I couldn't shape the words.

My stomach heaved. I handed the phone to Merkin as I jerked to the gutter. I planted both hands on the ground.

'Hello?' she said, into the phone. Merkin caught my hair, gently holding it from my face as I heaved. 'Yes, guards, please. This is Miss M. I'm at TRASH, the club, with Fi McKinnery. This is her phone. There's been a murder.'

Chapter Three

Thirty minutes later, back in the club, a uniformed guard stood at my shoulder, beside the puddle of blood. I looked at the dead woman's face. Her hair was short and dark, longer at the front. She wore earrings, silver hoops in both ears. A necklace swung from her neck, a pendant of some kind, the piece obscured by a fold in her shirt. Her trousers were loose cotton and she wore high lace-up DMs on her feet, the kind that cost a small fortune.

The guard looked at me. I shook my head. I'd never seen her before.

Merkin was wrong, it could only have been an accident. It was easy enough to see how it might have happened. The lighting pole was under the balcony rail and anyone who leaned too far . . .

The weird thing was why she was here at all. And who she was.

I frowned, trying to make sense of the puzzle, but the pieces were all different shapes.

'I don't think she was a cleaner?' I said.

She wasn't a TRASH regular, anyway. I was sure of that.

I reckoned the body had been there a while. The skin was glossy, strangely waxy, the highlights on the nose and the forehead pronounced with blood loss.

The guard muttered about the homeless situation in Dublin but the dead woman didn't look as if she'd lived on the streets. Her hair was stiff with product, and her clothes were relatively new, the type seen on any university campus in the city.

There might have been other reasons she'd broken into the club, I suggested. After all, it wasn't out of the question that she had been drinking, seeing as there were two glasses there on the bar. Then maybe she'd gone upstairs looking for a bathroom or something and leaned over from the balcony for some other reason and . . .

Two glasses . . .

Mind you, I rambled on. The front door had definitely been locked because I watched Merkin use the key, and as far as I knew there were no windows broken, or fire exits opened so it made sense she got in the usual way. There was a basement and I hadn't looked down there of course, I said. But anyway the door code had been deactivated so—

I stopped talking.

'Sorry,' I said quietly. 'No. I don't know who she is.'

The dead woman's face was frozen in shock. Her dull eyes were staring at nothing but the more I looked at her, the more I felt like I should know her from somewhere. She looked familiar, and yet I couldn't place her.

I recognised most people at TRASH, since Robyn started working there as Mae B, even if they didn't notice me. I liked faces. I noticed people. How they stood, how they walked. I loved to see the strange magic that happened when two people met for the first time and their sparks lit up a room, their pheromones already dancing wild, their auras connecting.

I started toward the glasses. The officer cleared his throat.

I could see through the railings to the balcony. There was no sign of a struggle, no broken glass or even a chair kicked over. Just the body speared on the lighting pole. Stuck.

Very, very dead.

The officer took out his phone. Calling someone, he looked away, lowered his voice. I leaned a bit closer to the body in case I was missing anything.

There were more guards at the door. Any second, someone would make me leave. I peered around the room, looking for something that might make sense of the poor woman's death. The dressing-room door was closed. The stage was untouched. Nothing else had been moved except the light and the two glasses.

There was no sign of a fight on her face, no bruising on her knuckles. The blood on the floor was untouched, the flow a perfect, smooth, dark stain. No footprints, no smears. No note. But then, even if it were an act of suicide, why would anyone try to kill themselves that way?

The pole was sharp but half an inch to the left or right and it would have caught on the woman's spine or her ribs. Probably damaged her, maybe jabbed at the softer flesh on her side, but she might have lived. Even a thick denim jacket might have been enough to stop the pole from passing right through her body.

No. It really must have been an accident, I decided. Murder wasn't very common. And anyway, people didn't kill one another by spiking them on lighting poles. That was ridiculous, even for TRASH.

I frowned.

The door opened. A fresh batch of guards started in. They were excited. Another weird death – and this one was a corker, one said to his friend. He saw me and bowed his head.

The pack muffled their words as they marshalled one another through the set procedures, but behind the bravado, not one of them looked the dead woman in the face.

Two broke off and started toward me. I tried to answer their questions.

No, there was no CCTV at TRASH. I started to explain that Thora'd been meaning to get a new system. She was off work for six weeks. Broken ankle, I said, helpfully pointing to my own ankle as if the guards wouldn't know what I meant.

I looked around for Merkin, or for anyone else to answer their questions.

Yes, it was true that the club hadn't been doing that well, I told them, what with all the drama we'd had that year. I gestured vaguely toward the outside of the club and started to tell them how a young queen had been murdered there only a few months before, how the detective in charge of the case had decided it was an accident when it clearly wasn't. One of the guards lifted his eyebrows.

'I know, right?' I said.

Anyway, security systems cost money, I went on. And it wasn't that Thora didn't care, because she really did.

And she did, I thought. She cared about TRASH more than anything in the world.

Her ankle wasn't the only reason she'd moved in with her aunts. By the end of the summer, the funds were so low at the club, Thora had sold her own house just to keep TRASH running. But I didn't tell them that. They could work that out themselves.

I don't suppose new cameras were on the top of her list, even after Eve's death, I said. I was fairly sure there was one in the office and he was welcome to see that just as soon as Mark arrived to unlock it. No one was stopping them, of course, I said. Just that I wasn't in charge and—

I was talking too fast.

'Miss McKinnery?' My original officer was done with his phone. 'If you will?'

We traipsed back along the thin paper carpet the forensic team had put down from the door.

Back out on the street, Merkin was crying into her hands. A tall guard stood beside her, patting her shoulder like one pats a horse.

I started toward them, but my officer grunted and put out his arm. His phone bleeped again. More cars came, more guards, all shiny and keen to see the gore-fest on their doorstep.

It was like a tableau of gothic horror.

As soon as my officer looked away, I nipped between the guards and hurried over to Merkin. Her face was ravaged with grief, her make-up ruined.

'Fi.' Her whole body shook as she passed me the big ball of keys from her pocket. 'I have to . . .'

She gestured to the street.

'Sure,' I said.

'Please,' she hissed. 'Think about what I said?'

'Which was . . . ?'

'Umm, ma'am?' said a deep voice behind me.

I watched Merkin slip between the flashing cars and disappear into the night, then I turned.

'We really need to speak to the club owner,' said a short man in a white coat. 'Is he . . . she . . . they here?'

'Oh, Thora, she's um . . .'

I breathed deep, trying to settle my stomach, horribly aware that the man stood right next to where I threw up.

The white-coated man was called away. Then another came by. They'd interview all of us this time, I thought, after the way the last investigation went. Every part of this messy little community.

Messy.

What was the woman doing at the club, to fall off the balcony? What was she doing there at all?

I wondered if Merkin had gone back to the shop. I hoped there was someone with her. That she wasn't alone.

Frankly, I didn't feel that great, either. You just don't expect to see a body spiked on a lighting pole. It's . . .

Weird, I thought. Yeah, for all Robyn's teasing about my making things weird, this was already really, really weird.

He was wrong about the rest, though: I was no expert on anything. Certainly not on something like this. The only person I knew who was an expert on death was Patrick, and he was a gazillion miles away in some jungle.

I huffed out a long breath.

It turned out Robyn's mum, Edna, was right; we could have done with a doctor in our group. Although she was probably thinking of someone who could help with her digestive disorders, not someone who spent his days cutting up dead people.

Ugh, I thought. I was so over weird.

Still, at least the gardaí would make sure they got it right this time, after being so publicly, embarrassingly wrong with Eve's death. And surely a different detective would be put in charge . . .

A sleek black Audi pulled in beside me. Detective Darrel O'Hara stepped on to the pavement. He stood for a moment, taking in the scene. The club door, the guards, the forensic team, me. And the long alley where he and I had met over another dead body – a dead queen, lying in the gutter.

'Miss McKinnery,' he said. 'Two bodies in the same year? This is becoming a habit.'

'It's hardly a habit,' I said. 'Two is hardly a habit. It's barely even a thing.'

When the homicide detective knows your name, it's a thing.

'Oh and it's Ms,' I added, figuring I might as well start as I meant to go on.

'Stay there,' he said, without reacting. 'You' – he pointed to a young guard – 'watch her. And I want no one in or out of the club without my say so.'

He spoke like the kind of man who would walk two paces in front of his wife.

'I don't suppose it was a murder this time, thankfully,' I told him, following. 'Horrible accident, really. Quite gory.'

'How gracious of you to determine the scene.'

'I mean, there are a hundred ways to kill someone in a club,' I said. 'Without doing *that*, you know? You'd never be sure that they'd die, for a start. And—'

'I think that's up to the experts to figure out, don't you? You two' – he gestured to more guards – 'I want a thorough search of the building, all entrances and exits, all rooms . . .'

In a flash, I remembered the dartboard in the queens' dressing room with O'Hara's photograph from a newspaper stuck in the middle, pink darts each marking a spot.

I turned around to hide my untimely grin.

O'Hara was a knob, even if you ignored his snooty expression and big ears. Everything about him annoyed me. His shoes annoyed me. He walked with the click, click of moneyed footwear, his fancy suede lace-ups pointed with an extra inch. And it would take more than an extra inch, as Robyn would say.

O'Hara dropped his voice as he spoke to a huddle of officers. His jacket opened in the night breeze and I saw a toffee wrapper stuck to his jumper underneath. Maybe not quite as sophisticated as he'd like to think.

Then I felt sick again as I remembered the poor woman inside. The blood.

The death.

I looked away.

'No Thora Point today?' the detective asked me. 'No line of queens to greet us?'

He smirked. Who smirked at a death scene?

'Thora's broken her ankle,' I said, my voice dull.

'You're all alone, Fi,' he said. 'There's a surprise.'

I opened my mouth to tell him that Merkin was there, then closed it. He'd find out soon enough. It wasn't my business.

'TRASH won't be open for another hour,' I said. 'Del is on his way. Thora Point is staying with family.'

I wrapped my arms around my stomach. The dead woman's family wouldn't know yet.

Somewhere, they'd be sitting around a table, or watching the telly, or making tea. They'd have no idea. They'd be eating a sandwich or just turning on the TV when the knock came at the door, and from then on, nothing would be the same.

I checked the text from Del again.

Merkin would surely have called everyone as soon as she was out of sight of the officers. She'd have told them what we found. What happened.

My head was spinning.

'I think I need to sit down,' I said.

O'Hara was still talking to the officers. He had all kinds of opinions and he hadn't even gone inside the club yet. He hadn't even looked at the poor woman, stuck up there. None of them had. They saw the club first, the stage first, and then the dead body.

'So who am I supposed to talk to?' O'Hara grumbled.

'Mark will be here soon,' I told him. 'You'd recognise him. Tall guy, well built. He was there when Eve was murdered and you said it was just an accident and th—'

O'Hara grunted and walked away.

Game, set and match to the rats in the gutters.

I huffed. I probably shouldn't be such a jerk to a guard, but he annoyed me. There were some people in life that got under my skin. The worst of them stayed there like the scar of a festering sore, and

O'Hara was captain of that putrid heap. I had no problem with the force, there were lots of nice guards in Dublin and all kinds of humans being all kinds of competent and so on, but Detective O'Hara was a wanker.

I texted Robyn again, but he hadn't seen the last text yet.

The officers around me kept muttering about the owner but sure, there was no way in hell I was going to be the one to call Thora and tell her there was a body in her club. She'd never forgive me.

Mark's number was written on the wall in the office. I started for the door but a scary-looking lady in a white forensics jumpsuit glared at me and a guard stepped back into the way again, barring the door.

Right enough, so, I told myself. It wasn't my place, even to go creeping up the stairs to find a phone number. The guards and the forensic scientist people were trained for this kind of death malarkey. I was just a shop worker and part-time photographer of other people's pets and – occasionally – of drag queens. Frankly, apart from the fact that I happened to be there when the dead woman was found, the entire thing was none of my business.

I concentrated on the cars, the lights flashing in the darkness. The damp trees behind the fence.

A young man watched from behind a lamppost. Beside him stood a man in an anorak. A woman pushed an empty buggy right up to the gardaí tape while her child climbed between people's legs, staring with the same gawkish intensity as his mother. People had started to congregate behind the tape as if the unknown dead had suddenly gained celebrity status in their sudden demise.

It was a sad little scene. If the circumstances were different and we'd been looking at a murder, then any one of them could be standing right alongside a killer. A murderer often returns to the scene of their crime, the TV shows taught us. But there was no killer here, just grief.

There were two glasses on the bar but that meant nothing. Anyone could have left the glasses. There would be fingerprints . . .

I wondered if they'd already dusted the bar and if we'd all have to give our fingerprints for testing. I also wondered if we'd be taken into the station this time or just questioned on the street.

The club door opened and O'Horrible burst back on to the street, complete with the toffee wrapper still stuck to his jumper and a deep, deep scowl.

'Get that child out of here!' he shouted. 'You!' He pointed at a young garda and let off a tirade of orders, gesticulating wildly as he made his demands.

I stepped back toward the fence.

'So,' said Mark from behind me. 'This is fun.'

'I think we can safely say you'll not be opening tonight,' I said.

'Not tomorrow either,' said Del as he and Robyn dipped under the tape.

'Robyn!'

Without waiting for the invitation, I rushed into his arms, holding on, pressing my face into his jacket, my eyes closed. He held his arms tight around me.

'Hey, baby,' he whispered. 'It's OK.'

'She's dead,' I said. 'This woman. I don't even know who she is but she's in there and she's on this pole and—'

'Hush.' Robyn soothed the back of my head with his hand. He kissed the top of my ear. 'Look at me. Breathe. You're OK. We're OK.'

I nodded. 'But she isn't. Oh,' I added, 'and our favourite detective is here.'

Mark growled.

'What's the situation?' said Del. 'Anyone else on the scene when she was found?'

I shook my head. 'Just Merkin and me.'

'Merkin was here?'

'Didn't she call you?' I said. 'I didn't recognise the woman. She was on the . . .' I shivered. 'Ugh, it's horrible. I guess she slipped and fell. It must have been an accident, though, I mean—'

'A bloody strange one,' said Mark.

'TRASH is good at strange,' said Del. 'It's what we do.'

By the time Robyn got hold of some coffee, my stomach had nearly settled. We stood together in the drizzling rain and watched the men coming and going from the club.

'Six,' said Robyn.

I nodded. 'Seven, if he'd lose that look on his face.'

'His face is still there under the look,' said Robyn. 'What about that one?'

'Mmm, eight?'

'Just because of the beard?'

'I like beards. That one?'

'Ugh, three,' said Robyn. 'Oh now, look, see here, check out this pair of legs! I'd climb that . . .'

'Are we objectifying men?' I said.

'Absolutely. That one is a solid nine.'

'Really?'

'Really.' Robyn winked. 'You should see him without the uniform.'

'You didn't! You never told me!'

'Well, no, I didn't, actually. I got close. It was a long time ago. Anyway, I am now a reformed character and I have a boyfriend.' He preened, his coffee lip accentuating his smug grin. 'Yeah,' he said dreamily. 'Definitely a nine. Patrick was a nine.' He darted me a look.

'Patrick is in South America,' I reminded him. 'And you agreed to stop hassling me about him.'

'I'll stop when you admit that you should have told him how you felt before he left.'

I finished my coffee, leaned over and stole Robyn's cup from his hands.

'Hey!' said Robyn.

'Less talking more drinking,' I told him. 'You bitch, you lose.'

'You can't make up new rules on me like that.'

The club door opened. They carried out a stretcher.

'Do me a favour,' I said to Robyn quietly. 'Don't die. OK?'

He put his hand on mine.

'I'm not planning on it,' he said.

White sheets covered the poor woman but nothing disguised the shape of her death. I leaned against Robyn and he wound his arm around my shoulders. Along the street, Mark bowed his head, and Del stood alone, his face lined with pain and loss.

We didn't know her but she had died at TRASH. Which meant she was, in her way, one of us.

It was late by the time we trudged down the cobbled streets in Temple Bar and up the three flights of stairs to our apartment. I rubbed my eyes, trying to rid myself of the gory picture that would not leave my brain. Robyn flicked on the heating, and I made toasted cheese sandwiches. He hung up our coats. I put away the breakfast dishes. We moved around each other easily. Every now and then he caught me staring at nothing and he patted my arm, or squeezed my hand.

The whole evening had been bizarre. Merkin's shop. Her worries about Niall.

And then the dead body.

Definitely not an average night.

Merkin's words ran round and round my mind, how Niall told her everything. How that was why she was so sure there was something wrong. And she really didn't believe that text was from him. She was shaken even before we got to the club. She needed Niall; she clearly relied on him. Her personal assistant, she called him. He represented her in Paris and London and New York, at fashion shows and bridal fairs. And yet suddenly, with no warning, he stopped coming to work and fell off the map.

I'd seen Merkin throw a full-blown tantrum over someone moving her clothes to another hanger, but this was different. She was sure something was wrong but she wasn't panicking. She was asking for my help, but I really couldn't see what I could do.

Robyn settled on the sofa to call Gavin.

In my room, I opened the window to see the Liffey. The streetlights cast their glow over the dark, muddy river water, picking up the green stain on the bank walls.

The bridge was busy. Some nights I would have picked up my camera and taken pictures for my blog, but I couldn't settle. My head was filled with endless pictures of the dead woman on the pole, and of Merkin crying. I had no energy for bridge pictures.

Robyn chattered on the phone, his soft voice shaking as he told Gavin what we'd seen. I eased my door closed. After a while, the washing machine clicked on, the water rushing through the pipes. In the road, someone's car stereo played an old jazz number. Two men walked past the corner, their conversation rumbling.

Time passed around me. A young woman walked the bridge slowly, looking into the water.

Merkin had never asked me for help before. She'd never asked me for anything, except to get out of her way.

A soft knock at my door.

'Fi?'

Robyn was shaking.

'The dead woman at the club. It was Merkin's niece,' he said.

Chapter Four

There are two sides to Dublin. There are the picture-postcard places, the bridges and the cobbled streets where the tourists gather, where the air is sweet with music and laughter, and the soft chink of money. These are the well-travelled ways of tour buses and hen nights. This is the Dublin of the theatres and the parades. Of students lazing around on the steps of the universities, preaching hope and bemoaning love. Of culture and comfort walking hand in hand.

And then there's the other side, where no one is laughing, where the hopelessness and the anger seep from the shadows, and where fear festers and rots through the thread of survival for the hidden souls in the shade.

I checked the list Thora had sent me and lifted the heavy shopping bag on to my shoulder. She was fine for food, she'd said when Robyn called. Not a bother at all, she told him. She was quite happily staying with her aunts, resting up until her ankle healed, she said. Nothing to worry about. Of course, she added, if we *were* going to Dunnes . . .

Even away from the madness of the city centre, the square was quiet. In the green, a few of the residents walked along the path, braving the chill inside the long cast iron railings.

It was cold for the beginning of October. The leaves on the trees were brittle, tinged with the light gold of autumn.

I gripped my coffee cup in my spare hand, forcing my breathing to slow. I tried not to walk down that way anymore. The street held too many memories.

Over there, that was where Mark had run up to the corner. And there, on the step, was where Del's husband Ben was shot and killed.

And there, that was where the killer stood, just inside the park, in the shadows. Robyn's sister, twisted by hate.

I shivered.

Still, I thought, that was then. And now, Karen was in jail. We were safe. And the tragedy of the young woman in TRASH, and the drama with Merkin and Niall, that was up to the guards to sort this time. Delivering vegetables and biscuits was my job. Food for the soul.

I sipped on the cheap latte. It wasn't as rich or as creamy as the stuff we sold at Jenkins and Holster but while I really didn't mind picking up Thora's shopping, I was determined to stay firmly away from the till-pinging of overpriced artisan foodstuffs at Jenkins and Holster on my day off.

I took a long drink; I winced, blinking my eyes as the bitter taste coated my throat.

My phone buzzed. Robyn checking in again. I sent back a quick reply confirming there were no problems and I'd be home right after I'd delivered Thora's shopping.

I glanced at the time, double-checking.

I shivered. None of us who had been there in the summer would see the quiet street in the same way again, but it was just a normal day in a normal park in a normal square. No one was out to kill us. And if we had to remind ourselves of that ten times a day, then Robyn's therapist said that was OK. It was a healthy coping mechanism. For now, she'd added.

I juggled the cup and the shopping, and tucked my hair behind my ears.

A paper-thin leaf broke from a branch above my head, making me jump. It slowly drifted down to the pavement. In a dart, I checked the parked cars and the people walking over the grass, and the gutter, and the man in the red Skoda down the way.

The steps where Ben died.

I drained the last of the coffee and started along the row of tall nineteenth-century houses. One step at a time; that was the way. Deliver the shopping to the elderly queen with the broken ankle, take a few minutes to check she's OK, and then go home. Close the door. Hug Robyn, because that was also a healthy coping mechanism, and maybe open the cheap bottle of Aldi merlot in the back of the cupboard . . .

I could do this.

Seeing a flash of colour I looked up. Del waved to me from his third-floor apartment window. He had his phone to his ear. I smiled as he shook his fist to the unseen caller. He held up his hand to me to wait, then dipped out of sight, reappearing wearing a massive orange wig. Still on the phone to whoever was annoying him, he flicked the flame-coloured bangs, making me laugh.

That was the other thing, I thought. I couldn't keep avoiding visiting my friend in his apartment. If he could walk over those steps every day, I had no reason not to.

I checked the house number from Thora's text. Black paint peeled from the metal gate. The basement door was boarded up. Thick net curtains hung at the first- and second-floor windows – the kind that let through very little light.

I lugged the bags up the steps. The front door was impressive, tall and imposing. A small peephole was set at around my shoulder height. Time had crusted the edges of the metal surround.

I shifted the groceries to my other hand to ring the bell. Far away inside the house I heard a thin and reedy voice. Then another, stronger. I stepped back to wait for the slow footsteps to come closer.

I looked along the row. Back when they were built, each house would have been owned by a single family, but in our time of insanely high property prices in Dublin, only the very old or the very fortunate still clung to an entire house. Some, like the neighbours on the other side of the railing, had closed off the basement and let the top floor as flats. No one except the aunts had the lot.

I started for my phone to take a photograph, but this street wasn't somewhere I wanted to think about too often. I'd stick to bridges, I decided. No one I knew had been killed on a bridge.

A key jangled behind the door. I pulled my sweater over my hips. The door creaked open, slowly allowing light into the house.

From the outside, it was a hell of a house. Del's apartment, three doors down, was stunning enough, and he only had the top floor. When Thora told us she'd moved in with her aunts on the square, I'd pictured some kind of place similar to Del's but number thirty-nine was a whole new level of fabulousness. Classic, dark – it was like walking into a Hitchcock movie.

Lit by a dusty chandelier, the figure who greeted me was split into two very different halves. Their bottom half was in jogging pants with an ugly plaster cast over the right ankle and an old man's slipper on the left foot, and their top half was wonderfully busty, in a sequin baby doll dress and ruffled red lace gloves. Full drag make-up with high brows, fake lashes, slick red lipstick and huge diamanté earrings finished off the look, with the biggest silver wig I'd ever seen.

'Fi. You're early,' said Thora Point, framing the words with her big red lips. 'That seems out of character. I was so sure you'd be late.

It's not my house, before you look at me like I'm minted. It's my aunties' place. Come in. I'm on in two minutes.'

I looked back down the hall. There was no audience. Thora grabbed her crutches in both hands. She set off in the uncomfortable lope she'd developed since she broke her ankle.

'You can leave the stuff here,' she said. 'I'll get the money and—'

She turned into the first room on the right.

I stared around in awe of the sheer dilapidated grandeur. 'I can wait.'

'Just give me thirty seconds,' she called to someone else. 'Sorry, Fi, I . . .' Then, into the room: 'Yes, darling, the bloody internet is giving me shite again, it's . . . No, I'm here, ready when you are . . . No, it's only Fi and—'

I leaned against the big front door and heard it click shut, closing off the real world outside.

The kitchen would probably be downstairs. The cold stuff needed to go into the fridge and it would save Thora carrying it down there.

'Yes, I'm here,' said Thora. 'Fi, pet, leave the receipt and I'll sort you, OK? Can you let yourself out? I'll th— Yes, absolutely, darling, bring it on . . .'

Thora's door closed.

In front of me, a wide staircase swept up and up. The landings of all the floors were carpeted in the same musty red. The walls hadn't seen a paintbrush or a duster for some considerable years. Gilt-framed portraits glared down at me, each one with Thora's nose and sharp disapproval.

Music boomed out from the room. Further into the belly of the house, *Countdown* suddenly blasted from a television in reply.

I picked up the groceries, went along the hall and started down the stairs. It was warm enough, for an old place. I'd drop the food into the fridge, I figured. I could let myself out.

On the last step, I stopped.

The kitchen was huge, running the entire length of the building. Every surface was filthy. Plates stacked unwashed, dirty mugs and glasses piled two or three high, food stuff growing thick with mould in trays. A mountain of full rubbish bags in the corner waiting to be taken up to the wheelie bins on the street. By the sink, someone had started the process, but a few washed knives and plates were only the tip of a grim iceberg.

She'd got everything all under control, Thora had told Robyn. Just a few groceries needed. That was all.

I texted Robyn that I'd be late but I would be definitely, absolutely home by six. Tying back my hair, I walked into the battlefield.

The water ran hot, the pipes knocking and banging long after I'd filled the first bowl. There was plenty of detergent and bleach under the ceramic sink. I worked quickly, tackling the nearest stuff first. I carried out the full rubbish bags and I swept and mopped the floor. It wasn't so bad, really, once I had the first few rounds done.

Thora's music finally faded. Hearing *The Chase* start up from the aunts' room, I put on the kettle. I found a tray and set a teapot to warm on the stove.

Thora's heavy footsteps crossed the hall above.

'Fi?' she called. 'Is that you? Are you still here? Don't you be doing what I think you're doing, girl!'

'Not at all,' I shouted up the stairs. 'I'm an apparition. A ghost of kitchens past.'

'You're an aberration . . .'

The floorboards creaked in the sitting room.

'Tell her not to make the tea too soft,' called one of the aunts.

'I'm telling her nothing,' Thora bellowed. 'And don't you be telling her either.'

Well, now I was told, I thought.

I stuck another teabag into the pot.

One of us should have come over before. It had been weeks since Thora tripped over her aunts' dog. Judging by the cardboard boxes of ready meals and empty packets of Taytos, she clearly wasn't coping.

Upstairs, a door banged open with force.

'Tell her not to give us the plain biscuits,' the other aunt shrieked. 'I'm too old to eat a plain biscuit.'

'I'll take the plain,' the first aunt chimed at full volume.

I pulled out a packet of Mr Kipling's Almond Slices from my bag and laid them over the plates. There wasn't an old lady alive who couldn't be tempted by their almondy yumminess. I had bought them to eat at night whilst lying in bed, watching old black-and-white movies on Netflix, but I could get more.

'Fi?' called Thora again. 'I hope you're not—'

'Oh, I'm probably not,' I said, starting up the stairs.

I emerged on to the landing, the tray in my hands. Thora was leaning against the wall. Her face was wracked with tiredness behind the make-up, her good leg clearly unsteady as she gripped the doorframe.

I kept my eyes on the tray but something in my belly gave a soft wiggle of fear under her hard stare.

She frowned. 'Girl . . .'

'I made tea,' I said. 'And I'm not sorry either so you can stop looking at me like that.'

She clocked the almond slices.

'You shouldn't listen to the aunts,' she said. 'They're bullies. They'll have you run ragged, Fi.'

A tiny old lady edged her walker out to the landing, a small white dog cowering by her feet, snarling at me. 'Fi? Who's Fi?' she said.

'I am. It's nice to meet you.' I smiled, trying to wave my fingers from under the tray.

'Daniel, who is this?' said the old lady. 'What is she doing?'

'This is Fi,' said Thora with a long sigh. 'Fi rarely does what we ask of her. Right now she would seem to be carrying a tea tray. Fi, this is Aunt Flo, and at her feet, the essence of all evil, my arch-enemy, my adversary: Douglas.'

The little dog wagged his tail.

'Is she one of the lesbians from next door?' said Flo.

I kept my face straight. 'No,' I said. 'I'm very sorry, I'm—'

'She dresses like a lesbian.' Flo looked past me with abject disgust.

'I'll alert Ellen,' Thora told her in a dry tone. 'Now—'

'Well, I hope you pay this one properly,' snapped Flo. 'The last one only left because you didn't pay her – and because of the spirits. Did he tell you about the spirits, girl?' she said to me. 'And really, Daniel . . .' The elderly lady looked Thora up and down, taking in both the drag and the slippers. 'Are you surprised they leave? Would you look at yourself?'

'Are my lashes crooked?' said Thora. 'Or is it the earrings you don't like?'

'How about some tea?' I said, stepping between them.

'It's after five.' Flo turned and walked back into the room. 'Come along, Douglas,' she said. 'We haven't had a thing since lunch you know. Agnes gets awful dry.'

'It's very late,' muttered Agnes.

'I brought you tea earlier, but you were both asleep,' Thora sighed.

'I was not,' Flo argued. 'Don't be ridiculous, lad. I never sleep in the day.'

The dog blinked up at me. His tail spun in delight, and he looked at the door.

'Again?' said Thora. She started to the front door. I had visions of the little creature darting out around the traffic.

'Hang on,' I said. 'I'll take him.'

'I can do it,' said Thora.

'And so can I.' I grinned. 'Go on, catch me.' I moved to the aunts' room. 'Let me just— blimey!' I said, as a wall of heat hit me.

Stepping into the sitting room was like entering a tropical glass house at the botanical gardens. The heat filled my lungs and stole my breath. My eyes seemed to steam up the closer I got to the enormous gas fire in the chimney breast.

'You make sure he pays you enough, now,' said Flo, as she lowered herself into her seat. 'This is Agnes.' She waved vaguely to the even smaller old lady tucked in the other chair under a thick layer of blankets, on the far side of the raging fire. 'Now, you tell Daniel—'

'Fi isn't working here,' said Thora, from the door. 'Aunties, could you keep the volume down just a smidge, please, while I'm online. I—'

'What in heaven's name do you think you look like?' Agnes steamed. 'Look at him, Flo, look at our nephew making a show of himself like this . . .'

'Tea?' I said.

Agnes gave a deep *harrumph*, and pursed her lips together.

I heard Thora head back into the hall, working her crutches around Douglas's fidgety paws.

'I'll take him,' I said again, ignoring Thora's protestations. 'You have a garden, right?'

'You're a stubborn girl,' said Thora.

'It's fine,' I told her, truthfully. 'I like dogs.'

More than most humans, I wanted to add, as the old ladies grumbled.

The cold garden air was a relief after the stifling humidity of the sitting room. Douglas scuttled down the path. He squatted against a low-growing weed as he emptied his bladder. I watched him wander over the lawn, flattening the long grass. It was some house. It would have been some garden too, I thought, if they could manage it.

The little dog scampered back inside.

Putting away the last of the washing up, I took one more glance around the colossal kitchen but there wasn't much more I could do to help without at the very least talking to Thora first.

Douglas led the way. I knocked at Thora's door. She let me in before lurching back to her chair under the beam of three Zoom-friendly lights. Behind her, a black-and-silver poster board had been taped between two standard lamps. Thora held up her finger to me, fluffed the top of her wig and blinked, setting her eyes bright as she clicked her laptop.

'Next up,' said a gritty voice from inside the screen, 'we are back to Thora Point from Dublin!'

And the show was live!

Thora's eyes sparkled. Her tiredness was completely gone – a well-seasoned star, she ruled her tiny laptop screen just as she did the stage at TRASH. She opened her mouth, and I believed.

Her sequinned baby doll was made from ten or fifteen layers of sheer satin tulle, fluffing out from her perky boobs. Her red gloves shed glitter. Her huge wig was piled in curls, complete with a tiny birdcage on one side with a goldfinch rocking on the middle bar. Her earrings were so big I had to wonder if she had loops catching them over the entire ears, but it was her make-up that I loved. Classic old-school drag. She looked amazing.

I watched in delight as, with another click, Cher's voice soared into the room, the words framed perfectly by Thora's sparkling red lips. Thora kept her eyes on the screen. She matched 'Strong Enough' exactly and as the chorus came, I found my shoulders moving, and my own mouth silently shaping the words along with her.

The sheer joy of the performance was infectious and, for a split second, Thora smiled at me before she was back to end the performance, sinking lower and lower and lower in her chair as the song finished, folding over her extended leg until she finally clicked on the mouse and ended the lip-synch out of view of the camera.

I waited until she had the laptop closed before clapping my hands together in quick applause.

'Oh, stop,' she said, batting the air. 'And before you say anything, I don't know what you've done down there in the kitchen but from the damp splodges on your knees and sleeves I can guess. I'm mortified, Fi. I'd never have asked—'

And we would never have known, I thought.

'I'm sorry I butted in.' I sat down, perching on the very edge of a scruffy Georgian chair by the bookcase. Heavy crime hardbacks leaned over me with their thick covers and dark roots. I thought suddenly of Merkin, alone in Bride of Life. Frightened. Of the body of the young woman, Merkin's niece. Pierced by the light.

'It was bad, was it?' said Thora.

Had I spoken aloud? Did she mean the death or the kitchen?

'I probably shouldn't have gone in.' That covered both, I figured. 'I'm sorry.'

With a weary laugh, she hitched herself back on to the chair.

'Presumption is the mother of many.' She smiled. 'You're sweet,' she said. 'Whatever you did, thank you. Just don't do it again. I can manage.'

Right, so. The kitchen, I figured.

'It's fine,' I said. 'I really don't mind.'

She pulled out a stool, resting her ankle in its heavy cast. Her toes were grey and grubby and the nails unkempt in strange contrast to the glittering top half of her body. Breathing hard, she tugged the red gloves and peeled them down her forearms. She took each finger one by one between her teeth and loosened them from her hands.

'I had someone due to start this week,' she said. 'Niall, from Merkin's shop – you know him?'

I nodded, my stomach sinking as I guessed the real reason she'd asked me to bring over some groceries.

'It was only two hours a week. Bits and bobs. I needed someone to tide us over until my ankle gets better,' she said. 'The aunts like him and I paid in advance, but he hasn't shown up. And when I tried to talk to Merkin?' Thora shrugged. She laid the gloves on the table, stroked them with her finger. 'I mean, I wouldn't mind but he was down to perform at TRASH all of next week too, and Merkin really relies on him.'

And here we are again . . .

Congratulations, Fi, I thought. *You walked right into this.*

'No note, no text even,' Thora went on. 'Merkin was gutted. She took him in, you know. He was just at art college when she met him! She taught him everything he knows.'

I nodded.

'Now they're facing Friday at TRASH with just Del and Merkin and this Stan she hired, and—'

'Mae B will do it?' I offered quickly, knowing Robyn would grab any excuse to be in drag.

Thora smiled. 'Sparkle McCavity was booked and Sparkle McCavity will bloody well be there if you have to go over to her flat for me, drag that silly boy out and shove the wig on his head!'

Thora pulled off her earrings with a snap and then winced as she removed her wig.

'It was bad, wasn't it?' she said slowly. 'Francesca, I mean.'

I nodded.

'Merkin is broken,' said Thora. 'She loved that girl. She's such a mother hen. I'll be honest, Fi, what with Fran dying like that and Niall going missing, I'm worried.'

I didn't know what to say. 'I'm worried too,' I told her.

Behind me, a clock bonged.

'I should go,' I said. 'Sorry, only Gavin is cooking and I said I'd be home and . . .'

'She'll lose it with him on Monday if he doesn't show at the shop,' said Thora. 'And now this other business, and in my club too!' She grimaced, ran her hand down her leg, smoothing out her muscles. 'That poor girl. Francesca was such a darling! If I can't perform, and now Merkin . . . It's a mess. The whole thing is a mess.'

Messy . . .

'Is there anything I can do?' I said.

Thora smiled. She reached her hands to me, beckoning me closer.

Caught.

'You're a good girl,' she said, pulling me into an air kiss four inches from her cheek. 'I know you'll help Merkin if you can.'

Dammit, I thought.

'You're a blessing in a bad knit, Fi McKinnery,' she said. 'Go do whatever it is good girls do on Friday nights, and tell my Mae B I love her.'

At the door, I looked back down the long hall.

'Daniel?' shouted one of the aunts. 'Tell the nice lesbian she can come tomorrow if she likes.'

I grinned.

'She's not—'

'It's fine,' I said. 'I'll pop by tomorrow.'

'Go home, little girl,' said Thora. 'Before the resident ghosties get you . . . or that bloody dog.'

I peered up into the darkness at the top of the stairs. The banisters caged the long space behind them.

'Are there really ghosts here?' I said.

Thora blew me a kiss, and the door closed.

Chapter Five

I couldn't concentrate.

Everywhere I went, I kept seeing the woman on the pole, like some bad-taste kebab. And then all the rest.

Flash: dead woman on the pole.

Flash: Merkin.

Flash: dead woman on the pole.

Flash—

There would be an autopsy, Del said. They'd come back to us if they needed. After the clean-up crew had finished and the new dance floor was put in, there was pretty much nothing else we could do.

The club would open that weekend, said Thora on the group video chat. They had to open. They had to show up. Do Cher the whole night, she said – do Celine Dion if you have to – and hire anyone available. Whatever else was going on, someone had to be on the stage lip-synching, and someone had to be behind the bar mixing cocktails, or there would be no TRASH to come home to when this was all done.

No TRASH for her to come home to, was more the point.

'So, we have a plan,' Robyn said.

'The show must go on,' said Del, throwing up his hands.

But Merkin had said nothing. Nothing then, and nothing since.

I walked past Bride of Life on my lunch break. Voices hissed behind the open door.

'Miss M is in a meeting at the moment,' said someone.

'That doesn't work for me,' came the irritable reply.

I leaned in. A woman turned to me. Starched, frighteningly clean with perfect hair, she looked like a press-out cardboard doll. She raised her eyebrows as I stepped on to the carpet with my soggy boots.

'Oh, sorry,' I said.

'Can I help you?'

'I, umm . . .'

'Well, can we at least book an appointment with Miss M?' said the lady with the cross voice.

'The next one I have isn't until the second week of April,' said the cardboard doll. 'I can take a deposit?'

'Is Niall here?' I asked, interrupting.

'No,' said the woman.

She waited.

Right, so. That was a no, then.

Apologising, I backed through the door. I shifted my feet on the uneven pavement.

I looked up. At the top window, Merkin stood, watching me. Rain streaked the glass. Her face was drawn.

Her assistant had disappeared. Her niece was dead. And the club, in all its faded glory, was falling apart. She'd come to me for help—

Me.

Mind you, outside of yelling at someone to get her a drink, Merkin was the most self-reliant person I'd ever met. The Miss Merkin up at the window was frightened.

And Del was grieving, Thora had her ankle, Mark was terrifying, and Robyn was in love.

Time to get myself a beige mac.

◆ ◆ ◆

Saturday nights kicked off early since Robyn started performing as Mae B. Most of the drag queens got ready at TRASH and Robyn now had a locker for his drag stuff, alongside Del and Thora, but that didn't include the hours of discussion at home over which outfit he might wear, with which shoes, or which song he would do out of the three he'd been playing back-to-back for days while he learned the lyrics.

Merkin got dressed at home. As she told anyone who asked, she had never been one to play well with the group. More importantly she hated Del's getting-dressed playlist. The last thing anyone needed was Little Pick and Bloody Mix, she would hiss through her teeth.

If they were honest, though, this weekend none of them wanted to go into TRASH at all. But, as Del said, the show did have to go on and – silver lining – seeing as Merkin had finally finished Del's new costume, he'd get more wear out of it on stage than in Tesco.

With Robyn taking two hours to do his face and Del going in early to dress his wigs, it fell to me to meet Miss Merkin outside the club and help her carry in a fully extendable, enormous peacock tail.

A new outfit like this was a Big Thing in the TRASH family. Even on a good day, Merkin may have been a little short in sugar, but she was certainly handy with the threads.

She arrived in a minicab driven by a worried-looking man. Merkin leaned toward him to snap her orders. He pushed himself into his seat, his eyes widening as he stammered the price of the fare.

Merkin snapped back to face the club.

She lowered herself down from the van seat, heels first, twisting her tightly laced frame. 'Fi! You're here,' she said. 'I suppose that means Del is still trying to contour his nose?'

'Happy to help,' I told her. Not that I'd been much help at all, with anything, as yet.

'I'd drop the Pollyanna act. No one else appreciates it,' she said. 'That's why we pay someone to do the heavy lifting.'

'Were you planning on paying me?' I lifted my eyebrows but Merkin shot me a mean glare. The nerves in my chest grew antlers, prickling discomfort all over my body.

She pulled out a huge laundry bag filled to the top with something shimmering and flimsy. 'Don't touch that,' she said. 'That's mine. No one touches my stuff.'

She gestured instead to the cab. The giant tail lay across several seats like beautifully feathered roadkill. Leaning right in, I extracted the costume extremely carefully. It was heavy. I held it as high as I could from the road, silently cursing all costumes and costume makers as my arm muscles burned taking the weight.

There should be a support network for the friends of drag queens. Spending every weekend trying to get the queens and their outfits from one building to another. Hours of stuffing tulle into bags, apologising to drivers for their cars being coated in glitter. Lacing up waists and zipping frocks, spending your Sunday night steaming a Little Bo Peep costume, and waking up to tights dripping on the shower rail every Tuesday morning.

I eased myself and the enormous tail through the door and started up the stairs. Mark came out on to the landing.

'That tail will have to go straight backstage,' he said. 'There's no room up here. Where the bloody hell is Sparkle? Who's that behind those feathers?'

'Del wants it upstairs,' I said. 'I was just—'

'Del can get himself into it down there.'

The long pole started slipping through my fingers. I felt the first of the feathers fall out of my hold. I stuck my head over the top bits. 'Could you grab th—'

'Fi?' he said. 'I thought you were a guy, with those legs and boots.'

'Oh good . . . is that Fi?' Del peered around Mark. 'Merkin, my lovely, lovely Merkin, honey, you made my tail!' He squeezed his palms together in delight. 'Even with everything else, darling, you did it!'

'Never has there been a nicer tail in all of Ireland,' Merkin said dryly.

'I'm losing it,' I warned them, adjusting my hold.

'Welcome to TRASH,' said Merkin. 'We've all pretty much lost it.'

'No, I'm serious,' I said. 'Can I just—'

I edged up on the step but Mark held out his hand to stop me. He bit his lip, looking down at Merkin as if searching for the right words, clearly trying not to say the thing he really wanted to say. Behind me, the sharp tones of Merkin's stage voice filled the hall, lashing against someone trying to get in for free, declaring themselves to be Thora's friend. By the time Merkin was done, the young girl had run out of the club, crying, and I was still holding the tail.

Please, I thought. *Please no one mention Francesca. Not now. Not yet. Not tonight. Let's just get through the show.*

'Um, folks?' I slipped my knee under the tail to take the weight, accidentally brushing the top feathers on a poster.

'Mind the bloody wall, girl,' cried Merkin. 'Hag's cocking head, my feet are in ribbons and it's not yet eight o'clock. Someone tell me Sparkle has shown up tonight? Has anyone at all heard *anything*? I'll— Christ, girl, would you get up those bloody stairs before someone mounts you and sticks you up on the wall!'

'Honestly I'm not sure I can,' I said, referring as much to Mark as to the weight.

I made one more step before Del got to me, his strong hands reaching under the giant semicircle. He popped his head around the side and blew me a kiss, whispering a quick hello. His eyes were wide, his face lit up at the sight of the new creation.

'Let's take a proper look in the dressing room,' he said. 'The dress is stunning, I can't wait to try it with the tail— oh, it's perfect, Miss M!'

'No. That thing has got to go down,' said Mark.

'Darling, we all have to go down in the end,' said Merkin. 'But your backstage area is filthy. This masterpiece is going straight into the dressing room where it will stay so I can check that it fits young Del's backside. I am too old to get down on my knees, stitching behind the bloody curtain. From then on it is his responsibility and not mine.'

'We have an entire basement filled with empty space, can't y—' said Mark.

'The basement is filthy.'

'It's not my job to clean!'

'Run for it, Fi,' Del whispered to me, giggling.

I crept down the stairs.

Flash: dead woman on the pole.

Flash: Merkin.

Flash: dead woman on the pole.

I took a breath.

I could do this, I told myself. I could push open the door and walk in . . .

I took three steps into the club. Suddenly the air around me became icy cold.

The room faded. The crowd disappeared. In my mind I saw the body. I saw the blood. I heard the shadow of Merkin's voice beside me.

My hand shot to my mouth, holding in the scream.

'Fi?' Someone stepped in front of me. 'You're Fi, right? Is Mae here? Only—'

'I, umm . . .'

'Is Mae B here tonight?'

'Yeah,' I said. 'She's . . .'

'That's great! Hey, Tina, she's here!' The man hurried away to tell his friend.

I stumbled toward the bar.

My heart crashed into my chest. I saw a movement above me. I looked up – away from the floor, from the space where the lighting pole had been. Up to the balcony. Merkin stood, gripping the railings.

She saw what I saw. I could feel it.

She took out her phone. In my pocket, mine buzzed. She'd texted.

So . . . who's next?

I looked up to the balcony, but she was gone.

All around me people were moving. The majority of them probably didn't know someone had died there only a handful of days before. They walked on the new floor. They laughed, they danced; they carried on as if nothing had happened.

I rubbed my eyes.

It wasn't in the news, after all. Mark had put a sign on the door saying the club was closed for cleaning. Even if people had heard someone died, no one outside the group knew the state of the poor woman when she was found. It really was just a horrible, tragic accident. And what's more, it was private, as Merkin said. It was family.

'Shit,' I muttered. It would be really nice not to have to think about death for a while.

Now I looked around, I could see the place was packed. All different ages but a lot more young people than usual.

I slid in behind a large crowd of students. The bar was three deep, but I was in no hurry for a drink. On Thora's request I tried to count the customers so I could report to her that the club wasn't 'going to the dogs' under Mark and Merkin's rule. As much as I longed to give her good news, no one wanted to hear their business was better without them at the helm. And I knew one night's takings were just the tip of a very, very large iceberg.

I recognised a fair few faces but there were new people too. More women hanging out on the soft chairs in what Del fondly called Lesbian Corner. A group of young men I hadn't seen before gathered near the stage, excitement rattling through them as they waited for the show.

Behind the bar Chris lifted their hand in a V for vodka and I grinned, nodding my thanks. They didn't ask me if I was OK, and I didn't reply.

None of us were OK.

Dead bodies aside, even in the two weeks since Thora had been off her heels, the club space looked different. Posters lined the walls. Not just one or two as before, but loads of them. Really old posters from all over the world, as well as the new ones advertising upcoming drag gigs at the club.

I tried to remember if I'd ever seen a club poster in the bar before, not just on the door, or dotted around Dublin, peeling from thin panels of plywood surrounding construction in progress, and lost planning sites around the city.

I turned to the back wall. I liked it. Not too much, just enough to distract from the faded paintwork. Perking up the room, like a new wig with an old body suit.

The queens I knew were there on the posters, along with plenty I didn't recognise from the past. There were also pictures of all the drag kings who had performed in TRASH over the years. Like a 2D fashion show, it was a cohesive collection, each drag queen and king representing their time on the TRASH stage.

One of the newer photos was mine, taken only a few months before. Mae B on the Ha'Penny Bridge. I grinned. She looked good, but then it was impossible to photograph Mae B and make her not look good. She was a stunner.

The house lights dipped. The music changed. A light touch caught me round my waist and a whirl of colour blinded me as I was spun around. I looked up into my best friend's face.

Mae B stood tall in her five-inch heels, the magnificent foam padding sculpting her exaggerated curves. She breathed in sharply and her new breastplate moved with her chest.

'You disappeared,' she said.

'You look stunning,' I told her. I nodded to her immense pink-and-purple wig. 'Have you been raiding Del's drag room again?'

'This hair is bigger than his.' She touched the soft curls with the back of her fingers. The ice-cream twists. 'Gavin got it for me.' She blushed under the thick drag make-up, her dimples carving deep, the red warmth just showing at her ears. 'Come on up,' she said. 'I want you to meet Stan.'

'Sure. Who's—'

The dance floor parted. Mae took my hand and led me through the crowd and up the spiral staircase. I watched in wonder at how she took the steps with those heels. She squeezed my fingers.

'Don't look,' she said. 'Trust me, it doesn't help.'

I fixed my gaze to her back, and not to the new patch of floor. Her words came to me in snatches as she pulled me up the stairs.

'I've been searching for you all over,' she said. 'Del told me you came in with Merkin—' She bent to air kiss a passing friend as they moved past one another on the thin steps with an 'Oh hey, girl,' without breaking her stride. 'I wanted you to meet Stan all week, and he said—'

On the balcony, the same two fans from the other week were standing at the back, trembling with excitement. Mae B drove us through the dressing-room door, pulling me almost off my feet in her excitement.

Del was half in or half out of a pair of purple tights, his naked fake boobs bouncing up and down as he struggled, his short gold bob shedding on the floor.

'You might want to cover your eyes,' said a voice as smooth as Irish cream.

'Oh, Fi's seen it all before,' said Mae B, swiping the air with her hand. 'Stan, this is Fi.' She tugged me forward. 'My flatmate and best friend,' she added. 'Fi, honey, I want you to meet Stan the Man.'

Something in my belly flipped over.

Blimey, I thought.

I put out my hand.

'H-hi.' I was grinning like an idiot. 'It's, umm . . . Hi . . . Great to . . . uh—'

'Hi.'

His hair was short with a slight quiff at the front. His suit and shirt looked vintage and perfectly cut. He wore a black moustache and short beard, his brown eyes framed with kohl. He had an open tie around his collar, his shirt buttons undone at the top.

He held my gaze until my brain did a little dance all by itself.

'So, you're, um . . .' My mouth was dry. I fought to remember words – any words – or just *a* word that made sense.

67

Stan pulled me into a hug. His arms were strong; his body felt solid, like armour.

'It's good to meet you,' he said.

'I, um . . .' I tried again. I blinked.

'Del?' Mark looked around the open door. 'Are you ready, love?'

Del looked up, still one leg in and one out of the tights, the tail on the floor beside him, taking up most of the room. 'Almost completely there,' he said.

'I can see your arse!' said Mark.

'Just two minutes—'

Mae B giggled.

I started toward the chair, then stopped, then looked up. I couldn't remember what I was doing or why.

'Can I get you a drink, Fi?' said Stan.

'Oh.' Drink. I frantically searched through my brain for some kind of sensible response. 'Sure. Thank you,' I said. Then I realised I was already holding a full glass. I blushed. 'That is, I mean, no, thanks, but . . .'

Mae B took my glass. She looked from Stan to me and drained the vodka.

'Problem solved. What's your fancy?' Stan asked me.

'I, um . . .'

He was truly, truly gorgeous. I'd seen drag kings perform before but there was something in Stan's eyes I hadn't seen in anyone. Something different. Intoxicating.

He was a good-looking bloke, and I'd never been very good at talking to people I fancied. I'd only managed to talk to Patrick because I got to know him before I realised how much I liked him. I usually just dribbled some garbled nonsense and ran away.

And Stan was a man in the very best sense. In the way he stood, the way he held his shoulders. The way his moustache tipped up when he smiled, curling in the corner. The way he looked at me . . .

Shit, I thought. I was screwed.

'Del?' Mark warned.

Finally hitching the waistband of the purple tights over the other three pairs he had on, Del stuffed his feet into his red dolly shoes and grabbed a shimmering purple corset from the back of his chair. He turned, adjusting his wig with a tug, and Mae B pulled up the zip.

Mark tapped his finger on his watch. 'Thirty seconds,' he said.

The tail fitted perfectly.

'Twenty-two,' said Mark. 'Twenty-one, twenty—'

Slicking on another layer of his bright pink lipstick, Del turned for us. He posed, just for a second, and blew me a kiss, and then scuttled after Mark's massive disappearing frame.

The rest of us moved on to the balcony. Del made it to the curtains bang on time. Mark was ready with the bright circle of the spotlight in the centre of the stage and Del ran up on to the boards to a roar of applause. Under the lights, the purples and pinks shimmered. He clicked his red heels together and pursed his lips, then chuckled with the cheering crowd.

'This old thing? Thank you, thank you,' he crooned into the mic as if it were just a normal night and no one had recently died a hideous death right there beneath the balcony rail. 'All my trash and all my treasures! Such a good evening, my lovelies. How are you all doing tonight, hey?'

I felt someone standing just behind me. Stan stood the same height as Del, but somehow he seemed to take up more air around me in his sharp suit and tie and the trousers that clung a little too well to his thighs.

I kept my eyes on the stage. A woman had died in the club only days before, and a young man was missing. This wasn't the time to notice anyone's thighs, suited or otherwise.

And anyway, we'd always had drag kings and non-binary drag performers in TRASH, along with the queens. Drag was an art form, as Miss Merkin would say, and art was whatever we wanted it to be.

Stan's legs really were strong . . .

On the stage, Del had risen to the challenge of a Thora-less night with a track by a nineties grunge band Thora would have hated, and several new moves of which the older queen would not have approved.

As the last notes faded away, Stan strolled down to the stage.

The crowd met him with a huge cheer of love and delight. He stood under the lights like he owned the space. The mic in his hand, he spoke easily, that same smooth voice sending ripples through the audience as he teased and joked. The first guitar chords of Jace Everett's 'Bad Things' came through the speakers. Leaving the mic, Stan spun once and slid straight into the song.

Mae B came to watch with me.

'Ever seen two hundred people turned on at once?' she said.

Stan lip-synched perfectly and he moved well, but the performance was more than that. I glanced down to the audience. Mae was right. There was a connection in Stan's eyes, as if he saw every one of them. As we went into the middle hook, people moved with the music, lips framing the words, hips feeling every beat. Stan looked up to the balcony and just for a second I forgot everything.

'Phew,' Mae B teased me. 'Umm . . . earth calling Fi?'

I shot her a look.

As soon as the last guitar chords faded, Stan went straight into an upbeat, classy jazz number I didn't know, before delighting the crowd by spinning into a song with Del, both of them working the stage together, hamming up the moves and playing the lines.

The show ran smoothly with quick changes and snappy handovers. From Gaga to Gershwin, it was well put together. Still grinning, I took my balcony seat at the end of the row. There was a new fire in Del and Mae B. Even Mark was having a good time. But as Stan came back up, and Mae B and Merkin set off down the stairs for a group number, no one backstage could deny that Merkin was still clearly upset. On each step she snapped out a tirade of fury, her words biting and sniping at anyone in her way.

I moved over for Stan to sit down.

'Sparkle hasn't shown up – again,' he said, leaning close to my ear so I could hear him. 'What with that and Fran, Merkin's heart is broken. Del said someone was helping her look into it all, like a PI, or—'

Nope, not a PI, I thought. And so far I had found out nothing.

'Does anyone know what's going on?' I said.

His mouth was next to my ear. I focussed on the balcony railing. On the stage. On anything . . .

'That's the peculiar thing,' he said. 'Niall – that's his boy name, right? He's been out of touch with everyone. It's not just Merkin – no one has heard a word. I went over to his flat on Thursday and his car's still there, the curtains were open, and I've rung and texted loads, but nothing. Only that weird reply Merkin got.'

'You know Niall then?' I said.

Stan nodded. 'Sure.'

Stan's breath was on my neck.

'He was the one who introduced me to Merkin the other week when she was looking for more performers to fill Thora's slot,' he said. 'And he really loves that job at the shop. He lives for it. I kind of thought Merkin was getting a bit overdramatic at first, and then Del tried to find if he had any family or people. But what with Francesca dying like she did and Niall disappearing . . .'

Stan's thick eyebrows rose.

71

'It's messed up,' he said. 'If Niall's just done a runner for some guy, I hope whoever he is, he's worth it, because Niall'll not work for Merkin again, not here or at the shop, not the way she is. She's heartbroken. She'll slaughter him.'

The number finished and we both clapped and cheered with the crowd.

One of the posters on the wall announced Sparkle McCavity headlining for the following weekend, the other performers all in smaller letters, their names taking second place. Miss Merkin, Gloria de Bacle, Del Peen, Mae B and Stan the Man.

Sparkle was young to headline but she had a massive following on Instagram. She performed regularly at the other bars in Dublin – the more successful drag bars, Robyn might add, somewhere between his third and fourth vodka and lime – and she was clearly popular with the young crowd. She did all the high kicks, and the death drops and so on, but she wasn't one of the TRASH girls. Not really. She was too . . .

I searched for the right word in my head.

Too successful. And kind of plastic.

The opening brass chords of Shirley Bassey's 'Goldfinger' filled the little club. Merkin danced over the stage in a shower of tiny gold tinsel pieces.

I grinned. Merkin had a way of using her wide mouth when she was lip-synching that worked perfectly with Shirley Bassey's huge voice, and she knew every word and every breath as if she'd written the song herself. The audience was a hundred per cent sold, right up to the last powerful high note. Merkin's body twisted as she leaned back, her arms wide.

I pulled out my phone and took a picture. I moved forward along the rail. Without thinking, I leaned just a little, letting my body rest against the strong metal bar as I took the shot.

Stan grabbed my shirt, held me back from the rail. In horror, I realised where I stood.

I looked down, at where Francesca's body had been.

'You OK?' said Stan.

No. I was really, really not OK.

'Sorry,' I muttered.

'No, I'm sorry,' said Stan. 'Only . . .'

I nodded.

'You can't resist taking a picture, can you?' said Mark, from behind us.

'If Sparkle had been here tonight, that would have been her number,' said Stan.

'If Sparkle had been here, she'd still have a job,' Mark snapped.

◆ ◆ ◆

The city centre was busy as I walked home through the dark streets. Groups of young people, men calling in drunken yodels to their tribe, guards parked on the corners. Taxis weaved through the wobbling hoards. I walked quickly, my keys pressed into my palm. By the side of the church, three more tents had appeared since the day before; those with no safe bed in the bitter chill were now wrapped in the cold.

The air hung heavy with rain but my mind raced with the night's show, the huge peacock tail, Del and Mae B's new songs, Stan's great routine, and Merkin's fabulous 'Goldfinger' number. The music was still in my head, the same lines repeating behind the show reel.

There was a time I'd have kept to the shadows but that was before finding things in the dark. Now, I darted from light to light. When there was no traffic I took my path down the middle of the road, and when men walked toward me, I crossed to the other side.

I cut down Exchequer Street. Somewhere, someone was cooking a curry, the smell thickening the air with its rich spices.

At the crossroads that led to Merkin's shop, I caught my step. I hesitated. It was late. It was really dark, and no one was around, good or evil. I turned down the thin street.

Even at night, Bride of Life had a quiet, perfect elegance. The window was softly lit. The single dress stood out under a spotlight.

I turned my phone on as a torch and took another look at the door.

OWNER: MISS M

MANAGER: NIALL ASH

Stan said it was weird that he'd apparently done a runner, and he knew Niall.

It was a job Niall obviously loved and an exciting drag career . . . and he was throwing it all away with just a single text? No reason, no explanation. He'd found a new friend and that was it.

From Sparkle.

Even if he was angry at Merkin he could have called one of the others. Mark wasn't shitty all of the time. Stan seemed like a nice guy, and Del was lovely. Niall could have picked up the phone to at least apologise for not showing up, and then when he wanted to return to the stage, he'd be welcomed back with open arms.

As it was, not a single one of them would work with him now. He wouldn't get booked anywhere. First and foremost, drag performers were professional. They showed up, they performed. They worked hard on the crappy little stages they were given, and they didn't mess around when it came to bookings.

I frowned. It didn't make any sense, and things that didn't make sense bothered me like an itch.

The top window was dark.

Merkin would be home by now.

First her assistant, and now her niece – and still, that night she had painted her face and she had pulled on her drag, and not a single person in the audience would have known how she really felt, inside. She was a professional.

That, or she was playing me. But what would she gain? What was the point? It wasn't like I could do anything anyway, even if Niall Ash was actually missing.

I flipped up her text.

So . . . who's next?

I ran my hands over my arms, trying to calm the goosebumps that popped up on my skin. I shouldn't even be here. I couldn't do anything to actually help. The guards were the ones to call if there was an actual problem.

Yeah, I thought. *And look where that got us last time.*

Enough, I told myself. It was late and the very last place I wanted to be right then was a bridal shop. I was done with romance, and done with men. All men. Especially very tall, good-looking pathologists with nice hair and big feet and a way of looking at me that made my belly go squiggly. I was done, done, done.

I walked back to the main road and darted between the crowds. A couple came toward me, hand in hand. I stepped into the gutter.

Anyway, I didn't need a man in my life to be happy. If anything, I had too many men in my life, although admittedly most of the ones I knew looked better in a frock than I did.

I glanced behind me at a scuffle along the street. Hurrying down through Temple Bar, I turned just past the vintage shop. I ran to the last house at the end of the row, unlocked my door and stepped inside, closing away the night, my heart still banging in my chest.

But as I walked up the stairs it wasn't the tall pathologist on my mind. It wasn't even the fine-looking drag king with the smooth voice and the strong thighs. It wasn't the woman on the pole.

It was the face of the young drag queen already fading from the middle of a poster, and the fear in an old one's eyes.

People didn't just disappear.

Chapter Six

The club was to be closed for the day of Francesca's funeral and wake.

It had been a horrible, horrible accident, everyone agreed. Or rather, everyone agreed except Merkin.

The young dead woman's bag was on the balcony and the guards had said it looked like she'd got the key and code from somebody, and since she had clothes with her and make-up in the bag, maybe she was planning to leave her partner. Maybe she was just staying there overnight, to figure out what to do in the morning. But she'd let herself in with someone's permission, they said, even though no one was admitting it.

When we found her, Francesca had been dead since the early hours of the morning but there was no sign of foul play, they said. She had a job and people who loved her. She had no history of mental illness, no debt, no addiction issues. She didn't even have a student loan. There was seemingly no reason for her to take her own life, even if that had been her intention. The death was officially ruled as accidental, and quietly noted as a bit bloody weird.

The best we could reckon, Thora said, was that she'd maybe hidden in the bathrooms or the basement as Mark and his team closed up for the night, and then for whatever reason she was there she had – tragically but entirely accidentally – tumbled over the balcony. If not for the unfortunate placement of the old-fashioned film light, she might have escaped with a broken leg or wrist. It must have been a really unlucky fall.

Everyone apart from Merkin was absolutely sure that was what it had been. The whole messy thing was sad and awful but it wasn't a threat. No one was coming for us. We were fine, we said to one another. Fine, I said firmly, to Thora. Absolutely fine, Robyn said to me.

And every time I saw Merkin, she looked away.

The next day, I walked up the steps to Thora's aunt's house and dug into my bag to find the spare key Del had cut. The neighbour next door flicked back the curtains. A second later his door opened, and he stepped out.

'Nice day,' he said. He brushed his long fringe from his eyes.

'Not bad,' I told him.

'It will rain later.' He peered at my bags. 'You're doing the shopping for them now?'

'Just today,' I said. 'They usually have a delivery, I think, and—'

'Every Tuesday and Friday,' he said. He smiled. 'They're nice old ladies. My mother used to have tea with them now and then.'

I got the key into the door, turned the latch. 'It was nice to meet y—'

'I was thinking,' he said. 'I've had some trouble with noises and the like. Coming through the walls. I was thinking maybe their kitchen . . .'

'Oh yeah. The pipes are noisy,' I told him. 'If you like, I can give Thora a shout—'

'No,' he said quickly, his fingers at his fringe again. 'No, don't bother them.'

He looked past me into the old house. Fair, I thought. Not everyone wanted to deal with Thora.

'I'll have a word,' I said. 'If it's bothering you?'

The man smiled, his relief clear.

Inside, the house was quiet. I headed down to their kitchen with my bags. The floor was clean and someone had started on the back door, wiping at the little window. I finished the washing up on the counter and then slid the frozen lasagnes, made by Del's mother, into the freezer. The pipes rattled even worse than usual and there was a high wail in the water, like a spirit stuck between the two worlds.

A chill ran down my spine.

It was normal, I told myself. Just because it was Halloween in a few weeks, that didn't mean a thing, and if my brain wanted to make up ten reasons why such a noise might be spooky then that was simply a by-product of watching too many scary movies with Del.

I stacked the lasagnes front to back, wishing I didn't yearn so much for a certain tall pathologist to be standing alongside me, telling me I was being daft about the spirits.

The kitchen looked a lot better. I wasn't to worry, Thora had told me on the phone. They had everything settled now – she'd worked out how to bum-shuffle down the stairs with her bad leg stuck out in front of her and even if she couldn't stand to cook much at the moment, she could microwave a dinner just as well as the next broken human. They were doing great, she said, and there was no need even to pop over unless I was already coming and then she wouldn't stop me of course because the aunts liked to see me, and if so then there were a couple of things. But only if I was coming anyway, she said firmly.

I double-checked the shopping list she'd sent.

I smiled, feeling strangely fond of the grumpy old queen.

I made tea for the aunts and carried the tray back up the stairs. In the hall, faint strains of music came from the house next door. Old-style music like Duke Ellington or Louis Armstrong or something. I was trying to work out what it was when Del opened the aunts' door with a flourish and Douglas dashed through, his arthritic little legs moving as quickly as they could as he ran to the door for me to take him out.

'Excellent, I thought that was you scurrying down below us,' said Del. 'The dog only wakes up when you're here! Oh, marvellous – tea. We can take a break from the sherry.' He took the tray from me and led the way into the hellfire-hot sitting room.

A table sat between the aunts that both women could reach from their chairs. They each held a hand of cards close to their chests.

Del grimaced. 'I'm in trouble,' he said. 'They're fleecing me.'

'He cheats,' said Flo fondly. She patted the arm of her chair as if he were closer. 'He's just like Daniel's brother, Paul.'

'I don't cheat,' Del grumbled as he settled back into the third chair. 'I couldn't possibly be cheating, or I'd win.'

The old-fashioned music drifted through the thick wall again.

'That'll be Milton next door,' said Flo. 'Nice man.'

'Good to his mother,' said Agnes, shooting a look toward Thora's room.

'Gentle,' said Flo. 'Tidy.'

'I just met him,' I said. 'He mentioned the noises from the pipes in the kitchen?'

'Nothing wrong with the pipes,' said Agnes. 'It's an old house.'

Flo looked up, her watery blue eyes worried.

'He wasn't making trouble,' I said. 'He was just asking, that's all. Checking if your pipes were OK, I imagine. You know . . . winter . . .'

Checking if he was due any compensation for the noise, I'd be guessing, but I didn't add that.

'So,' said Del. 'He's nice to his mum and nice in general and tidy and has great music taste . . . Where have I heard that before? Are you sure we don't know him? He sounds like my kind of guy.'

'Oh, you wouldn't like him,' said Flo, reaching over to pat Del's actual arm this time, and stealing a glimpse of his cards as she did. 'He doesn't go out much, never really has.'

Del took a card and slid it into his hand. He thought for a moment, then discarded a king of diamonds.

'You can do better,' said Agnes, pointing to him. 'He's no king of diamonds.'

'I never liked the king of diamonds,' said Del, stabbing at the cartoon red face on the card. 'I don't trust a man who displays his jewels. I once dated a Chippendale and it put me right off for life.'

I giggled. Flo smiled at Del with indulgence. Agnes plucked the king from the top of the line and laid her cards on the table: ace, king, queen, jack, ten, nine and eight. All diamonds.

'Gin!' she said.

'Ah,' said Del.

'Shit,' said Flo. She laid her hand out and dug in her chair for her purse.

'Another hand to me, then,' said Agnes, delighted.

'You want in?' Del asked me.

'I'm not sure I can afford the fees at this school,' I told him. 'I'll take Douglas for a walk and—'

Flo caught my sleeve. 'They've been screaming again,' she said. 'Did Daniel tell you?'

'Sorry?' I said.

'The spirits,' said Flo.

A cold shiver ran over my skin.

'They've been screaming all through the night. They're upset, you know.' She gestured to the next room. Thora's room.

'Don't you worry about that,' said Del. 'There's no spirits here, Auntie.'

'It's your mind that's upset,' Agnes told her. 'That's the third round you lost in a row. You owe me another tenner.'

'It's probably just the chap next door walking up and down the stairs,' said Del. 'Or, I don't know . . . tap dancing along the hall to his jazz?'

'You shouldn't joke,' Flo warned him.

'Good point,' he said. 'I'm sorry. Tap dancing is a serious issue.'

I moved to pour the tea. Flo grabbed for my sleeve.

'I hear them all the time. I hear them all night, whispering and moaning,' she said. 'You have to believe me, girl.'

'Oh, umm . . . of course,' I said. *Not in a heartbeat*, I added in my head, as I gathered the dog and hurried out of the room.

Seeing a flash of movement, I nearly screamed.

A figure stood by the door.

A shadow of her drag self, Thora looked stooped and broken as Daniel, with his ankle in the cast and his weight leaning on the crutches. The long red wall behind him cast purple bruises under his tired eyes and his thick body seemed somehow frail in a crumpled checked shirt and blue jeans.

'How is she?' he said.

'Flo? Oh, she's—'

'No. How's Merkin doing?' he said. 'That poor girl. She must be heartbroken.'

I nodded. I chattered away about the shop and the club, and I tried to say the right thing, to make the right noises as I clipped the dog's lead to his collar.

'She asked you to help her,' he said. 'Did you have any luck? Any leads as to why her young lad has disappeared like this?'

Thick, prickling heat spread over my face and my chest. 'I did ask around a bit, but . . .'

'Oh,' said Daniel. His voice was flat. 'Right, so.'

'I mean, there wasn't much I could do really—'

'No,' he said. 'Of course. Well, as long as you tried, pet . . .'

I put my hand on the door.

'It's not really . . . I mean . . .' I squirmed on the step.

Had I tried? Had I really even bothered at all?

'After last time, that is . . .' I said.

'I'd have thought that *after last time*, as you put it, Fi, you'd be the first to understand how it feels to be convinced of something when no one else will listen,' said Daniel softly.

Chapter Seven

I slunk around the square with the dog. Douglas sniffed at every fallen leaf, every stick and every parked car. He was a pretty little dog. Not coiffed or adorned like some of the precious canines I photographed for pet portraits, but his tail wagged and he stuck out his tongue when he was really happy. As much as the square still freaked me out, there was something wonderful in strolling along and watching Douglas enjoy this quiet, shadowy corner of Dublin.

Away from the strange old house, I let my thoughts settle.

Thora was right. (I couldn't think of her as Daniel.) I hadn't exactly tried to help Merkin at all. I'd put the whole thing as far from my mind as possible, so I could go back to normal.

The truth was, I didn't want to be looking at another death, intentional or otherwise. I didn't want to be looking for a missing person. I wanted to go to work and come home from work and to watch Mae B and Del on stage, and to maybe get some decent takeaway coffee now and then between, and the occasional pizza. I wanted to post pictures of bridges on my blog, and to take a few photographs of other people's pets. And to worry about paying the electricity bill. Not about death.

As I rounded the far corner I saw Del coming out to meet me. I skipped the last few steps. I tucked my arm through his. We set off for a second lap.

It was a funny little square, really. Not posh like Merrion Square, but it had a quiet elegance and a history to it. Like much of the city now, it was split between those who had the most and those who needed the most. At the back of the park, a single blue tent crouched under a willow tree. On the other side was a hotel with a long, glass-fronted restaurant. A poster advertised an afternoon tea that would cost more than my day's wages and make even Del blink at the price.

We stopped by the last bench, facing the steps in front of his apartment building.

'He was a shit,' said Del, staring at the space where Ben died.

I squeezed his elbow. 'You want to sit for a while?'

'No,' he said, but he sat down anyway. 'And I don't want to talk about him, either. But he was an absolute shit.'

It was cold and wet. I sat beside him, and Douglas jumped up to my knee. A woman walked past us, keeping to the edge of the pavement. A taxi rumbled down to the other corner. In the distance, a church bell rang.

I wanted to ask Del about Merkin's niece. Where she'd lived. Who her girlfriend was. What the rest of Merkin's family were like. I couldn't imagine anyone being related to Merkin, young or old. I'd never met anyone like her in my life.

I pictured Merkin at the shop, sitting by the little fire, or at the window. She'd be working. Drawing, stitching, fixing. Merkin was a perfectionist. Bridal or drag, she'd throw herself into the grind to get through whatever was going on. That much I didn't need a beige coat or a giant magnifying glass to detect.

I put my hand over Del's.

'Is it happening again?' he said. 'They're coming for us again? Niall has been missing for weeks now. No word. Nothing, and then Francesca . . .' His eyes drifted to the steps outside his apartment. 'It's happening again, Fi.'

'No,' I said. I gripped his hand. 'Definitely not.'

'But you think it's odd too, don't you?' said Del. 'You think something has happened to Niall. I know you do. This is out of character for him. It's been too long now and no one has seen him – not at work, not at home, not even answering his phone. Just that one quick text to Merkin that frankly I don't believe was him either and—'

'It's not like before,' I said. 'And people are rude in texts sometimes when they're upset.'

'No, it's worse than before,' said Del. 'Francesca was lovely. She didn't deserve . . . Shit, Fi, no one deserves a death like that. Not even Eve deserved her death. No one deserves their life to be taken from them.'

He stared at the steps.

'Come on,' I said. 'Let's get you h—'

'Was she really stuck like they said, on the light?' he whispered.

I nodded. 'It was an accident,' I told him. 'It must have been – she probably just slipped.'

'But why her? Why there?'

'Why anyone?'

'No, really. Why her?' said Del again. 'What was she doing there? Why Merkin's niece, and why Merkin's assistant? You know there's . . . *something*?'

Del wiped his hand under his eyes. He shot me a look. 'Oh, come on, our Hagatha Christie,' he said. 'Don't tell me for one second that you don't think there's something weird going on with Merkin because I won't believe it. I saw her last night, just as you did. This isn't just grief. This is—'

'Maybe grief takes different forms?' I said. 'When my dad died, I thought about taking up miniature golf.'

He smiled. 'The important thing was that you only thought about it. You didn't do it,' he said.

We stood up, started to cross the road.

'Niall will show up,' I told him, reaching up to kiss his cheek. 'Go on inside now,' I said. 'I'll watch and make sure no scary beasties jump out and get you.'

'Then who will watch you?'

'I have Douglas.' The little dog wagged his tail at the mention of his name. 'And anyway, no one will come for me,' I said. 'I'm not that interesting.'

'Don't you believe it,' said Del.

I watched until his light came on upstairs. Three doors down, the curtains flickered in the aunts' neighbour's place. As I unlocked the big front door, the neighbour nodded to me from behind his window pane.

'Hi.' I waved.

He smiled, his eyes piercing, his head tilted a little.

Along the road, Del looked down from his window. I waved again, and then let myself into the old house, thankful that at least I lived in a street where no one cared a hoot what time people were coming or going. And no one had been murdered in my street.

I closed the heavy front door, but the cold had snuck in with me, clinging to my bones. Somewhere in the walls a high-pitched squeal came from the pipes. I hurried to get my bag from the kitchen. I didn't believe in ghosts. It was almost certainly the pipes . . . but either way, I was going home.

◆ ◆ ◆

Our flat was buzzing with the sound of laughter from the kitchen, but I needed a minute. I dumped my work clothes into the linen basket and took a shower. I washed my hair and I rubbed nice-smelling moisturiser into my skin. I moved slowly around my room as I mulled over the day.

I pulled on some grey leggings and a thick fluffy fleece. I opened my laptop.

Francesca's death had to have been an accident. There was no reason for anyone to kill her. At least that I knew. The question was, as Del said, why was she there at the club? Who let her in? Who gave her the key and wrote down the security code? And why did she have a bag with her?

And if she knew the club so well as to hide out there at night, how come none of us had ever seen her at TRASH before?

There were the two glasses at the scene. Who was she drinking with?

I crossed to the window and picked at a flake of peeling paint on the sill. The rain had stopped, and the wet pavement was a mirror. Away over the water, the people crossing the bridge were cast into silhouette against the iron lights, like shadow puppets in a play.

I picked up my camera and focussed on a couple. They stood watching the river. The woman had her hand in his, her shoulder leaning to his, her head tilted, just a little, toward him. The man stood straight. He wore a leather jacket, and the shine from the lights cast tiny stars over him. As they turned, he put his free hand through his hair. I caught the shot, his fingers, his body language as he looked away, seeing something, or someone, who wasn't there.

I uploaded the pictures to my laptop. I set to editing the last shot, cutting, softening the shadows, checking that none of the people could be identified.

As I worked, my mind shifted.

My fingers hovered over the keys.

Flash: dead woman on the pole.

Flash: Merkin.

Flash: dead woman on the pole.

Flash—

Maybe Francesca had been in the club with a friend? A lover? Maybe they'd been messing about, or one of them was hiding something there for another reason . . .

A soft knock at my door interrupted my thoughts. I pressed upload on my blog post, publishing the picture of the couple on the bridge.

Robyn slid into the room and closed the door behind him. He sat down on the bed. 'Hey,' he said.

I smiled. He looked happy. 'Hey, yourself.'

I dug out a box from my bag with a cream cake from Jenkins and Holster, the very last one left.

'It's probably a bit squashed by now,' I said.

'You're good to me.' He leaned around to see the picture on the laptop. 'Nice shot.'

'I wonder who they are.'

'Let's call them Henry and Delilah.'

'Let's not.'

'She looks like a Delilah.'

'I love the light,' I said. 'Look here, the way the rain just catches on the back of her heel.'

Robyn rested his hand on my shoulder.

'Come on, eh?' he said. 'Come and eat with us. It's just spag bol and garlic bread but Annie brought wine. You didn't eat yesterday or the day before.'

'I did.'

'Cheese sarnies don't count, now,' he said. 'We're adults.'

'No one sent me that memo.'

He kissed the top of my head. 'Consider yourself told, by all of us. Come on, Fi, put it away for the night and don't think about any of it, not Henry and Delilah or Thora or Merkin, or . . . any of it.'

'I've been thinking, though,' I said. 'It doesn't make sense. I mean—'

'And it still won't make sense tomorrow. Come on, this is an intervention, and it comes with wine.'

He led me out of my room. I was nearly at the kitchen when I realised he'd mentioned another person, an Annie . . .

The woman standing at the kitchen door looked familiar, but I couldn't place her.

'Hey, Fi,' she said. 'Good to see you.'

The smooth voice twigged my memory. I grinned. 'Stan?'

'Not tonight,' she said. 'Annie. How're you doing, girl?'

I looked around the tiny room – the wine, the dinner, the actual cutlery . . .

'We're alive,' said Robyn. 'And we're OK, Fi. We're fine. All of us here, right now, are actually fine.' He smiled. 'So we're just remembering how good that feels before something terrible happens and we end up dead.'

'Drinkies,' said Gavin, lifting a pint glass and a half glass. 'Big drinkies or small drinkies, m'dear?'

Slowly, I felt the steel cage that had gripped my insides start to loosen.

Robyn was right. We were OK. I was OK. Or maybe I was *nearly* OK, and that was something.

Chapter Eight

Even before I opened the door to Jenkins and Holster, I could hear Mr Jenkins ranting, my name peppering his choice phrases.

'I'm so sorry th—' I started.

'Nearly an hour late,' Jenkins snapped. 'An hour, Fi McKinnery! It's really not good enough, even for you.'

My head throbbed. I left my stuff on my peg, took my money tray and slid behind the till, my face burning.

'Tell me, are you an hour late when your friends are onstage? Do you just expect them to wait too?'

'I'm really sorry,' I said again. I gestured to the next customer. 'Yes, madam, this till, please.'

'Well, is there an actual reason?' said Jenkins, following. 'Do you have an excuse or are you just rolling up to work when you feel like it now? An hour, Fi! A blooming hour, and—'

He put his hand to his chest, and I tried desperately to think of an excuse that wasn't the truth – that even when I was in bed, I couldn't sleep because of a missing queen and a dead woman on a pole. Not that I was in bed for long.

Jenkins was still talking. 'Just because your best friend is dating my son, that's—'

The wine hadn't helped, of course. The first couple of bottles weren't so bad.

'—and I'm docking your wages this time,' said Jenkins.

Mind you, the next two bottles hadn't been awful either. The reduced merlot was quite nice . . .

'I'm taking two hours' wages off for today!' he ranted. 'And if it happens again, Fi . . . Yes, sir, just down there on the right-hand side, we have salty and non-salty. Here, I'll . . . Fi, you can't . . . Yes, sir, if you—'

I pinged through another customer's food. I smiled sweetly, though the lights over the till felt like an axe through my skull, and I asked her if she'd tried our coffee.

The customer coughed and held up the takeaway cup she'd just paid for.

It wasn't even that I'd drunk that much of the wine – or not as much as Gavin and Robyn. But it was so long since we'd kicked back like that, playing music, chatting and laughing. It was ages since Robyn had been home for the whole evening and not had to run off to TRASH to perform. By the time the vodka was opened, I figured to hell with getting up for work. By about three, or maybe four, I decided to hell with all of it. If I got myself fired then I'd get another job. I'd been sending off more job applications and, sure, something would stick soon.

And in the end, Robyn had been right. We were alive.

We cranked up the volume. Mrs Harper downstairs had been away with her sister and there was no one living in the buildings either side of us. Robyn put on Madonna. Gavin and I held our voting cards, scribbled with my cheap eye liner on the back of a cereal box, while Robyn and Annie were vogueing between the kitchen and the sitting room, dipping and switching, twisting their hips, dropping to a duck walk and then to the floor, narrowly missing ornaments and furniture as they spun and flicked—

Tens, tens, tens across the board . . .

It was gone five when I made coffee with Gavin for what seemed like hours. We debated if Thora would keep hiring more diverse drag performers. Next, we went on to whether the rumours were true that the Welsh queen Carol Singer was coming to Dublin to do some show no one seemed to know anything about. Then, an impassioned argument as to whether *The Rocky Horror Picture Show* was strictly drag or burlesque. And if burlesque was actually the grandmamma of drag. And then Robyn sang some silly song that made us all laugh . . .

Then when I finally made it to bed, I lay there.

Flash: Merkin.

Flash: dead woman on the pole.

When my alarm had gone off, I could barely move. Probably more from doing the Time Warp with Annie in our little kitchen than from drinking the wine . . .

I beamed up at the next customer, asking them how they were, and nodding as their voice rumbled back to me over the conveyor belt, their words not even making a dent in my sleepy brain.

Right at that moment, I didn't care, as I pinged their overpriced wholemeal pasta salad. I didn't care about work, or money, or about any of it. I'd care tomorrow. And sure I was grateful to have a job at all, and to pay the rent, but just for one night I was glad to kick back and have a laugh with my friends.

The problem wasn't just being tired. It wasn't even the wine, or the Time Warp. The problem, the glaring big problem, was that as soon as Annie had gone home, and Robyn and Gavin were in bed, I was alone with my thoughts, and all I could think about, over and over again, was Merkin's face at the window, and Merkin's niece, Francesca, dead on the pole. And Merkin's assistant, gone. And I had done nothing to help.

Who's next?

What did she mean by that?

Did she know something else? Something she wasn't telling me?

I took my shortened lunch break outside on the wall, hugging a coffee mug the size of my head.

Robyn texted me. He was also in the doghouse for turning up late to his job at the phone shop. He WhatsApped me when his boss was with a customer – photos of the night, and then one of him in the back room of the shop with a series of skull emojis. He posted a video on Instagram of all of us vogueing, waking my hazy memory, and within minutes Del had also messaged me, and then Thora, so she could disown me forever for my attempt at a death drop which had me bruising both Gavin and Annie and nearly knocking myself out on the corner of the kitchen cabinet. As I sat on the wall trying to stomach my coffee, even Robyn's mother, Edna, was texting me and teasing me for my sorry dance moves.

I grinned. It had been fun.

Gradually, my brain began to settle. Still exhausted, I finished my coffee feeling almost human.

The thing was, aside from all the jollity and the silliness, Thora was right. I should have listened more to Merkin. I knew what it felt like to be frightened, and for no one else to listen to me. And if I were honest, the more the days went on and Niall still wasn't showing up, the more I thought Merkin might be right.

The guards weren't interested. Francesca's was an accidental death, sure, but they were done with that now, and they couldn't care less about the disappearance of a young queen with a promising career in selling haute couture wedding dresses.

It all felt horribly familiar.

Zipping up my jacket, I started on the chocolate bar I'd bought from the out-of-date box.

What bothered me more than anything wasn't the facts. It was Merkin. Thora was worried too, and she'd known Merkin far longer than any of the others – longer than either of them would admit.

The older queens still terrified me. Their quick snap-fire wit could bite hard, and they ruled the little club with more than a pinch of shade. Whilst Merkin was all for diversity on the stage, she never hid the fact that she felt the club shouldn't be for *people like me* in the audience. She had no time for me, or for my sort—

Yet, as Thora reminded me, Merkin had come to me for help.

And a little voice in my head wanted to know why.

Why did she bring me to TRASH? Why was I there, when she found Francesca? Was that coincidence?

A smart man once told me that a coincidence was rarely a coincidence. But then, the man in question had gone off to work in South America so . . .

But was it really just chance?

I headed back inside, still mulling over the same thing. I helped an older lady to find our wheat-free organic dog food, and I took over on the coffee station for Mickey so he could take a break . . .

When Merkin walked out on to that stage in TRASH, she was always in charge. It didn't matter if she was wearing a cheap wig from the fancy dress shop or the most expensive lace-front creation; she held herself as true drag royalty. She'd performed with the best, with Lady Bunny and Regina Fong.

Like them, she had something stronger behind her eyes, like a bitch trained to fight and now unused to a fluffy bed.

Merkin tolerated me. I was under no illusion that we were friends, however kind she'd been with me recently. If I had to be there, then she would use me to carry things and take pictures, but I had neither Mark's muscles nor Robyn's pretty boyfriend. Merkin made no bones that she preferred the days when straight girls were not allowed in her clubs. When gay bars were gay bars and the hidden, the edgy, the bitter triumph of drag was as it should be: a protest and a political statement, and not, as she regularly told Del in my hearing, an opportunity for selling merchandise to young women.

I winced as the overhead shop light flickered. I was exhausted; what I needed was about nine hours' sleep and for no one to be killing anyone else for another week at least.

Slowly the afternoon trickled by.

Our customers were mostly regulars with the usual smattering of tourists, including a group of young women from Spain, their accents making our artisan products sound fabulously exotic and nearly worthy of Jenkins' high prices.

Sadly, as with anywhere, there were also the stupid people: the racists and the bigots. Whoever came through the shop door, it was my job to smile just the same, and to ask them if they'd tried our coffee. To wish them a good day. And if Jenkins still hadn't realised that I charged the racists and the bigots thirty cents extra for being arseholes, then that was maybe for the best. A stupid tax was the very least they deserved.

I grabbed another coffee, hiding it under the counter between sips. I pinged eighteen bananas and a jar of vegan relish.

If coincidences were rarely coincidences, then Merkin was right to be scared. She was the connection.

I wondered if she had any contact with the rest of her family. If they were nice, like Robyn's family – homicidally insane sister aside – or if they were like Thora's. Not just old and bit grumbly, like Thora's aunts, but mean, nasty bigots like Del said Thora's mum and dad had been. Thugs, like Thora's brother Paul, who definitely deserved the stupid tax.

Merkin lived on the outskirts of Dublin in a small house set high from the pavement. The path tucked between two tiny patches of garden, the herbaceous borders well behaved and the weeds banished before their first breath.

Her house and garden, like her shop, were exquisitely decorated, but it was a home for someone who lived alone. She had a reputation for tending and collecting pretty people as much as pretty plants, but I had never heard her talk about a partner of her own, or even friends, outside of the club. In fact, the more I thought about her, the more I realised I didn't really know Merkin at all.

I rolled over the thoughts in my head, and took another thirty cents from a woman who'd snapped at Mickey that her coffee was too hot.

If the connection was Merkin, then would she be the next to disappear . . . or worse?

◆ ◆ ◆

The apartment was empty when I got home. I opened my laptop and googled *Miss Merkin drag queen Dublin*.

I touched Play for the first video. An hour later I was still watching a small stage in East London, the velvet backdrop curtains nearly hidden by huge plastic palms, the lights flickering and the sound croaking through tinny speakers into my headphones. From Tina to Streisand to Cher, Merkin worked all the classics. Even back then she had been terrifyingly good.

I clicked to the next link, a video from the mid-nineties. Merkin was thinner but had no lack of strength. Her wigs were smaller too. One was long and glossy, like a really good version of her own hair. She'd drawn herself thin brows and used a thick white line that ran over her lids and swept up to her temples. But it was her dress that hypnotised me. Clearly a nod to the classic safety-pin frock of the time, the cut-away black panels were held together at the sides with huge gold safety pins hiding very little. As she turned, the back of the dress was also split, the massive pins doing nothing to cover the two-inch gap that ran down the middle of her back and over her perfect, naked arse.

I watched as Merkin danced and sang to a club filled with people, half of whom paid her no attention at all, while the front two rows were barely cheering. The audience were mostly men but there was one woman on the left, by the wall. Recognising her from another video, I clicked back to that one again, and then further back to another from London Gay Pride in ninety-five. The woman stood to the side of each of the performances.

I took a screen shot. She looked like Francesca, but softer. Less dead.

The safety-pin dress returned in the next video – a short clip of Merkin in Berlin, walking through a club with a drink in her hand. As the camera pulled back, she turned her hip and posed, just once, her eyes boring through time into mine.

She wasn't the most beautiful queen. She wasn't the best performer or the best dancer. But she had that incredible force, somewhere between fury and excitement.

She stood like a warrior.

I wished I could have photographed her back then, in her prime.

Would the Miss Merkin of those days have made me coffee and asked me about my own life before she asked a favour?

After the drama, the sadness and the tragedy of the summer, it had been such a relief for all of us to go back to normal life. To the safety and comfort of boredom.

It was dull. I liked dull. Dull was safe.

I moved to the window, watching the river.

But what if a coincidence really wasn't a coincidence? And what, if anything, could I do to help?

I pulled my laptop toward me and started writing a new blog post.

Chapter Nine

'CALLING SPARKLE?' said Del. 'You titled your blog post, Calling Sparkle? Who are you, Jessica bloody Fletcher now?'

Del stood between the sugar-free biscuits and the crackers for cheese. He had on his most expensive suit that screamed quiet class and superiority, the suit he only brought out to intimidate his most obnoxious clients. Behind him, Jenkins frowned.

'Good morning, sir,' I said to Del. 'May I help you? The hazelnut flour is actually on offer this week, and—'

'I'm more interested in toothpaste for my *cavities*,' said Del.

'We have a lovely bamboo range of toothbrushes, just this way, sir . . .'

I led him past the toothbrushes and over to the coffee station on the opposite side of the shop to my boss, pointing at various things while I talked. 'I think sometimes someone has to say things out loud,' I whispered, jabbing my finger at the new dark blend of Columbian coffee. 'If someone says what needs saying, it starts a conversation. And you were right. It's weird. We had a dead body in the middle of the dance floor there, and now no one is saying anything out loud about Niall disappearing. And someone has to, just in case he's hanging out with some gym god in Mayo then—'

'And do tell me, have any of those someones listing the strangeness online actually checked their facts first? I'd hate to have to represent them in a case of libel . . .'

'He's not shown up to work in two weeks now,' I said. 'That's a fact *and* it's strange. Even Merkin thinks it's strange.'

'She's the expert—'

I scowled at him over the handmade ravioli.

'Merkin asked me to help her,' I said. 'And so I'm going to.'

Del rolled his eyes. 'Well, while we're talking the demands of the elderly, I have a message from Aunt Flo. She says she thinks that young Niall might be trying to contact her from the dead.'

I blinked. 'Is he dead too, then?'

'Shit, I hope not.'

'Does Flo know him?' I said.

'She says she's sure it's him. Anyway, she wants to do a séance. Are those also glutton free?' he said loudly, as Jenkins drifted closer.

'Gluten, yes, but glutton, no, I'm afraid,' I said. I dropped my voice to a low hiss. 'All our séances are chock full of organic gluttons . . . Del, I'm not doing a séance.'

'You do remember what happened last time you wrote a blog about a missing drag queen?' Del returned.

He looked over to Mickey, who was eavesdropping from behind the counter. Del fluttered his eyes and shaped his hands into a heart.

'One large latte, double shot, and a chocolate hazelnut twist, please,' I said to Mickey. 'And yes,' I added to Del. 'Last time we found the bad guy. Or the bad girl, rather.'

'That was Robyn's plan that worked, though, not your blog.'

'That's nine euro fifty,' said Mickey.

'Can you stick it on her tab?' said Del.

'She doesn't have a tab,' Mickey sniped.

'It's fine,' I said. 'We're all fine and—'

'Yeah, except the latest drag queen who's gone missing, of course,' Mickey said in his low growl. 'How terrible to lose another one, so soon, yeah? How . . . careless.'

'Oh bless, was that an attempt at humour?' said Del. 'Well done for trying.'

Jenkins was coming closer. I grabbed the coffee, handed it to Del.

'Well, thank you, kind miss, who I clearly have never met, and I don't know at all,' said Del sweetly. 'I'll be sure to come back again.'

'And thank you, good sir, who I have also never met before,' I replied. 'And who doesn't pop in here all the time when they're passing.'

'Bye, Del,' said Mr Jenkins. 'If you see Gavin, tell him it's his mum's birthday next weekend – he should pop in.'

I sat behind my till. No one said anything.

I wanted to check how many people had clicked on my blog, or if anyone had answered. Not that it had any weight to it. As Robyn regularly pointed out, blogs had died long ago. But there I was, still taking photos of people on bridges and posting them, as if anyone cared.

But grumbling aside, this business about Niall really did bother me, and if I could do nothing else, I could write about it. In my own lame, quiet way, I could shout about it online, and maybe in writing, my scrambled brain would figure out what was going on in the process.

Niall missing really irritated me. I couldn't let it go. It was all wrong.

I pinged a big bag of organic artisan meat-free dog food and a pack of reduced fat frozen vegan curry for the next customer.

'Have you tried our new blend of dark roast Ethiopian coffee, sir?' I said. 'It's really amazing.'

Merkin hadn't hidden anything from me, so much, but there was something more to it, I was certain. I realised, as I pinged a string bag stuffed full of organic apples, that somewhere along the line, I felt used. And I didn't like feeling used. If there was something more going on then I would find it and put the matter to bed, and then if nothing else I might get some sleep.

◆ ◆ ◆

I clocked off bang on time.

The rain had become a solid Dublin downpour. My stomach was growling, but at the crossroads I turned south. Bride of Life was open, the lights on. The window shone with newly strung fairy lights draped from the white ceiling. The dress on the mannequin had been changed to a delicate ice-white gown, the skirt flowing over the floor like the sea meeting the shore.

Voices were coming from the other side of the door. Upset voices.

'But it's the only time I'll ever get married,' said a woman's voice. 'It has to be perfect.'

'It will be,' said her friend. 'It's everything she promised. It's the one . . . it's *the* dress.'

'So, to confirm the new dates,' said another voice. 'The dress will be ready on—'

The door pinged as I pushed it open. All three women shivered in the draft of cold evening air. I stopped on the mat, dripping rainwater.

'Are you here to see Miss M?' said a woman dressed all in cream. Like the shop, she was really, really clean. Her clothes, her shoes, her hands – everything about her looked plastic. She blinked in a slow sweep, foundation hardly cracking at the corner of her eyes as it worked to keep up the tension.

'Miss M?' she repeated, prompting me. 'You're . . .' She looked me down and up, as if whatever she saw was self-evident and displeasing. 'Fi?'

'Oh, um, yes?' I said.

I had no idea why I was there. I had been on my way home when my feet betrayed me. Now faced with this plastic perfection, I couldn't seem to explain myself at all.

After an uncomfortable silence, the clean woman waved me through. I hurried into the long room of bridal gowns, then on through the bridesmaids' frocks, and up to the drag. I couldn't help myself but to touch. I was halfway through the silks when I heard crying.

Not a light crying – not soft, gentle, delicate crying – but deep, guttural sobs.

I ran up the stairs, following the sound through the maze and down the long corridors, the crying getting louder and louder.

I could smell petrol.

Merkin knelt on the floor of the staff kitchen, a scrubbing brush and a bucket of foaming water beside her, the floor soaked, the air thick with petrol fumes, two more rags by the sink, and she sobbed and sobbed, her heart clearly breaking.

She held her hands over her face. I dropped down beside her and pulled her into a hug, holding her tight to me as she cried. She shook in my arms. I waited, still holding her, and after a minute she clung on tight and I soothed her back, rubbing her skinny shoulders.

Soft fairy-like footsteps along the corridor brought the plastic woman from downstairs.

'Miss M,' said the woman.

Merkin broke from my hold. She snapped around. The woman started backing away.

'Go,' said Merkin. She pointed to the stairs.

Merkin sat back on her heels and scrubbed her hands over her face. Her make-up was smudged.

'They tried to kill me,' she said. The tears done, she pulled herself up from the floor, leaning heavily on the counter. 'No,' she said. 'I'm not making this up, Fi. You can choose to believe me or not. I'm sure the guards think I'm raving at this stage. But I know what I know, Fi, I really do . . .'

Her clothes were soaked, the knees of her silk trousers sagging, her shirt cuffs dripping. The floor was drenched with water and the petrol swirled over the surface. The smell got to the back of my throat as the rainbow colours swam over the beige kitchen tiles.

'Shit,' said Merkin, in a long sigh.

'Here, I can clean this up,' I said. 'It won't take a minute . . .'

'It's not the mess,' she said. 'It's not even the broken window or the stupid note . . .'

I started for the scrap of paper she plucked from the counter, but she whipped it back, stuffed it into her pocket.

'No,' she said. 'You're not having this. I know who it was.'

'Then who?'

'It doesn't matter,' she said. 'It's not even the things they said. I *was* responsible for Fran. She was my family. And I'm responsible for my TRASH family too. And look here, that's my girl down there, Fi. All my girls. They work here. I'm *responsible* for them. And look at this street. If this place went up in flames, who else would lose their homes or their jobs? Or worse? If that match had—'

She stopped. I took the note from her hand, opened it. *Back off or I will destroy the one thing you love.*

'Who sent this?' I said.

Merkin shook her head. 'They're just words. Words I've heard too many times,' she said. 'It really doesn't matter, darling. A Molotov cocktail without a match is just a glass bottle with a bit of petrol in it and an old handkerchief stuffed in the top.'

'How . . . ?'

'The window was broken by a rock thrown in from the fire escape. It's there, see. I didn't touch it, but the guards weren't even . . . They didn't . . .'

'You called them?'

'Sandra called them before I could stop her,' she said.

So Sandra was Miss Plastic, I took it.

'And did you tell them you knew who did this? Did you give them this note?'

Merkin pursed her lips. She turned away but it wasn't anger that stopped her talking, it was fear. Sheer unguarded terror.

'I can't,' she said. 'If I tell them, I can't protect any of you. Like I couldn't protect Fran. I won't do it. One little broken window – I won't do it. My family is worth more.'

I cast my gaze around the little kitchen. The damage didn't look like much, a bit of water, a bit of petrol, broken glass, but she was right: it was everything if those you loved were on the wrong side of that window.

I took out my camera.

'Step back a minute?' I said.

'You're not putting this on some blog,' she warned.

'No.' I shook my head. This was way more important than a blog. This was going to the guards. I focussed on each part of the room, on each broken piece. I took ten, twenty shots, carefully stepping around the mess as much as I could, my feet sloshing.

'You never know when you might need a picture,' I told her, making a mental note to send them to Del as soon as I was home.

Merkin glared at me.

'Go on,' I said, dismissing her with a wave of my hands like she'd dismissed me a hundred times. 'You're soaked. Go and get changed. I've got this.'

Rolling up my sleeves I picked up a freezer tub and scooped up the rock without touching it, and the remains of the glass bottle.

The guards should be the ones bagging the evidence. They should be there, listening to what Merkin was telling me. Detective Darrel O'Bloody Hara should be sitting in Merkin's old-fashioned office and holding her bloody hand until she tells him what it is she knows, and he should be the one easing her fears.

I racked my brain, trying to think who could have done this to her, but I had nothing. No one I knew would hurt her this way. They'd all get mad at her, sometimes daily, but not one of them would do this.

After a few moments I could hear Merkin snapping at one of her girls as she spun out more orders. I didn't understand why the guards were ignoring this. Even if Sandra had rung and not Merkin, this was serious. This was dangerous. O'Hara was an idiot but the guards were smarter than this.

I cleaned up the floor and, when I was sure she wasn't watching me, I took another good look around. It didn't make any sense—

Unless, I thought, suddenly, there was a reason the guards weren't talking to Miss Merkin. Unless they knew something I didn't know.

Fear like hers wasn't fake. The window had been smashed with real anger too. Merkin was upset and frightened, and she knew who did this, and yet she wouldn't even tell me . . .

I stood at the window, looking at the broken glass. So fragile.

Now why would anyone attack her? What had they meant by telling her to back off?

What had Merkin done?

◆ ◆ ◆

I stopped in the drag room on my way down the stairs, at a purple-and-gold striped corset and a matching skirt on the far end of the rail. The corset was piped and had tiny threads of gold exquisitely shot through the fabric, with gold sequins to catch the light.

I took a picture. Robyn would look incredible in the colour and it would fit him like a dream if I could afford to get it for Christmas.

I held it out from the line so that the sequins glittered and shone.

She was good with light, was Merkin. She knew just how to show what she wanted an audience to see and how to hide the rest, but she lived in shade in more ways than one.

Chapter Ten

'Fi?' said Robyn.

He placed a tall takeaway coffee in front of me. His face was drawn and serious.

'Who's dead?' I said.

'No one.'

I picked up the mug and sniffed. He'd made the good coffee, the stuff we only used when things were terrible or awesome. I took a long drink.

'You're sure no one is dead?' I said.

'Well,' he said, 'maybe your vagina?'

Coffee spurted from my nose and from my mouth. I swore, making Gavin giggle from behind the bedroom door.

'Way to go, taking the smooth approach, Rob,' he said.

Cleaning my jumper with the tea towel Robyn handed me, I glared at them both.

'It's good coffee, though,' said Robyn. 'Shame to waste it.'

'I know it's good,' I said. 'It came from Jenkins and Holster.'

'Which shows that I care about you. I'd like to note th—'

'What about my vagina?' I said. 'Why do you even . . . Why are we even . . . God, Robyn!'

'The thing is,' he said. 'It's just that . . . the thing *is*, Fi. And I don't want you to take this the wrong way . . .'

'I'm not sure there's any other way,' I said.

'I get that, but if you think of it like I was you, and you were me and, if you were thinking what I was thinking, and then I had to say what you were saying, and then you made the good coffee so I would listen to you, and—'

'Who has the vagina at this point?'

'Forget I said anything about a vagina,' he said.

'I wish I could,' I told him.

'The thing is, it isn't really about anyone's vagina, so much, just—'

'It's about more than just *my* vagina?'

'No!' Robyn threw up his hands. He dropped down on the sofa next to me. Took a breath. 'Patrick is gone,' he said. 'For whatever reason, he's not here.'

'He's not gone, though.' I shifted around to pick up my coffee again. 'He's not dead, I mean. He's working in South America for three months, that's all and then he'll be back and—'

'And at what point were you planning on picking up the phone and telling him that you messed up?' said Robyn. 'And that you really do love him, even though you kind of accidentally gave him the impression that you didn't care he was going away, when you really meant to just be supportive of his work, or whatever was going on in your head behind your moment of insanity, and that you'd quite like him to know that?'

I held the mug to my lips. 'Can't reply,' I said. 'Drinking.'

'I'm just saying,' Robyn went on. 'You liked Patrick. You still like him. If you'd tell him that, then maybe he'd come home?'

'I can't tell him. He didn't ask.'

'He asked,' said Robyn.

Gavin wandered through the room, nodding. 'He asked,' he said.

I sighed. 'He didn't. He said he had been given an opportunity to work abroad for a few months and did I think he should take it? That's him telling me he had a work opportunity. That's not asking how I feel.'

'It's asking,' said Gavin from the kitchen.

'How?' I said. 'If he wanted to ask me how I felt, why didn't he just say those words?'

Robyn rolled his eyes. 'For someone who takes an extraordinary amount of pictures, honey, how can you not see what's right in front of your face?'

I glared at him. 'I see a coffee and a so-called friend who seems to be telling me my vagina is dead,' I said.

'I put it badly.'

'I'm not sure you have put it at all yet,' said Gavin, at the door.

Robyn waved his hand again. 'So,' he said, 'you're absolutely, definitely not going to call Patrick, right?'

'No.'

'Not even to tell him that, actually, you had no idea why you said what you said and did what you did, but now you realise you're in love with him and—'

'No,' I told him. 'I'm not. Not at all.'

'And you don't want, for instance, a friend to call him and tell him th—'

'Christ, Rob,' I hissed. '*Definitely* not.'

Robyn nodded. Stuffing his hand into his pocket he drew out a piece of paper. 'Right. So,' he said.

'What's this?' I asked him.

'You need to get a life,' he said gently.

'I have a life,' I told him. 'I'm fine.'

'Yeah.' He rubbed my leg. 'And you have a v—'

'Please, Rob,' said Gavin. 'Will you stop saying that word to her? You're not helping the cause.'

'There's a cause?' I said in a high squeak. 'My vagina is now a cause?'

Robyn handed me the paper. It was a flyer for a speed dating night. *Find love. Find that connection. Meet new people.*

Robyn scratched his chin like he did when he was nervous.

'You think I should go speed dating?' I said. I turned over the page but the words were scrambling in front of my eyes, each one messier than the last in its rush to be more irrelevant.

'The thing is, Fi . . .' said Robyn.

'Look, I know you mean well but—' I started.

'I kind of bought you a ticket,' he said.

'Why?' I said. 'And please, please don't say the word vagina.'

He giggled. 'Because you need to meet a guy who fancies girls,' he said. 'And before you argue with me, I know you're happy as you are, and I love you – we all love you, honey – but—'

'But you're worried about my vagina?'

'I'm worried that it's too easy to stay at home and watch Netflix, and it's a lot harder to go out and meet someone. And we all love Patrick and we're very aware that you do too, but if you're not going to tell him that and if I'm not allowed to go over your head and tell him for you, then maybe it's time to meet someone else.'

'And this is your plan? Either you call up my ex and tell him I'm too pathetic to talk to him or I go *speed dating*?' I announced the words with sheer disgust.

'Where else are you going to meet straight single men?' said Gavin. 'Tell me three who you even know.'

I opened my mouth, and then closed it.

I didn't have time for this. I had to find a way of helping Merkin. I couldn't leave her there on her own, with a petrol bomb being thrown into her shop, and her crying like that. I had to do something.

And apart from that, speed dating sounded like my idea of hell. I really didn't have time to worry about what I was going to wear, and to get my hair done and to work out what to say to the men.

'If you do this for me, I'll get you Niall's keys so you can take a look around his apartment,' said Robyn quietly.

He looked at me with that same determined flash as his mother when she knew she'd already won.

'That's illegal,' I said.

I held his gaze. He was serious.

'When is this nightmare?' I scanned the flyer.

Gavin laughed and ducked back into the kitchen.

'Um . . .' said Robyn.

'There's no date on here,' I said. 'I'll have to get my hair cut at the least, and—'

'The ticket is in your email inbox,' said Robyn. 'It starts in an hour.'

◆ ◆ ◆

I closed the door of my room and opened the window wide. It was cold and damp and it smelled of home.

Dull browns and murky greens clung to the river walls, dirty with life, the light dulled by the rain and the people who walked over the bridge moving quickly, hurrying to their homes or to their work or to the bars and the clubs, hurrying to be away.

Gavin ordered a pizza, but the smell of petrol from Merkin's shop still clung to the inside of my nose. I felt sick. I really, really wanted to get inside Niall's flat, but Robyn wasn't changing his mind and the idea of sitting at table after table, of being rejected over and over . . .

I shivered at the window.

If Niall was there – if he was home and everything was normal – then there would be nothing to worry about. It would be just a silly quarrel between an assistant and his manager.

But if he was really missing. If the flat was empty, if there were signs, or . . .

He drew a hard line, did Robyn.

I groaned, resting my forehead on the wall.

Robyn didn't get it.

People like Patrick didn't just appear at speed-dating events. He was one in a million.

He was one in four point nine million.

And if I missed him more than I ever knew it was possible to miss someone, then that was my fault. I screwed up. I didn't grab the moment, I got scared—

And whatever the guys said, Patrick didn't tell me how he felt, either. He was offered a job, and he took it.

On my bed, I'd laid out three pieces of paper to write a plan to help Merkin. My pen was still, the paper untouched.

It was really, really bad to go breaking into someone's home, even if your best friend somehow got you the keys.

The blank pages fluttered in the light breeze.

But if I had Niall's keys, then I had somewhere to start . . .

My phone beeped. A message from Del telling me definitely not to go to the speed-dating event.

Del is typing . . .

The next said that he hoped by telling me not to go, I would find myself compelled to do so.

The next message pinged on to my screen in block capitals.

TALKED TO ROBYN. I'M COMING WITH YOU.

'Shit,' I muttered. 'Robyn?'

The door opened instantly.

'Are you serious?' I said. 'You can get me Niall Ash's keys, so I can get into his apartment?'

'Yes, but I can't go with you. The keys are at the club. I can get them out for an hour while I'm on stage, but I'll only do it – and I'm deadly serious here,' he said, 'because I am absolutely using your need to be nosy about stuff in order to get what I want!' He grinned. 'I will get you the keys for an hour if you do this one tiny thing for me. I'm asking as your best fr—'

'Overruled,' I said. 'And you know that I won't meet anyone I like at this thing. I will be rejected fifteen times and . . . you'd really get me the keys?'

I could actually do something to help.

His beautiful mouth spread in a wide, self-satisfied grin.

'You want help to pick out an outfit?' he said.

'You being gay doesn't mean you're automatically better at picking out clothes than me,' I grumbled.

'It's nothing to do with being gay. It's a case of opening my eyes. You have terrible dress sense.'

'I do not,' I said.

'And anyway, TRASH is closed tonight . . .'

He opened my wardrobe.

I'm doing this for Merkin, I told myself. I can show up, say hello, go through the pain, and get takeout on the way home. And then, with any luck, Robyn would shut up about my vagina for another few years, and give me Niall's keys.

And if there were any sign of something bad having happened to Niall then the idiot detective would have to actually listen to us. If there had been a struggle, or there was a note on the kitchen counter saying, *Help, I'm being murdered*, or if Niall was lying dead in the bath, or—

Robyn was still talking.

'. . . and Del needs a night out,' he said. 'I need something to think about that isn't strange deaths, or visiting my sister in jail, or wondering if my drag career is grinding to a halt before it's even started—' He raised his voice to reach the other room. 'And Gavin needs to stop eating the last piece of pizza because he's eaten four and I'm still hungry!'

'Sorry!' said Gavin.

If I had Niall's keys, it wouldn't really be breaking and entering, either. It wasn't like smashing a window.

'So, actually,' Robyn went on. 'You're doing three bored gay men a favour. We haven't been out in ages.'

'You went out last n— Wait . . . you guys are coming to this hell hole with me too?'

'Of course we are,' said Gavin. He stood in the doorway. 'The black dress is good,' he said to Robyn.

'That's Del's,' I grumbled. I had been meaning to return it.

Gavin grinned. 'Perfect,' he said.

'I hate you both,' I told them.

'No, you don't,' said Robyn. 'You love us.'

'I'm rapidly going off you.'

The room was already buzzing with people talking to other people. A woman laughed with a pretty tone. Two men looked over to her, their eyes running up and down her body. They liked what they saw.

It's all for Merkin, I reminded myself. Get in, get out, get the keys. Go commit probably-illegal breaking and entering . . .

Del took hold of my arm.

'No one else has brought an entourage,' I grumbled. 'Are you even allowed in here?'

'Because we're queer?'

'Duh, because you're not part of the evening. Although, yeah. Possibly that too.'

'She thinks we're too gay,' said Gavin.

'I know I am,' said Robyn.

'We're your friends,' said Del. 'I wouldn't miss this for the world. Now you stay here and register. Hi!' He waved to the woman behind the desk and gave her a beaming smile. 'I don't know about you darlings but I'm feeling gayer by the minute.' He winked at me. 'I will find us a drink.'

'I think it says no alcohol?' said Gavin, pointing to a poster.

'Don't be ridiculous,' said Del. 'Fi, try to smile, sweetie. You look terrified.'

The registration woman was cut from the same cloth as the one working at Merkin's shop. The same hair, the same smile, the same make-up, the same figure-fitting jumper and skirt. The same tights and perfect shoes.

I took a breath. 'Hello,' I said.

Merkin . . . Merkin . . . Merkin . . .

'I, um . . .'

Del slipped through a door to the next room.

'Name?' said the woman.

'Fi McKinnery?'

'Are you asking me or telling me?' She laughed.

I hated her.

'First time?' she said. 'Don't worry, we're all friends here. You'll soon find like-minded souls.'

I turned for the door.

'No date night, no keys,' Robyn whispered into my ear.

'You're a sick man,' I snarled.

'Here's your name label and your match card,' said the woman. 'If you'd like to mingle, we will be sitting down in just a couple of minutes. You're only a little bit late for the mixing part of the evening so not to worry. Soon catch up, eh? That's a great dress there . . .'

She moved her hand. A shiny engagement ring shone from her finger.

'Right then,' she said, standing up. Everyone looked at her. And then at me. 'If all the women would like to take a seat? One per table.'

The other women started to move around the room. Without exception, they all looked stunning. None of them looked like they wanted to throw up.

'Gosh, it's terribly exciting,' said Del as he came over.

A man behind us laughed with a deep rumble. He stood with his back to me. Nice suit jacket, well-cut blue jeans. I looked down. His shoes cost more than Del's entire outfit, and that was saying something.

'Just for the record,' I hissed to Robyn, 'you're not allowed to ask anything from me *as my best friend* for at least another month.'

I slunk over to one of the tables. I sat with a start, not realising the chair was as low as it was, wobbling my boobs. A bell pinged and a man sat down in front of me. He smiled with perfect teeth. He started talking. When the next bell pinged, I hadn't said a word.

'It was great meeting you,' he said.

'Yes, um . . .'

I'd take my camera to Niall's apartment. I'd wear plastic gloves so I didn't leave any forensic evidence that I'd been there . . .

At the back of the room Del lifted a glass that looked a lot like it might hold a gin and tonic with ice, even though I couldn't see a bar anywhere.

Focus on Merkin, I told myself. I'd start with Niall's apartment. Then go to the guards with the pictures from Merkin's shop. No one should have to suffer threats. No one should be frightened.

The next man to my table was quite sweet, but he clearly had a crush on his neighbour at home. He mentioned her six times in our short conversation. I told him, firmly, to say to her how he felt. To tell her, out loud. Then I told him again as the bell pinged, and another time as he tried to walk away.

The following chap was as bored of me as I was with him, although I guessed his grey clothes would have fitted with mine in a wardrobe, and I kind of liked his Dunnes dad-jumper.

As the bell pinged, Del slid into the chair opposite me.

'Wow, you're gorgeous,' he said loudly. 'I'm so glad to meet you. What's your name, Fi?'

'Why can't all men be like you?' I said, laughing.

'Because then there would be no more babies, dollface. Now stop being quite so capable and start laughing at my jokes. Straight men like that – and then I can loudly say things like, YOU CAN DO *WHAT* WITH YOUR TONGUE?'

Two men at nearby tables looked at me, and I blushed a deep chestnut-red.

The bell pinged.

Del stood up. He glanced over at the next man coming around the circle. 'Oh shit, actually, Fi—'

'What is it?'

'Do you want me to stay?' said Del.

Detective Darrel O'Hara sat down at my table. 'Oh,' he said.

'Oh,' I said, at the same time.

Del's smile had dropped. Grief filled his eyes. 'I, umm . . .' He turned for the other room.

O'Hara sat back in his chair. He raised his eyebrows. 'Ms McKinnery,' he said.

Nice jacket. Nice shirt. Overpriced shoes. Wanker.

Great detective he was – he hadn't even noticed Del. O'Hara sat with the same smug expression on his face as always. And all I could see was a dead queen, face down in the rain.

Eve.

And Ben.

And Francesca.

And Merkin, tears rolling down her face.

I looked away.

'Shall I go?' he said.

'Sure,' I said. The very last thing I needed right now—

But then I stopped. I was wrong. He was exactly what I needed. He was the one person who might actually be able to help me. I had so many questions—

'Wait. Is there any news on the case?' I said.

O'Hara lifted his eyebrows. 'Case?'

Good point, I thought. As far as he was concerned there wasn't a case.

'The damage to Miss Merkin's shop. And the missing young man?'

'I'm not aware . . .'

'Would you rather we discussed the weather?'

'You could say it's nice to meet me?' His voice was like sharp gravel. 'We could try to tick one another's boxes, as it were. Isn't that the kind of joke you like?' he laughed. 'And then I could call you, maybe. We c—'

Call you maybe . . . It had been a while since anyone around me had said those words without singing them like Carly Rae.

'Is Francesca's death suspicious?' I asked.

'Fi, can we just do th—'

'No.' I crossed my arms. 'No, we can't.'

Robyn and Gavin were watching me. I nodded to them, barely moving.

'You have babysitters?' said the detective.

'They're friends,' I told him. 'You might not know how that works because it involves caring about someone, and them caring about you.'

'Ouch.'

Robyn started toward my table. I had to focus, to ask the right question.

'So, Francesca—'

'Accidental death,' he said. 'You know that. You called the station obsessively until they told you.'

'Have you looked into why she was in TRASH?'

'I can't imagine why anyone would go there,' he said.

'But—'

He exhaled, clearly bored of me. Then he leaned forward, and I found myself stuck in his weird, intense gaze. 'Come out with me, Fi,' he said. 'You're a good-looking woman. I'm not a bad bloke. I can show you a better time than these—' He stopped, suddenly aware Robyn was standing behind him.

'Go on,' said Robyn, leaning down. 'Finish that sentence, detective.'

'These men,' said O'Hara, without flinching. His eyes didn't move from mine. 'Is this what you want, though, Fi? A bloke who wears a dress? I can do that. I can be a drag queen if you like, put on a tight frock and show you my legs. Sure, can't any of us here be drag q—'

'You will never be a queen,' said Robyn quietly. 'You can wear anything you like and you will always be exactly what you are.'

The bell rang but as the next man came to my table, the detective still hadn't moved. I had to find some way of keeping him. I had to ask him about Merkin. About Niall. I had to make him see what Merkin was saying, make him help her.

'Ah, go on,' he said. 'You're single. I'm single. How about it, eh?'

'*How about it?* Is that how you talked to your ex-wife?' I said, taking a wild guess at his marital status. 'Maybe not such a surprise why you're here then, is it? Or was that more how she talked to the other guys she was shagging while you were at work?'

It was a stab, an angry bite, but as the words fell from my tongue, I saw the mark hit.

I stood up. 'Sorry,' I said. 'I should go. This was a stupid idea.'

I looked around the room at all the men and women talking to one another, having normal conversations, smiling and laughing, enjoying the few minutes for what it was. Then at my friends, standing with me, through their ridiculous attempt to help.

The receptionist woman started toward my table.

O'Hara hadn't moved from his seat. There was so much I wanted to say, so much I wanted to know . . .

'Tomorrow night at eight?' I said.

The detective blinked, then smiled in surprise. 'Tomorrow at eight?' he said.

'Sorry, sorry, my loves,' said the receptionist. 'That's not how we do it here. If you'd like to tick the box on your card and then—'

'Does the lady have any favourite restaurants?' said the detective.

'Fi,' said Robyn, his tone warning me against taking this any further.

'Your place,' I said, staring right at O'Hara. 'You have my number, I presume, in a case file somewhere. You can text me the address.'

'We really don't advise—' said the woman.

Sweeping my coat over my arm, I walked to the door, my heels clicking, my heart pounding. My friends were right behind me.

'That was either incredibly cool or incredibly stupid,' Robyn muttered in my ear. 'Tell me you don't like him, Fi.'

'I loathe him,' I said. 'He's an absolute arse.'

Del stepped forward. 'And now tell us you're not going on a date with him just to find out what he knows about Niall, or Fran, or Merkin?' he said.

Taking the steps at a skip, I grinned at all three of them.

'Shit,' said Robyn. 'That's a really awful idea, Fi.'

'One of my worst, I thought,' I said.

'Not quite,' said Robyn. 'But with any luck this one won't end in someone trying to kill you.'

Chapter Eleven

The estate where O'Hara lived was nice.

The houses were nice. The pavements were nice.

It was the kind of place I imagined getting a lot of DPD deliveries. Where everyone would be in their front rooms of an evening, watching *Line Of Duty* reruns on their moderately sized televisions. Deliveroo would find them, no bother. There were well-tended trees and plain iron garden gates. Each border was a monument to planting out flowers that would never survive the wet Irish winter and replacing them the following year.

I'd taken the DART. As the train rattled along, so my confidence and determination weakened.

I stopped outside the house.

I texted Robyn as arranged.

I'm here. Call you later. Xx

The reply came in seconds.

Any issue, leave. Or maybe leave now anyway xx

The drive of number 143 was freshly gravelled. No weeds grew close to the house. I went through my intentions in my mind.

Firstly, to find out what he knew about Merkin.

Then to press him about Niall, and to check, one more time – to make absolutely certain – that he thought Francesca's death was an accident. Even though I was almost a hundred per cent sure it was not.

And lastly, not to get thrown out of the house, forcibly, for telling the detective he was a giant wanker.

O'Hara opened the door. He looked past me.

'I came alone,' I said.

O'Hara smiled. Not the cocky, self-assured smile of the other night but a softer, gentler, more humble grin. Surprised, I smiled in return. *OK*, I thought, *I can do this. I can pretend to like him for a very, very short amount of time.*

'Hi,' I said.

'It's good to see you.'

'You too.' *Detective Big Ears*, I added in my head.

I stepped inside, firmly ignoring my nerves and Robyn's warning, and the list of reasons I should not be there that Del had messaged me.

Lieutenant Columbo would be there, I thought. And so would Jessica Fletcher. And Morse.

Del couldn't be calling me Hagatha Christie when I ask too many questions and then expect me to stay home and keep quiet when it might actually matter.

Anyway, there was a tiny, tiny bit of me who wanted to see if I could make O'Hara squirm.

The hall smelled nice. The carpet was clean. Only two coats hung on the coat rail. One hat and one umbrella. One pair of leather gloves on the windowsill. There were no pictures and no rugs, but it was warm, and the lighting was comfortable.

O'Hara took my jacket, leaving me feeling exposed in my new dress and high boots against his beige Aran sweater and blue jeans.

I smoothed down the back of my hair, wishing there was a mirror to check my make-up and feeling suddenly ridiculously grateful that there wasn't. I didn't need to see myself through this charade.

I had every right to be there. He invited me to hook up with him – he suggested we got together. And he was a detective. He was a guard.

What was the worst that could happen?

At least he wore shoes in the house. In a sudden burst of panic I realised that if I had to take off my borrowed boots, I'd be stuck in the thick woollen walking socks I wore on Edna's farm.

I'd never really understood why some women liked to wear high heels; I left the foot pain to the men. They could keep it.

'Would you like a drink?' said O'Hara.

Drink. *Yes*, I thought. *I'd like a very, very large drink.* Columbo and Fletcher may be able to work their magic without a glass of wine in their hands, but I had neither his eyebrows nor her bold earrings, so I would have to make do with alcohol.

I followed him down the hall.

'Oh, nice carpet,' I said. 'You can never go wrong with beige, can you? Beige is great. Thank you. Yes, please, a drink. I'm really parched, actually. Dry as a—'

Stop talking, Fi, I told myself. Especially stop saying the word beige . . .

'Great house,' I carried on, seemingly incapable of stopping. 'Nice area too. I don't get down here often. It's the kind of place not too near the city but then also you could be outside Trinity in no time at all. Like the sort of area you imagine you'd get when you grow up but no one actually ever does, although clearly you have, and . . .'

Shut up shut up shut up—

I followed him past an empty-looking room with a single chair in it, to the kitchen. He'd cooked. The table wasn't set and a single wine glass stood ready, as if O'Hara wasn't quite sure that I would actually show up. But there was music on in the background and as he reached into the cupboard for another glass, I saw the draining board was clean, and a pair of well-used oven gloves waited by the stove.

The windows were closed. I stood, uncomfortable in the stillness of the strange, quiet surroundings.

Start as you mean to go on, I decided. Good manners were everything, Edna always said. I handed O'Hara a bottle of overpriced organic red wine from my bag. He read the label.

I was so far out of my depth. Edna would have known exactly how to start a conversation about nothing and then end up talking about a missing drag queen, a tragically dead young woman and an unlit petrol bomb.

Every time O'Hara looked another way, I glanced around the room. I wondered if he'd keep a big whiteboard in his house, like the murder detectives did on the TV. Or maybe stacks of files, or notes he'd been writing.

'You look lovely,' he said.

'Thanks,' I said. I searched my brain for something to say. 'Oh, so do you,' I said.

He moved around the kitchen, chatting easily as he did. We talked about nothing and everything – about the weather and the trains and the wines and the meal. Maybe this was how people lived when they weren't sharing three small attic rooms with their drag queen best friend, upstairs from an old lady who didn't like noise, in Temple Bar.

'You've had your hair done?' said O'Hara.

'Yeah. Umm . . . it was, you know. Probably time. Every year or so.'

He was being nice. It freaked me out. But it was easy for him to be nice when he wasn't being honest at all. He didn't like me, but then I didn't like him. He didn't want a date, he wanted to win. To prove a point. To smarm me into submission or something. He wanted to show me what I was missing; I just wanted him to listen to me. As Gavin had pointed out before I left the flat, it was probably the recipe for a perfect marriage, if O'Hara hadn't had that one tiny personality flaw of being an absolute arsehole.

He chattered away to himself, comfortable with small talk while I tried desperately to think of a way to switch the conversation from the local GAA team to Bride of Life. I laughed at his jokes, and I sipped on the wine but as he turned on a pan for the rice, I knew full well that the real Darrel O'Hara wasn't this man in a Chris Evans sweater.

O'Hara was the detective who had miscalled Eve's death in the summer. He was the detective who arrested the wrong man for Ben's murder. And whilst those are both human mistakes to make, O'Hara hadn't just misdiagnosed a situation. He had strutted through the wet streets behind TRASH, looked down his nose at the queens and told me I was wrong at every turn. He'd snapped at the queens and told me that I was interfering.

Anyone can buy a nice jumper. Detective Darrel O'Hara was a smarmy, self-satisfied jerk.

He had no interest in me as a woman; he was playing with me as a cat played with a mouse, right before it slashed its throat.

I turned, realising he was still talking.

'I went with chicken,' he said. 'I hope that's OK? I don't remember you being vegetarian in our notes.'

'How do you do it?' The words shot out before I knew I was going to say them.

'You don't mean the chicken,' he said slowly.

I held my glass against my stomach to hide the tell-tale shake suddenly in my hands.

'How do you separate it all?' I said quietly. 'This. Life. Cooking, chatting, and . . .'

And death. Murder. The very worst of human behaviour. The darkest hours.

He didn't answer for a minute. The rice was bubbling.

He had big hands, strong forearms. His knuckles looked red and bruised. I wondered who he'd punched, and if they'd punched him back.

He hadn't answered my question.

'Sorry,' I said. 'I'm told I ask too many questions. I'm just curious how you work in the job you do. And—'

'It's work,' he said. 'Work is work, and when I get home and close the door, then it's done. Do you still think about Jenkins and Holster in the evenings? Do you think about it more, now young Gavin is living with you? He's Jenkins' son, isn't he?'

'He's not living with us,' I said. 'They're really just dating. Although—'

I closed my mouth. Score one to him. O'Hara nodded; a jerk of his chin.

'You should go out more,' he said. 'Out out, I mean. Not just that drag club and those kinds of people.'

My friends.

His eyes showed the sneer he left from his voice.

He opened a warming oven, took out naan breads, and laid them on the wooden board. It was all so strangely domestic. There was he, in his comfortably smart trousers and his I'm-so-muscly jumper, and on the other side of the room I stood with my back to a kitchen cabinet, my hair done all fancy, my body squeezed into a frock, a glass of wine in my hand. It was . . .

Yeah, congratulations, Fi McKinnery. You hit weird, again.

Still, in for a penny . . .

'So,' I said. 'Did you figure who was drinking with Francesca the night she—'

'Let's not talk about that,' he said. 'Let's see if we can get to know each other.'

'Oh, I don't mind . . .'

Frankly, he already knew too much about me. I didn't mind one little bit not getting to know him.

Columbo would go in from the edges, I thought . . .

'Right,' I said. I imagined myself raising one thick eyebrow. 'Get to know each other . . .' *Come in slowly*, I told myself. Adjust the collar of your imaginary beige mac. Raise the topic, then ease into the nasty stuff. 'Umm, have you worked in homicide for long? Or murder squad . . . or whatever you call it . . .'

'Crime,' he said. 'It's not New York, Fi. I joined straight after school. My da was a guard, my brother the same. How about you, what did your folks do? Your mum was British, right?'

Two points to him. I was not talking about my mum.

'Yes.' I set down my drink. 'So what made you do the whole murder . . . thing . . . rather than maybe one of the other departments?'

'Honestly, we don't get much murder,' he said.

Really?

'I'm not saying we're the heroes,' he said, 'but I like to think we make a difference. We stand where others cannot.'

He mostly stood looking down at everyone else. I caught at the rage in my chest. Let it hold me up.

He used his hand as he talked, as if he were talking to an assembly of school children. 'I think most people go into the guards because of some kind of need to help others,' he went on. 'Not to stand back. We want to see what's really happening.'

Shit, I hated him.

He chuckled. 'After all, if there are bad guys, then there needs to be good guys – or good people, I suppose I should say, before the pronoun police get me!'

Line. Crossed.

I felt the anger spin through my veins. I wanted throw something at him. Something hard. To stamp on his feet. I wanted to scream into his face—

I had to keep it together. I had to try, for Merkin's sake, for Niall's sake. I looked at his self-satisfied face.

He knew exactly why I was there.

And he was right: I couldn't do it. I couldn't be fake-nice to this utter arse.

I was unlikely to make it until the dessert without being forcibly ejected in one way or another.

I put my hand over my eyes. O'Hara left the drained rice on the counter and came over. He wore some kind of aftershave that made my eyes itch. He took my hands. He leaned over me like I was fragile or something.

I froze.

I never minded how Patrick was tall. I liked it. I loved stretching up on my toes to kiss him, the few times we'd kissed, and how his long arms wrapped around me and how mine fitted around him, and—

O'Hara's entire body seemed to surround me like I was his china doll. He gathered me against his chest.

He pressed up against me. I should have known. Some people took every chance they could to lead with their dicks.

My stomach rolled. I bit on my tongue. I definitely didn't ask for this, I thought. I showed up. I brought him wine. I came for dinner. I played the bloody game—

He kissed the side of my neck, then my temple. I edged very slightly out of the way of the obvious.

'So, little Fi,' he whispered, 'how far are you willing to take this?' He chuckled again, the same low, irritating laugh.

I moved back, pushing away. I felt sick. I wasn't hungry anymore. I wasn't sure what I was doing there at all. I was no detective. I was a phoney. I was pathetic—

I realised with a flash of horror that I was actually going to be sick.

'Can I use your bathroom?'

'Sure, it's—'

I ran for the stairs.

I locked the door behind me. I closed my eyes until the nausea passed, then breathed slowly, in and out.

I sat on the edge of the bath and took out my phone.

I texted Robyn.

This is weird.

The reply came instantly.

Stan here. Mae B is on stage, gave me her phone and said to watch for messages in case anything. You ok? You need rescuing?

I gulped back the tears that had washed into my eyes.

I'm OK. But thanks.

I'm not OK, actually, I wanted to say. I made a mistake. O'Hara was a creep. A manipulative, nasty creep. I was an idiot.

But they already knew that. That's why Robyn had given Stan his phone when he went on stage. That's why Del made me take a photo of the house and send it to him when I'd reached the close. And that's why Stan was asking if I needed rescuing.

I was so busy thinking I was capable, I forgot to figure out what I was actually doing.

I wiped the back of my hand under my eyes. I'd come all the way over here, and done nothing. No snooping. No questioning. Just a really uncomfortable guessing game with a man who'd been playing it way longer than me.

Help me, please, I wanted to write. Rescue me, please.

I wanted my friends. I wanted to call my dad to come pick me up. I wanted Patrick—

Everything Robyn had said was true. I wanted Patrick to come home. I wanted to hug him, to be with him, to see him smile, hear him laugh, to see the way he pushed his glasses on to his nose. I wanted to reach up and hug him. I couldn't say any of that.

How's the club going? I wrote, instead. All good? X

Merkin has hired Gloria de Bacle, came the reply. Hilarity did not ensue. Much yelling. Got to go, I'm on after this track – handing phone back to Mae B in a min. Scream if you need us! X

Inside, I was screaming, but I started to breathe more slowly. I hadn't lost the game yet. I was still there. I was still in the house.

After a few minutes, I opened the door and peered out along the landing. There were three rooms. One door was closed.

That would be it.

I tiptoed along the softly carpeted landing. I tried the door, half expecting it to be locked.

The handle turned.

The room was small, no bigger than my bedroom back at the apartment. The curtains were open, the window bare to the dark fields behind the house.

There was a chair and a table. And a massive stack of papers.

Bingo, I thought.

I glanced back toward the stairs. I could hear him draining the rice.

I moved the top sheet, a blank piece of A4 lined paper. A photograph of Merkin looked up at me. The next page, a hand-written timeline. The next, a photo of Merkin's shop. Of her, outside TRASH. Of what looked like a long blond wig hair on the pavement.

Then a photocopy of a note. Not the one Merkin had shown me, but another, capital letters written on Bride of Life headed notepaper. Dark brown stains on the corner looked a lot like blood.

Meet me at TRASH. Don't Tell anyone you're coming.

I said a bad, bad word.

I moved the paper. The next printed photo was the corner of the note sticking out from Francesca's pocket, a red pen line surrounding it, the tip of the shop logo on show.

I started to lift the photo when I heard footsteps in the hall. My heart racing, I replaced the pages and hurried out of the room, closing the door as quietly as I could.

O'Hara was at the kitchen door.

'Are you hungry?' he said. 'I think we're ready.'

'Bring it on,' I told him.

He'd lit two candles in the middle of the table.

My mind was racing. No way did Merkin kill her niece – I could see the picture O'Hara was putting together, it was obvious, but there was no motive, and no reason. And to add to that, anyone that knew Merkin would know for certain she would never, never hurt her family. She'd do anything for those she loved.

The plates were ready.

I watched his hands as he carried the rice to the table.

'It smells amazing,' I said, trying to turn my shudder into something that resembled excitement for the meal, which made me look like I'd just wobbled my boobs for no reason.

Be normal. Make it comfortable. I had to get something from him. I had to help Merkin.

He had to relax – not fake relax, but really, if he was going to tell me anything useful. I had to make him think he'd already won.

'This is quite a treat being cooked for,' I said.

'Do you enjoy cooking?'

'Oh, shit, no. I mean, who can be bothered with that, you know?'

Ah. Well done, Fi. Way to go making him comfortable.

O'Hara laughed. 'Well, what kind of thing do you usually make?' he said.

I was good at toasted cheese sandwiches. And I could throw things into a wok. And I was really good at making any given situation really bloody weird.

'I, umm . . .' *Name a food*, I told myself, *any food!*

'Ice-cream?' I said.

Not that food.

I picked up my wine. Took a long drink.

'I found a few good recipe books, recently,' he said. 'The second-hand bookshop up the top of Parnell Street is great.'

'That's great.'

Actual conversation and not about dead people. Huzzah.

He spooned the food to my plate. We talked about music and then films. He talked about gardening. He talked about cricket.

And the whole time, upstairs, there was that picture of Merkin on his desk.

I tried to eat. The meal wasn't bad, although it lacked balls, as Robyn would say. But I couldn't taste the food at all. I could taste the petrol from Merkin's shop in the back of my throat.

With every mouthful, I saw Merkin, crying. And Thora alone at her aunts' place, and the mess she did not want me to see. The disgrace of old age, of not being able to look after herself. And I saw Mark, struggling to get a show together, to try to keep the club alive. Del, juggling his grief for his husband and his full-time job, with working on stage, making people happy.

And I saw Francesca, dead.

Niall Ash, vanished. The posters of his face in drag the only thing left of him.

A silence settled over the table. I realised I'd stopped eating.

'Look, Darrel,' I said.

'Don't.' He stared at his plate. He broke the remaining bread in two, held both parts.

'Sorry?'

'No, don't do that either.' He looked up and smiled, but it never made his eyes. 'You're about to say you only came here to find out anything you could about your friend's niece, and then I would have to tell you I can't talk about the case. I'd remind you that her death was ruled accidental. Then you'll leave, and that will be that, we will never speak about this again. Leave the case alone. Finish the meal, Fi. Stay, have coffee with me.'

The case.

'You like coffee,' he said. 'I know you do. I know how you take it.' He laughed. 'No sugar, right? The stronger the better?'

There was a case – the photo upstairs was from a case. Accidental deaths weren't cases. They were tragic accidents. Ignored missing people weren't cases.

Cases were for crimes. So they didn't think her death was accidental at all. That was a lie—

'And you even buy coffee from that place you work when you could drink it there for free,' he laughed.

He thought he was being charming.

'Nothing is free,' I told him.

'Do you know,' said O'Hara, 'no one I interview buys coffee from their workplace. They don't have to – even the Starbucks baristas don't have to pay for what they drink.'

My fingers felt stiff, angry. I set down the wine. My spine hardened.

'Mind you, everywhere you go you get coffee, don't you?' he said. 'Even when you're travelling. You should see your debit card bill!' He chuckled as he stuffed another piece of naan into his mouth. 'Honestly, I think it's the thing I liked about you first—'

'You liked spying on me? So, this was an interview?'

He rolled his eyes as if I'd said something cute.

'Of course not,' he said.

'You said, *no one you interview*. That means this was an interview. Isn't that against the rules, detective?'

'Oh, come on, Fi, I was just saying—'

I pushed back from the table.

'So, you were going to ask me about Miss Merkin, is that right?' I felt the heat in my glare. 'You asked me here to pump me—' Terrible choice of words, Fi. 'To get me to tell you all her secrets?'

'Why?' said O'Hara. 'What secrets does she have?'

I stood up.

I carried my half-full plate to the counter. I started to turn back but he was there. He was right behind me. He reached his arm around to the side of me and put his own plate on the counter. The smell of curry wasn't nice anymore; it was sickening and strange.

'Fi?'

I pushed away, but he held firm.

I closed my eyes. I started counting.

'Let me go,' I said.

He didn't move. He didn't speak.

He had the same smirk on his face as he had the first day I met him. He'd been standing over the dead body of a drag queen, murdered and left in the rain.

O'Hara had laughed at me when I told him Eve's death was murder. He told me I knew nothing, and I should go back to the shop where I worked and stick to selling cream cakes.

I was done with the frosting.

'Are you investigating Francesca's death?' I said.

'I can't talk ab—'

'You can stand here pinning me to the sink like some big man, but you can't talk about that then?'

He eased his hold, but he didn't step back. 'Fi . . .'

'Are you even looking for Niall Ash?'

'Who's Niall Ash?' O'Hara leaned in around me, his lips to my neck. 'Is this what you like then, Fi? You want to play detective? Is Niall another one of your little friends, so?'

'Niall is Sparkle McCavity,' I said. 'He has been missing now for—'

'Another bloody drag queen, then?'

Putting both hands on his chest, I shoved him back, hard.

'And talking of drag queens' – my knuckles were white where I gripped the sink – 'have you even been to talk to Miss Merkin yourself? Have you seen what was done to her shop, there? Did you get close enough to smell the petrol? Or do you prefer to wait until the queens are actually dead before you take their statements?'

'So you think I should be questioning Miss Merkin?'

'I didn't say that.'

'Your face does. Come on, Fi, you can't trust these people!'

'*These people?*' Anger filled me, overspilling.

'It's not right,' he said. 'And I don't care what you say, I see everything in my line of work and, trust me, you don't know who you're dealing with. Do you even know *her* real name?'

137

His eyes flashed. He clenched his fists. A vein pulsed in his neck.

'I don't understand all this,' he said. 'Men who are women and women who are men . . .'

'You don't have to understand anything,' I said. 'You just have to not be a dick about it.'

I could not have hated him more.

I moved to get my coat. 'I should go.'

'But—'

'Yes,' I said. 'Yes, I know her real name – and don't you come at me with that pronoun crap, you're smarter than that, even if you're determined to stay in the last century,' I spat. 'Her real name is Miss Merkin. Miss M. That's it, end of story. Names are a choice, detective. They're what we choose to represent who we are. You think anyone, *anyone*, calls you Darrel?'

He didn't answer.

'You want a name?' I said. 'You should hear what we call you behind your back. Goodnight, *detective*.'

'I'm sorry I couldn't be any more useful to your little investigation,' he muttered.

I opened the front door. My heels clicked on the path. I pulled on my coat as I went.

'Forget all of them, Fi. They're not like you. They're—'

'Thanks for the meal,' I said, without stopping.

He stepped on to the path. 'I'm not—'

I didn't wait to hear what he wasn't. I walked quickly, listening for his step. As soon as I was around the corner I started to run and I kept running until I was on the platform, my heart still pumping.

I didn't stop looking around me until I was right in the centre of the city, back in the crowds on the street. Home. Surrounded by the scent and the sounds of Dublin's nightlife: the burgers, and the spilled beer, and the drunken cries, and the soft, careful footsteps of those going about their normal business without following mine.

As my mind slowed, I stood and thought. I rested my shoulders against the wall of H&M.

I slipped through the alley to Exchequer Street, and along to the turning for Bride of Life.

I was missing something.

It took me a while to find a gap where I could squeeze through into the thin courtyard space behind the street. The fence was already bent. I took out my phone and photographed it before I stepped through, and then again from the other side. I walked into the dark courtyard lit by a single security light and warmed only by the fading glow from a few curtained windows, high at the top. I photographed them all, those who might have been occupied that day and those who might have been at work in the small studios above the shops. I photographed the yard, and as I worked, I let myself relax, and think.

The fire escape was easy enough to reach. Anyone could climb up and look into Merkin's kitchen, and beyond – just a hint beyond – to her study with the fireplace, and the books, and the old tatty chair. The light was on; a blinking security camera newly fitted at the window.

Well, hi, I thought. You're being careful, now, at least.

And she should be, seeing as O'Hara had it in for her.

Did she really know who threw the unlit bomb? Who wrote that note?

If so, why was she protecting them?

She wasn't just scared, she was terrified. She was so desperate she'd asked me for help – me, a woman she clearly didn't like. And yet there in the kitchen, her tears rolling down her face, she still wouldn't give me a name.

And whatever the verdict, O'Hara didn't think Francesca's death was accidental.

But what if there was a reason he knew that? What was I missing?

I looked down at my feet, to the single spent match stuck in the fire-escape grill.

Chapter Twelve

The club was pounding. The beat was coming through the walls. People were queuing up to get in, the line spilling on to the pavement.

Mark was on the door.

'It's really busy,' I said.

He waved me past the others with a grunt. A Dua Lipa number was just finishing as I pushed through the interior doors. I saw Mae B step back from the stage, passing the spotlight to Del with a sweep of silver glitter.

I breathed in the sweaty, male-drenched air. The crowd was pumped up, the lights spinning from the walls.

I felt the sordid unpleasantness from O'Hara's kitchen slide from my shoulders.

I squeezed through the crowd until I found a space at the edge of the dance floor where I could see the stage.

Del's make-up was different, his eyes bright with a thicker white line along the lower lid, his lashes even longer, and his lips a glossy pinky-purple. He had on his full Marie Antoinette wig and gown, silver and blue. Morning-sky blue, he called it. Lightly puffed sleeves ruffled like satin blossoms. His waist was tightly cinched. It must have hurt him to breathe, never mind move. If

Patrick were there he'd have told Del to loosen the ties, that it was bad for his innards.

The skirt covered the front of Del's hips in a wide circle right down to the floor, but as he turned around, the audience roared to see the folds tucked up as if stuck in his underwear, open to the latticed-hoop boning and long white bloomers beneath.

Del turned to the crowd with his hand over his mouth in mock shame, and then he grinned and winked. The next track was bang on time, and he started spinning very still, very slowly, like the tiny doll in a jewellery box my dad had given me when I was ten. Instantly he wasn't the showgirl anymore. He was precious. He was fragile.

The music had a sharp, quick beat under the fairy-tale pop and, as Del moved, the spotlight slowly centred over him, catching the glitter in his hair and the glint of his corset, and his static, pretty face. It was genius – it was pure wonder.

I watched the next number before I went to the bar. I didn't look at the place where the light stand had been beneath the balcony. I didn't think about the floor, or that Thora told everyone the club should really have been closed for two full weeks in order that Francesca's ghost be given her time to recover from whatever it was she'd gone through. I didn't think about O'Hara. I didn't think about Niall Ash.

With a pop and a whistle, Mae B came back on stage for a new number with Stan. They only just knew the words, but her dancing was pretty good: loads better than when it was rehearsed in our kitchen. Mae B wore the silver dress, one of my favourites, and her silver bob wig, and Stan was down to a waistcoat and shirt, and a red cummerbund over the top of his trousers.

I clapped and cheered with the others. Mae B waved from the side of the stage, and I pointed to the bar. Mae held up her hand in a V, and then three fingers. I ordered three vodkas, each with ice, two with a straw, and Chris grinned, nodding to the stage.

'It's so busy tonight,' I said, shouting over the music.

'Gloria,' said Chris, with a roll of their eyes.

'I've not seen her, is she—'

'Yes,' said Chris, interrupting me. 'Whatever you're asking, she's that and so much more. So, so much more.'

Another track had already started and it was too loud to hear the bar manager's words, so I smiled and nodded, and gestured vaguely at the spiral staircase, in the hope that my gesture said, *Thank you, I'm going up there now*, rather than, *Ugh, look at that, that's where that poor girl died the other week.*

I pushed into the dressing room, calling out, 'Knock, knock,' and keeping my eyes closed as I walked forward.

'You're so polite, doll,' said Del.

'I am not.' I pouted, pretending my offence.

'You are,' he said. 'It's your Englishness poking through.'

'I'm half and half,' I said. 'And you know that.'

'Yeah, and the Irish half of you comes around the back door bringing drinks and the English half of you has to knock, politely, but is coming in anyway whether we like it or not.' He leaned in to kiss me. 'Hey, Fi! I missed you tonight.'

'Hey, yourself! You were amazing down there.'

'Down there, or down there?' He wiggled his highly painted eyebrows.

'On the stage, you great tit,' I teased him.

'Nice coat. Any chance you're actually wearing a dress underneath it?'

I grinned, and tugged my coat belt a little tighter.

'Hi, honey,' said Mae B. She wriggled past and took two of the drinks. 'You survived the dick-tective! Pay you later? Oh, that reminds me, I may have done someth—'

143

Mark pulled her from the room. Mae grabbed a suck on one of the drinks, handing the other to Merkin on the way past as she ran for the stage.

Del patted powder on to his forehead. He scratched his scalp with a pen lid and then retouched his lipstick. At the far end of the room by the wigs on their stands, Gavin yawned. He was curled up in a chair, texting on his phone.

Family.

The hateful detective was wrong. We could be friends without being the centre of one another's worlds. I could just be there, and that was fine. It was easy.

I hugged my arms happily around my middle.

I moved out on to the balcony, but I didn't recognise any of the young men or baby queens there. On the stage, was the infamous Gloria de Bacle, an older queen in a big ruffled red frock with a blond wig, running a comedy routine. She had a thick Welsh accent, and she was quick and really funny, taking on each heckler and shooting them down. The audience were tight in her grasp.

Del moved past me, the Marie Antoinette retired for his little black Chanel knock-off. As Gloria ripped into the front row, Del was already laughing at the jokes. He made his way down the spiral stairs, his mouth wide with glee.

The show was good. Even Gloria was fantastic, whatever Chris had said. What's more, the place was packed.

Merkin did Tina and Whitney and Cher, and Stan did an old song I didn't know, keeping the crowd laughing with him as he over-acted the words, and then Mae B and Del teamed up for a number I hadn't seen before.

The air felt different. The club buzzed with new life, and Thora had never liked change. Under her rule, the club ran the same nights each week. They took it in turns to host. Then on weekends they were all together, all the drag performers.

People enjoyed it, no question. They loved the older queens like they were fond of an elderly relative who had always been in the family, but this was exciting. I'd never seen a performer like Gloria de Bacle before. She was faster than Merkin and meaner than Thora and funnier than Del.

And Mae was on fire.

And Stan was . . .

Yeah. I wasn't thinking about that. I had enough going on what with Merkin and the detective and Thora . . . but Stan was . . .

I blushed.

Stan looked out from around the door. I shifted to the side to make room on the bench. We watched the last couple of numbers with Merkin and Del as they signed off, and then the music changed and the lighting softened around us. I yawned, suddenly feeling as if my limbs were filled with lead. Gavin had the right idea being tucked up in the comfy chair.

'You're tired?' said Stan.

I nodded.

'Long night,' he said.

'Not one of my best ideas,' I admitted.

'You look great,' he said. 'Even with your coat on,' he added, with a wink.

The music swelled.

I laughed. 'I don't think TRASH is ready for me in a frock,' I told him.

'Pardon?' Stan leaned closer.

'The dress?' I said. But the music was so loud. I scrubbed my hands through the air. It didn't matter.

I stretched my spine. *Yeah*, I thought. *A really long night.* I should go. I looked around to the others. Del was surrounded by people. Just inside the dressing room, Merkin was lecturing Gavin about something, their voices even louder than the music. As Mae

145

B made it back up the stairs, a scattered group of young women were already after her with questions ready and phones out.

Suddenly, I felt shattered. All I wanted was to be at home in my little flat with my pokey kitchen and dark window-less bathroom. I longed to take off my bra and pull on a soft fleece top and embrace Netflix and have a cup of tea and a big bar of chocolate.

Stan leaned toward me.

'Great night,' I said, pressing my lips to his ear to be heard. 'You were brilliant.'

'You doing OK there?' he said.

The smell of his aftershave tingled in the air.

'Umm, Stan . . .' I started. Only I didn't really know what I was going to say.

Mark called from the landing, already struggling with a table he was trying to move.

I scrubbed my hands over my eyes. Stan was right, it had been a long, long night, and I was clearly overtired. I shook my head. I waved goodnight to the others. I was done.

Done with death. Done with disappearing queens. Done with all of it.

My head was spinning. Frankly, I wasn't sure my brain was able enough to shape the right words for an actual conversation, never mind one in which I had no idea what I was saying. I needed eight hours' solid sleep, not—

I was halfway down the road when I heard Stan call my name.

'I'm walking that way,' he said, nodding toward the river. 'May I – that is, if it's not intrusive – can I walk you home?'

'I'm fine,' I said. I didn't need looking after. 'Thank you, but—'

He started to nod.

It was so strange. As Stan, he looked nothing like he did out of drag. He stood differently, he moved differently. There was something about him . . . something neither male nor female, and yet at the same time incredibly sensual. It was his mouth, or maybe his eyes, or . . .

He smiled.

He slid one hand into his pocket and rested back on his heels, as if he had all the time in the world and I could just look.

'Sure,' I said. 'That would be nice.'

We fell into step easily. My mind quietened. At the main road, we moved together; I turned down the thin alley, I felt him walking with me. His body next to mine.

I ran my hand through my hair.

He was right there.

Confusion filled my mind with tiny bubbles, each one another question I couldn't quite form into words.

At the archway, I stopped. Stan leaned back against the wall.

We didn't speak.

I stepped closer. His eyes were beautiful. He held more power and more steady dominance in his gaze than anyone I'd ever met – his control was absolute. He didn't move an inch and yet I felt myself pulled forward toward him. I put my hand on his arm.

I stopped. I had no idea what I was doing—

'Fi,' he said. 'Tell me what you want here.'

There were people along the street around us, but I could only see Stan. I couldn't hear anything except the frantic beating of my heart, the sound of my breath – too fast. My lips were nearly touching his . . .

'I don't know,' I said truthfully. 'I think . . .'

But I was done thinking too. I didn't want to think anymore, not about any of it. Not about Patrick, or O'Hara, or Miss Merkin, or . . .

I wanted to kiss him. But Stan was Annie. And she was him. I had never thought of a woman in that way . . . Not that Stan was a woman, because he wasn't . . .

Annie was.

But when Stan looked at me, none of that seemed to matter.

'I d-don't know,' I said, stammering. 'I don't want to be a jerk about it . . .'

'You're not,' he said, in his beautiful, smooth voice. His gaze held mine. It was a slow burn, a promise burn—

Still, he didn't move.

'Well then, Fi,' he said. 'You have a choice there, don't you?'

He smiled again.

'You can turn away and we walk on by, and it comes to no matter at all,' he said. 'Or you can come here to m—'

I met his lips with mine. I kissed him slowly, at first. I found a softness, a sweetness, a power of sheer and absolute magic. His moustache tickled my upper lip. I grinned suddenly, and he laughed with me. He touched his fingers to the side of my face and then the laughter was gone and I leaned in to his body. I forgot where I was, and who I was.

I kept my hand on his chest, feeling the solid binder under his shirt. I leaned deeper, and as I broke from his lips, he sighed, a soft, sweet sigh. His arm came around to the curve of my back and he pulled me to him . . .

He was Annie and she was Stan; their magic ran through me.

We sat on the windowsill of an empty building. We talked for a while. Then the talking went back to kissing and then the kissing went back to talking. And all the time, neither of us looked just down the road to where my door might lead to my apartment. For someone who loved to ask questions, there was one question I wasn't ready to ask.

◆ ◆ ◆

When I finally opened my door I could still hear his words echoing in my mind.

'Sorry,' I'd said, as I finally turned for home. 'I don't . . . I mean, I—'

'Yeah, but maybe not *that* sorry, though?' he'd told me, with a sly grin.

I blushed deep, deep red, as I walked up the stairs. At Mrs Harper's door I kept my footsteps light so I didn't wake our elderly landlady. I imagined how Stan's footsteps would have moved alongside mine and—

And alone in the flat, I closed the door with a click.

'Blimey,' I said, out loud.

I left my jacket on the chair, kicked off my shoes by the electric fire. I was still smiling as I went for the kettle.

A letter had been propped up by the toast rack with a note.

Fi – this arrived this afternoon but Mrs H took it by mistake. She brought it over after you'd left. Rxx

The envelope was battered and torn, stamped *Airmail.*

It was from Patrick.

It had been sent three weeks earlier, by the date on the stamp. The corners were tattered, and the inked sender's name was smudged a little, but it was definitely Patrick's writing, and it was definitely Patrick's name on the back.

I looked away. I couldn't do it. Not again.

When he'd left, I'd lost days crying thick, hot tears – ugly tears – the pain wracking through my heart as I realised what I'd lost by saying the wrong thing, and then by not finding the right thing to say in its place.

I held the envelope closed.

It was too hard.

I never meant to get it so wrong. I thought I was doing the right thing. I really did think he knew how I felt. I hadn't told him in so many words but only because I didn't think we had to do so. It was too early to say those things anyway. And then out of the blue he had a call to go and help with a plane-crash site in South America, and he asked me if he should go. I could have said it then. I could have told him how I was falling for him and how much I didn't want him to leave. Then – oh, the power of hindsight – *then* I could have told him to go on anyway, to do the thing he wanted to do. Because he did, I could see how much he wanted to help, and I could have said that I would be waiting. I would always wait.

But I didn't.

I was an idiot.

I'd let the pause go on too long. I made a joke – I don't even remember what it was I'd said. But the joke fell flat. Then he didn't say anything. He left. He told me he'd call the next day, but I was at work and I missed the call, and then I didn't phone him back because I didn't know why it had gone so weird, and I knew if I did then I'd cry, and I'd ask him to stay—

And then he was really, actually going, and I was at home on my own.

And we'd broken up without ever really being together.

My mind felt like it was filled with a hundred thousand angry bees.

I told him there was no reason *not* to go, that was all – I mean, if they needed him over there, if his expertise could help identify bodies so the families of the lost people could grieve, then who was I to demand he should stay with me just because I'd fallen in—

I swore under my breath. I'd told him, without meaning to, that I didn't care.

And there it was.

I was a total idiot.

The flat was cold and quiet. I opened the window to feel Dublin's shoulder alongside mine.

Why was it down to me, anyway? I would have told him exactly how I felt if he'd asked me. But then Robyn had said guys didn't always say things out loud like girls did, and then Del added gently that, really, I should have at least texted or emailed Patrick after he left so he knew I was just trying to support him. And then Thora told me I was a fool and I'd thrown away the only man who would ever look past my terrible dress sense to the woman I was underneath, and Edna joked how we'd needed a doctor in our friend group. It was forward planning, she said.

And I tried to tell them that Patrick had never actually told me how he felt, either. Not really.

And then it hurt too much and I stopped talking to any of them about any of it.

I'd decided I would move on but it was easier to think that at midnight than it was to stop myself going through the stack of videos on my phone at three in the morning. To stop mooning over the texts he'd sent before the job even came up, and before the uncomfortable gap where I should have said the thing I didn't say. When I made things weird.

And I was right, Patrick could have said it. Then I'd have said it back and then no one would have kissed anyone else under the archway.

A picture burned into my brain of Patrick in the hot mountain jungle kissing some smart pathologist woman who, because my brain hated me, looked a lot like the one from *Tomb Raider*.

I ripped open the envelope.

Hey Fi,

> *I miss you so much – did you get my other let-ters? Not sure if anything is getting through so I asked another pathologist who is heading back to New York if he'd send this.*

I pulled my cardigan around my shoulders and drew my knees up to my chest. The night sounds curled around me.

> *There's no wi-fi here, just a satellite phone for emergencies and it seems like maybe – I hope maybe – this is the reason I haven't heard from you. I keep thinking about you and the stuff we didn't talk about and I'm hoping that maybe when I get back, we can have that conversation?*

I read the rest of the letter with smudged words and blurry eyes. I gripped the pages tightly in my hands as if they might fly away. As I reread them, my phone pinged.

It was Stan.

Just to say goodnight xx

Chapter Thirteen

Niall Ash lived on the third floor of one of the tall new apartment blocks along the river. His car was parked where Annie said
it would be, in the private car park. Each space was marked clearly,
one per flat, the gates closed to outsiders. Under the car, the tarmac
was dry. Wind-blown dust coated the windscreen.

I unlocked the door, doing my best to look like I was meant
to be there while also wearing blue medical gloves so I didn't leave
any fingerprints.

The keys had been left in the locker Niall had used in TRASH,
Robyn said, dropped from his bag, about three weeks earlier. Niall
had called to check they were there, and Mark had put them safely
into the desk drawer in the office for when he came back, which
he never did.

Robyn took them while Mark was on the door, and Gavin
brought them to me at the street corner. As long as they were back
before Mark shut himself away in the office to sort the night's takings, I was grand.

As plans went, it was great.

I looked up at the CCTV camera by the gate, then at the door.

'If you see me, Detective Big Ears, then you're doing your job,'
I muttered. 'And that I doubt.'

The door closed with a softly muted seal, the brushes tempering the solid lock.

I checked the mailbox but there was nothing untoward, no big sign saying *HELP ME I'VE BEEN MURDERED* on the front. No letters from a sick parent, demanding Niall's immediate attendance.

I took the stairs.

The building was massive. So many apartments together, row after row, each door another home, another life. At the third floor I came on to a long, well-carpeted corridor.

CCTV cameras peered at me from every angle. It was posh. The finish was good, the doors clearly labelled, the soundproofing fantastic, compared to ours. There were indistinct mumbles from a television behind one open door and a baby crying somewhere down the hall, but I passed no one.

At the door of apartment thirty-six, I knocked, the sound dulled by my gloves.

'Hello?' I called. 'Hello, Niall? Hello?'

I slid the key into the lock.

'Hello?' I called again as I turned the handle. 'Hi, Niall? This is Fi here. You don't know me but I'm a fr— I know Merkin?'

I pushed the door open, letting it glide over the polished wood floor. I left the main door open and touched nothing. The air felt undisturbed, as if the owner had just stepped out to go to work. I walked through to the little kitchen area and opened the fridge. There was no food in there at all. No milk, no food. Nothing. The shelves had been wiped clean. On the draining board, a vase of tired-looking flowers stood in stale water, their petals brown and dry.

I checked the bread bin and the food cupboard. There was nothing fresh. A selection of herbs and spices filled a shelf, suggesting Niall might enjoy cooking, and the oven had certainly been used in the past, although that too was sparklingly clean. The bin was empty. Clean. Even if someone ditched an old cheese or an open tin of beans before they went away, I might have expected mustard or sauces or something in the fridge.

The main room was lived in but tidy. Thin voile hung against the windows. Modern furniture stood as singular pieces. Ikea rather than Zaha Hadid, but nicely placed. One wall held a large piece of art I didn't really understand; on a shelf stood a bronze sculpture of a woman's body twisted and wrapped in what looked like real pearls.

I edged slowly to the bedroom, careful not to disturb anything. A paper-thin fern on the windowsill had been recently watered.

The bed was stripped, the sheets gone, no duvet or pillows or anything, just the bare mattress.

Something felt wrong. It wasn't exactly off – there were no dead bodies pinned on random lighting fixtures – but it was like seeing a photograph taken from the wrong angle.

A small desk on the opposite wall held a pot of pens, a few bills, a couple of books including the new queer romance Robyn had been reading recently, and a skinny MacBook. I opened the laptop. The password bar popped up. On a whim I tried *SPARKL3* and the lock screen disappeared to show the home screen, the wallpaper a photo of Sparkle in all her glory.

'First time. You may be pretty but you're not that smart,' I said. I clicked on the email, then on Safari, on search history, browser history, then on Facebook, on Instagram, on Twitter . . .

A sound from down the hall made me jump, footsteps pricking at my guilty conscience. What was I doing? Not only had I broken into Niall's flat, but now I was stirring through his private life? I was reading messages from Thora and from Del and—

I clicked on an email to Merkin, one of the last he'd sent.

Not to worry darling, I'll sort that. Nxx

What did Merkin need sorting?

The laptop pinged, emails downloading. Thirty-seven of them.

Merkin: All ok love?

Merkin: I can't seem to get hold of you?

Merkin: Where the hell are you? I have customers here.

Merkin: Everything ok? Call me, please.

Merkin: Darling, whatever it is, please call me.

Merkin: Please, love. I just need to know you're OK. I won't say anything. I know what you did. I found your earring. I know you must be hurting – whatever I did or said, I'm so sorry, lad. This isn't the way. I'm worried about you. Call me. Mxx

Merkin: I said I'd look after you, and I will. But you have to call me. I can't help if you don't call. Whatever has happened, we can sort it out.

I looked for sent emails from Niall to match them but nothing corresponded. Nothing for weeks.

What the hell had he done?

I rubbed my fingers over my eyes. I was overthinking, and massively overstepping the mark of what was acceptable.

By his mirror was an old poster, Sparkle McCavity's beautiful drag face looking down at me. Empty suitcases stood by the desk, tucked behind a bin. The double wardrobe was full of clothes. There was a gap in the middle of the drag rail as if something big had been removed but that might be a dress gone for cleaning or an outfit left at TRASH.

There were no notes on the bedside table suggesting a spurious meeting and nothing written on the slender calendar saying, *Leaving forever now*. He had a massage appointment for the seventeenth. He'd marked TRASH on all the nights he was due to work, up to and including the end of the month ahead. In the bathroom, his toothbrush stood in the mug. A newspaper rested on the edge of the sink, a crossword half done, a pen lying on top.

Something was very, very wrong.

I backed away. I shouldn't be there. What had seemed a bit ridiculous now felt creepy and almost certainly criminal.

My phone rang. Del's number.

'Tell me you haven't broken into Niall's flat on some strange mission to help Merkin?' he said.

'Um . . .'

Del swore. 'Get out of there,' he said. 'Now.'

'There's something wrong here,' I said. 'I don't—'

'Of course there's something wrong but, Fi, you really shouldn't be there. Maybe – MAYBE, FI – it's time to bloody well get out of there?'

I turned to look again at the bathroom. 'OK,' I said. 'Only—'

'Not only,' said Del. 'Not anything. You're breaking the law, doll. Meet me at the office and we can write up your statement.'

'I'm sorry. I'll be there in five minutes,' I told him.

'You'll be a while longer than that,' said Detective O'Hara, from the door.

Chapter Fourteen

An hour later, Del closed the door behind us.

His apartment was a huge relief after the stark grey of the interview room at the gardaí station. I wanted to roll myself into the carefully folded throws and hide my head in shame. I plucked my favourite blanket from the couch, the soft grey cashmere, and pulled it around my shoulders. I sank into the chair by the window, tucking my feet underneath me.

'So,' said Del. He lifted his finger to me. He was really, really cross, and really trying not to show it. He walked around the flat, turning on a heater, dropping his jacket on the back of the couch, kicking off his shoes beside it, pulling at his tie. 'So,' he said again.

His phone rang and in a second his soft, careful voice was gone, and his hard lawyer voice was back, snapping out numbers and letters, sounding in charge and chillingly capable. I wished I could sound like that.

I don't think I was born with an in-charge voice as part of my DNA. My dad had been well able to speak like Del's lawyer voice. Dad never said three words when thirty would do, and he could be heard half a mile away when he laughed. I usually came up with a smart retort three hours after a conversation was over. Dad told me that I was like my mum.

I watched the soft rain coat the window. The cold air tinted the glass. The lights of the square twinkled. The pavement was wet through. It had been too long since I'd come over. I'd avoided the steps, the pavement, the place, but Del was there every day and night, and it was his husband who was shot and killed on the steps.

He stood in the open doorway, watching me.

'Thank you,' I told him again.

He put his hand over the phone. 'You keep thanking me, honey. Don't. It's sorted.'

'Yeah, but th—'

'Hang on, Fi . . . Hi, yes, Del here at number forty-two. Can I get a number six, a number twelve, two number thirty-sixes . . . Do you want garlic bread, Fi?'

'Oh, um—'

'Yeah, a double pack of the garlic bread, please, and two number fifty-nines, oh and . . .'

Del disappeared into the bedroom as he made the order, still rattling off numbers as he pulled his shirt over his head, then returning a few minutes later in sweats and a t-shirt, his feet bare and his hair ruffled, still ordering more food.

I couldn't focus. Even through the guard stuff and the taxi ride, the whole time Del shouted at me for being stupid. I was there in body, but my mind was scrambling to stay connected. It was too much. And despite everything, a tiny part of my head was still in a dark street, under an arch, near my apartment.

Stan's hair had been perfect. Patrick ruffled his all the time, without knowing he did it, but Stan's hair was really soft.

I groaned, pulling the throw over my face.

'What?' said Del, as he hung up.

'I'm a terrible person,' I muttered.

'Yes, we've established that somewhere between running around the yard outside Merkin's shop in the middle of the night in my dress and boots, and being busted out of the gardaí station after breaking the law. But this is something else, isn't it, Fi? You've hardly said a word.'

'I, umm . . .' I blushed.

'What?' He smiled. 'You can tell me anything, dollface.'

'I kissed a woman,' I said.

Del laughed. 'You kissed a Stan,' he corrected me. He opened a cupboard, then stopped. He sighed a long, weary sigh. 'Shit,' he muttered.

'Can I help?' I got up, started toward the kitchen. 'Can I get out plates? Can I make coffee?'

'No, love,' he said. 'It's late and you've probably been drinking coffee all day – your hands are shaking. I just opened the same damn cupboard I open every time, and there's Ben's mug, looking at me.'

'Ah.'

'Big ah,' said Del.

'I—'

'No. No, it's not going anywhere any time soon.'

Ten minutes later, the doorbell pinged.

I hugged him, kissed his cheek, then grabbed my wallet and jogged down the stairs. There was enough food for five people – six if one of them wasn't Robyn. Sitting at Del's kitchen table, we picked and dipped between each box.

I stuffed a forkful of spaghetti into my mouth.

Del was frowning.

'The thing that gets me about Francesca dying,' he said, 'is if the light had been just an inch to the left or the right, chances are she'd have only had a few bruises and maybe a scrape or two, maybe a broken leg. But it was sheer bad luck that pole had been placed where it was and I can't for the life of me remember who put it there. None of us can. And even a thick shirt or fleece might have saved her, from what I could work out – just enough to blunt the spike.'

'Proof,' I said, 'as Thora's aunts keep telling me, that it pays to dress for bad weather in Dublin.'

'If not to dress for killer light poles.'

He opened another box. French fries.

'There were two glasses on the bar that night,' I said.

Del nodded.

'And Francesca's girlfriend won't speak to any of us,' he said. 'I've tried. Merkin's tried a few times now. She said she stood on the step and rang the bell until the lass looked out, but Ingrid didn't come down. She closed the curtains. And I don't blame her, she must be going through hell. But at the same time . . . I mean, I was out the other night and I walked right past her and she turned the other way.'

'Were you in your orange wig?'

'Shut up,' he said. 'You kissed a girl.'

I grinned and broke off more garlic bread. 'I kissed a Stan,' I told him, reaching for the fries.

He opened the last box, a cheesy pasta bake.

'But back to the Merkin and dead-woman-on-a-pole thing,' I said. 'I don't get why Francesca was in the club, alone, and no one seems to be finding an answer for that. And then there's Niall. There was no sign of him being there in his flat . . . Yeah, I know.' I flicked a fry at him. 'I shouldn't have gone there. But people don't just disappear, Del. And, like Francesca, he was really happy in his day job and doing OK in life. He enjoyed the work. He didn't even mind working for Merkin, which would drive me insane. And as Sparkle she lived her best life. Flying up the drag hierarchy and getting work in UK and in Europe—'

'She's a million times more successful than me,' Del grumbled. 'And she's been performing for half the time.'

'She doesn't have an orange wig, though.'

I frowned. The whole situation was weird.

I shouldn't have snooped through Niall's life but everything on his laptop had read as totally normal. Even the messages on Facebook and Instagram that I definitely shouldn't have read were talking about meeting up or about day-to-day stuff.

Nothing, until the emails from Merkin.

Coincidences are rarely coincidences . . .

The disappearance of Niall. The unlikely death of Francesca. The unlit petrol bomb thrown into Merkin's shop. Whichever way I looked at it, the only common denominator was Merkin.

I took another forkful of spaghetti.

Was it Niall who she was protecting?

I dropped my fork back into the pasta.

'Could Niall have killed Francesca?' I said.

'But why would he?' said Del. 'And why do it there if he had? And why on a pole?'

'But either way, what if Merkin thinks he did?'

He didn't answer for a minute. Then he looked sad. 'She'd do anything for him that she can,' he said. 'She'd forgive him, even through a broken heart.'

I nodded. 'And—'

'Merkin would never hurt anyone,' said Del.

'Oh, come on. I've seen her onstage when she's being heckled by drunk straight girls.'

He grinned. 'Well, OK, she'd never physically hurt anyone *that badly*,' he said, amending his words. 'Take her on and you'll find a cat with claws, but behind the scenes, Fi, she's just your average sweet old lady with a broken heart of gold and a tendency to take in a stray pussy.'

'And she'd do anything to protect her family. So, Niall . . . ?'

'She loves him. She thinks of him as her son. Whatever has happened to him, it isn't her.'

'But you definitely think something *has* happened?'

Del didn't answer.

I plucked my fork from the pasta.

'So,' said Del, yet again. Then he looked up at me through batting eyelashes. 'Are we talking about the kiss now?'

'Nope.'

'Why not? I just literally got you out of jail. You owe me.'

'It's complicated,' I said.

'Because . . . ?'

'Because Stan. And because Annie. And because Patrick sent me a letter,' I said.

'Ah,' he said.

'I kissed Stan before I got the letter but . . .'

'Yeah,' said Del.

'Which was fine . . . but then that . . . and now . . . this.'

I stabbed a piece of lasagne, driving my fork into the layers of pasta.

'See?' I said. 'Complicated.'

I closed my eyes. They were sore from trying not to cry while O'Hara had been yelling at me at the station and then from bawling the whole time in the cab with Del shouting at me – after he'd been so calm with the guards, telling them how I was only over there to water the plants and how the key I had was one previously lent to us for doing so, even though we weren't entirely sure where Niall Ash had disappeared to. And anyway, there were no reasons to charge me with anything, as I wasn't doing anything except plant watering, he said. And he made them let me go . . .

'It's OK,' said Del gently. 'Stan. Patrick. It's OK.'

'Nope, I'm pretty sure none of it is OK.' I smiled, my heart somewhere deep inside the lasagne, under the fork's sharp tines.

'Patrick thinks I don't love him, and I do,' I said. 'I always did. But on the other hand I don't know how he feels either. And then I kissed Stan. And it was amazing. It was one kiss and my whole world exploded.'

'Wow.'

'Yeah. Wow,' I said. 'Now there's Stan in my head, and then there's Patrick . . . and I'm pretty sure I shouldn't have kissed Stan, although maybe that's not cheating on either of them because we were definitely broken up – Patrick and me – but also somehow I still feel like it was.

'And then there was my stupid idea of going to dinner with Detective Beige-Sweater so that maybe I could find out what is going on with Niall, and then going to the apartment and now nearly getting myself arrested, if it wasn't for you. And meanwhile, Merkin got a petrol bomb thrown into her work kitchen and I don't know how to help her. And in the middle of all of this mess somehow Francesca got spiked and dead on a pole. And . . .'

I shivered and pulled in a breath.

'And most of all,' I said, seeing Del's face, 'worst of all, honey, I should be here for you, not the other way around. I should be supporting you. Cooking for you. Making sure you don't live off Italian leftovers all week. Shit, I'm sorry, Del. Perspective versus self-pity, eh? You're right. I am OK. I'm a mess but that's nothing new. It's you that . . . that . . . You lost your husband.'

I looked back to the place where the picture of Del and Ben used to stand on the side table.

Del picked an olive from the pack and slid it into his mouth, chasing it with a slug of cold beer. 'Shall we backtrack to the Patrick thing?' he said.

I grimaced.

'So, you do love him?' said Del.

'I messed up.'

'Oh, well sure.'

'Thanks!'

'No.' Del rolled his pretty eyes. 'I mean, you're human. We all mess up. Now, Patrick . . .'

'I thought you'd be quizzing me about the Stan thing,' I laughed.

'Oh, I don't need to,' he said, innocence slathered thick all over his face. 'I heard all about the kiss from Stan the second he got home.'

I made a strangled squeaking sound, and dropped my head into my hands.

Del giggled.

'Could there be something I go through that isn't talked about in the TRASH dressing room WhatsApp group before I have a chance to figure it out myself?' I hissed through my fingers.

'I haven't told the others yet,' he said.

'There's nothing to tell.'

'Annie said it was a good kiss.'

'It was.' I grinned. 'Fantastic.'

'She said you were the one who kissed her?'

I nodded, my face burning behind my fingers.

'So . . . ?' he said.

'Incredible,' I whispered into my hand. 'And Stan's a real gentle-man. And Annie is great, I really like her. But I shouldn't have d—'

'You hadn't heard from Patrick for six weeks, Fi,' said Del. 'You guys were broken up. You didn't make any promises.'

'I'm an idiot,' I told him.

'Yes,' Del teased me. 'And you're also hogging the lasagne. Gimme. But you didn't cheat. Annie knows about Patrick.'

'Does she?'

'Duh.' He took a mouthful, considered it, and then another. 'It ruins eating Italian food when your mum cooks it better,' he grumbled.

'Why not order it from her restaurant?'

'Because she sends me salads rather than pasta and sweet notes in empty boxes reminding me of the calorie count in each slice of tiramisu and how I should go to her for support and not eat my feelings, which is no help at all when I want to eat my feelings.'

'There are no calories in tiramisu when you're upset,' I said. 'Fact.'

'I know, right?'

We sat for a while together at the table as Del picked and grazed between the dishes, I washed up and he boxed away the leftovers. We made coffee, and we put on some music. We talked about other things. Anything. A movie we'd seen together the week before, a gig at The George he was looking forward to, a shirt I'd found at the second-hand shop.

We talked about everything except the things that filled our hearts, and gradually, the pain that had been crammed behind my eyes when I was crying began to loosen and to unknot, and when I finally put on my coat and hugged him, the crease in his forehead had eased and his eyes were less sad.

I walked quickly, but I didn't panic. I knew Del would text Robyn at the club, telling him that I was just leaving, and that Robyn would text him back when I got home, and even though Robyn denied it, that they'd both got me on the 'find my iPhone' thing on their own phones so they could trace me if ever I fell down a rabbit hole.

I slowed as I came past the bank and I almost didn't look at my phone when it rang, figuring it was better to wait at least until I was off the tourist trap before getting out my relatively new iPhone.

It was Del. He spoke quickly. 'The guards are at TRASH right now trying to arrest Merkin. I'll meet you there.'

Chapter Fifteen

I ran down the middle of the thin street. As the club door opened, I could hear Little Mix's 'Going Nowhere'. Cars filled the road. Three large guards crammed themselves into the doorway, two more directed the traffic, steering the lit-up garda cars to the front. More came around the corner.

Two men who'd been walking toward the bar turned around and slipped away into the night, and in the foyer three women pushed out past the guards and hurried down the road, two of them holding hands, the third walking close, her eyes darting back to the fleet of cars with their lights flashing.

Way to go killing the business, O'Hara.

I hurried up the steps.

'No entry,' said a guard.

The music switched to Tina Turner. The intro to 'Steamy Windows', one of Merkin's signature tracks. Ignoring the guard, I shook my head and started up the steps.

'Sorry—' he said.

'We work here,' snapped Robyn. Reaching between the guards, he grabbed my hand and pulled me inside, then straight up the stairs and past the coat check room to the dressing room, Gavin on my other side.

I looked back, hearing Del's voice in the foyer.

'I understand you have my client—'

'Right now no one has your client,' said Detective O'Hara as he came into the foyer from the loud main room. 'Your client h—'

Robyn swung me into the dressing room, closing the door. Gavin and Stan looked really serious.

'Who's dead?' I asked.

'I wish you wouldn't keep saying that,' said Stan.

'You'd be surprised how often it comes up,' Robyn mumbled. 'And again, I can only apologise—'

'We are not responsible for our criminally insane sisters,' said Gavin gently. 'You are not Karen's crime.'

Stan cracked open the door. Detective O'Hara had raised his voice. We could hear him over Tina. I started toward him but Stan placed himself between me and the door.

'Where's Merkin?' said Robyn.

'She's gone to ground but she can't have left the club,' said Stan. 'They came in the door while I was onstage. Gloria was on after me. Mark is refusing to close down the show. It's insane, all these people for one Merkin? It's nuts.'

'Precisely,' said Robyn.

'Merkin was in the wings with her, ready to do Tina,' said Stan. 'She must still be in the building somewhere . . .'

'Who's on now?' I said. 'This is Merkin's track, right?'

'Gloria's taken it,' said Gavin in a flat tone.

'I should go down there. There's a limit to how many numbers even De Bacle can manage,' said Stan.

'Don't you believe it,' said Gavin. 'She'd steal your face, never mind your number. If the world ends tonight all that'll be left are cockroaches, tax collectors and Gloria de bloody Bacle.'

We looked out into the club. The officers were merging with the crowd, but the show was still playing, the performers determined. Stan waved over the balcony rail, holding his hands in the air, and Gloria pointed to the DJ behind us, her finger in the air. 'Run it, bitch,' she shouted. 'Now!'

The music spun straight into Gloria's favourite, a big Barbra Streisand number, and the audience cheered.

Robyn flinched.

The bar manager looked up to us, their eyes wary.

'What can I do?' I said.

'I don't know,' said Stan. 'I can't stop her. She hates kings.'

'Bitch,' Gavin muttered.

'Fi?' said Robyn. 'Do you truly believe that Merkin is in danger? Do you think what's happened to her has anything to do with Niall's disappearance?'

A cold prickle ran over my skin. I put my hand on the balcony bar.

'She hasn't done anything wrong,' I said. 'She's frightened. But O'Hara won't care. He'll take what he can get . . . and the more Merkin that is, the better.' I looked at them all. 'Thing is,' I said, 'I'm not sure O'Hara is a good bloke.'

'You're not sure?' said Gavin, raising both eyebrows.

'Yeah, we're sure,' said Robyn.

'No, I mean—'

But it was one thing thinking it, it was another altogether telling people a detective in the guards might have killed, and might well kill again.

'He's setting her up?' said Gavin.

'Yes,' I said. 'I think so. He'll do whatever he can to pin her down. He doesn't need the truth, he'll twist whatever she says.'

And as long as he had her for something, he wouldn't care what it was. Murder. Kidnap. Wasting police time. He just wanted to win. He didn't understand, he'd told me – but it was more than not understanding, because saying that would imply he was trying. He didn't want to know. He didn't want to hear. He was pissed at us because he'd been humiliated over Eve's murder back in the summer, and he was ready to take the first opportunity he could to fight back.

'She'll do whatever she can to protect the ones she loves,' said Robyn.

'And he'll do whatever he can to lock her up,' I said.

'It doesn't make any sense,' said Gavin.

'It doesn't have to,' Robyn told him. 'It's happening.'

'Then we should give her a chance to get herself ready,' said Stan. 'Not let him haul her out of here with this mob, that's not fair. We have to find Merkin before he does.'

Gavin took the dance floor and the storerooms. Robyn took the office, the attic and the weird upstairs rooms, while Stan went to the stage. I got the basement. Down the thin and dusty back stairs, two floors below the heaving dance floor, the beat rumbled through the walls and into the handrails. Nothing was shiny down there; the building was like someone incapable of hiding their age once they'd removed their clothes.

I knew Merkin was there before I found the first feather.

It took exactly three minutes to follow the trail of sequins. At the door, a smear of body glitter ran over the edge. As hideaways went, it wasn't great.

I texted Robyn, then knocked. Inside, Merkin stood with her back to the wall. She didn't look up. Her nails littered the floor around her. Her wig was laid carefully on the small table in the corner. Her own hair stuck up where she'd run her fingers through it in haste, and there were flakes of glitter falling everywhere.

'You'd think a six-foot-tall drag queen would be easier to find,' I said.

I closed the door and leaned against it.

'You OK?' I asked her.

'Not really, no,' she said.

I winced at the stupidity in my question. Merkin kept picking off the glitter, faster and faster. Her skin was red and sore. I crossed the room, refusing to let myself falter.

She kept picking and picking . . .

I put my hand over hers. I could feel her shaking. She stood as strong as ever, but grief was written in the lines of her face, in every shadow in her eyes; as she spoke, her voice was snappy but she lacked her usual caustic bite.

She looked up. She was afraid. 'How long have I got?' she said.

'They're here,' I told her. 'They're looking for you now. Del can make them see you haven't done anything wrong. O'Hara's just willy-waggling. He's a bully. You have to stand up to bullies. He has nothing on you because you haven't *done* anything. If you just tell them what you know . . .'

'No,' she said.

'You haven't hurt anyone,' I said. 'I don't believe it.'

Merkin smiled. 'Guilt is a funny thing, Fi,' she said. 'You run around town thinking everything is black and white, taking lovely pictures for your blog and falling on the truths that everyone else can already see. But truth takes different shapes, depending who you are.'

I stood back.

'If I don't stop this, then who's next?' she said. 'Thora? Del?'

'No one needs to be n—'

'I've had a good time.' She swiped the back of her hand over her eyes. 'I'm not complaining. And it was my fault. I loved him like a son, too much to see what was happening. I don't know what I did but—'

'Please,' I begged her. 'Please let Del handle this. They can't shut you away for doing nothing.'

'Read your history books, little girl.'

'But we can make them see sense and—'

'Everything has a price, Fi,' she said, wearily. 'You remember the note? He'll destroy the ones I love. I won't let that happen.'

'You're being stubborn,' I told her.

'I'm doing the only thing I can do and I don't expect you to understand,' she said. 'And what's more, Fi, I refuse to let you or anyone else, stop me.'

The door opened a crack and Robyn came in. He brought clothes and wet wipes. He gestured to the door, and I moved to hold it closed.

'You don't have much time,' he said to Merkin. 'What else do you need?'

'My phone and my drugs,' she said quickly.

'I don't think they're going to let you smoke a joint in the station,' I said.

Robyn shot me a look.

'Not drugs as in the fun stuff – drugs as in medication. I have HIV,' said Merkin.

'Oh,' I said. 'Oh, um . . .'

'Don't tell me you're sorry, little girl,' she said. 'I don't want to hear it.'

Pulling wipes from the pack Robyn brought, Merkin set to her face, wiping until she was clear. Robyn took a brush and moved behind her, starting on her hair. When he was done he took another wipe, gently stroking it over on her shoulders. Neither spoke. Upstairs, the beat carried on. I turned away as she changed into the loose trousers, t-shirt and cardigan, and the simple slip-on shoes.

The walls judged me.

'I didn't mean—' I said.

'No one ever does.' Merkin brushed down the plain t-shirt, wrinkling her nose in disgust. 'Christ, I look like your one from *Prisoner Cell Block H* already.' She took a breath, stood steady. 'I have to take my pill every evening, Fi. Not a big deal. I take my pill, and I carry on. U equals U. *Undetectable is untransmittable*, see?' She plucked another wipe and scrubbed at her face again, running the soft cloth under her red-rimmed eyes. 'It's my status, not my life, honey. I picked up the new prescription the other day – it's in my bag upstairs.' She set Robyn back from her and brushed down her t-shirt again. 'Right, so. I think I'm ready as I'll ever be.'

Miss Merkin smiled.

There were a hundred things I wanted to say but none of them were right. I crossed the floor and reached up and kissed her on her cheek, ignoring the sheer horror in her eyes.

'What the hell was that for?' she said.

'Fi kisses girls now,' said Robyn. 'She can't help it.'

I spluttered.

'Come on. I'll get your bag,' Robyn said. 'You should h—'

Noises came from the stairs, angry footsteps pounding in angry shoes. Merkin's face blanched, fear rippling through her. She gripped Robyn's arm.

'Not here. I need to talk to Del first,' she said. 'I need two minutes, before they shut me away.'

'But you haven't done anyth—' Robyn tried.

'I'm going to jail, pet,' she said. 'Because that's what you do if you care about someone. If you know they would never have done what they did unless . . .'

She waved her hand through the air as if to scrub away her words.

'Please,' I said. 'If you know who it is who killed Fran and—'

'Not the time, darling,' said Merkin. 'That time is long gone now. I've made up my mind. I dare say you'd be doing the same in

173

my position.' She smiled, and touched her fingers to my hair. 'At least I'm not wearing a fleece, I suppose.'

Someone shouted along the corridor.

'Fi, can you—?' said Robyn.

'Sure, yes. Wait – can I what?' I asked.

'A diversion, honey? Just do something – make some noise. Stop them long enough for us to get around the back stairs. We can go up through the back of the stage. Del can meet us in the dressing room.'

I hurried through the door.

I had absolutely no idea what to do.

The footfall came closer.

'Shit.' I peered around the corner.

The detective led the way. The guards filled the staircase, pushing out over the banisters.

Taking a deep breath, I shot off toward the guards in a run. Behind me, I heard the storeroom door open and close, footsteps hurrying away. I spun my arms and shrieked like a banshee – I just had to be loud enough and annoying enough to stop him for a few minutes. It wasn't like Merkin was escaping. She knew what was going to happen. I was giving her time to do it gracefully, that was all.

Detective O'Hara rounded the bottom of the stairs.

'Where is he?' I said loudly, staring right at the big-nosed knobhead.

'Who?' said O'Hara.

'Hah!' I gave my very best affronted queen laugh. 'Is that you, then? Detective?' I let my voice whine and pierce the weird quiet of the basement. Behind the guards, Del peered around the corner. He stared at me, his mouth open, but I didn't take my eyes from O'Hara's. I could do this. I could make a scene.

My pulse beat hard in my neck, my mouth was dry.

'How could you?' I started crying, loudly, still shaking my arms up and down. 'How could you do this . . . ?'

'Out of the way, please, Miss McKinnery.'

'So, you're happy enough to try to shag me, then, but, oh no, heavens, no, you can't have a conversation!'

The young guards were smirking. They stopped on the stairs, looking between him and me.

'That's it, is it?' I shouted. 'You're just done with me? Just like that?'

I planted both feet in the middle of the corridor and waved my hands some more as I shouted. O'Hara rolled his eyes. He was clearly doing his best not to look as angry as he felt.

'You think it's OK to have me at your house for dinner?' I said. 'You're OK with dry humping me at your kitchen sink . . .'

One of the young guards giggled.

'You think you can just swan in here now, and . . . and . . .' I was running out of words. Out of ideas.

I saw Del nod, suddenly realising what I was doing. He turned and raced up the stairs.

I couldn't think of anything else to say.

'Argh!' I screamed. 'Arggghhhh!' I let the scream go long and loud. 'How could you?'

'Fi, I don't understand what you're asking me,' said O'Hara.

'Then do you even understand anything?'

I was making no sense whatsoever.

'It's like you're always here,' I said. 'You're always arresting someone . . .'

Getting lamer by the second.

'What?' he said.

'And . . . and . . .' I glanced behind me. Seeing my stumble, the guards started to move past the detective, past me.

O'Hara bent down, whispered into my ear.

'Never run from a predator, Miss McKinnery,' he said. 'Unless you want to get a charge of obstruction?'

The guards were searching the rooms.

O'Hara rocked back on his heels. 'Where is Miss Merkin?' he said. 'And please keep in mind I could be a great deal more upsetting to your little friend if I wanted. After your scene here, darling, I can make your life a living hell.'

He'd get her anyway. I sighed.

'She's upstairs,' I muttered. 'In the dressing room.'

'And that performance was, what, to give her time to get away?'

I didn't answer. He wouldn't understand, because he didn't want to.

'See here, Fi McKinnery,' O'Hara hissed. 'Don't flatter yourself that I have any interest in you at all.'

I let my eyes travel down his body, resting my gaze on his barely noticeable interest. Thora or Merkin would have known what to say, but O'Hara was long gone before I opened my mouth, and I found myself alone in the basement with the fallen sequins.

Chapter Sixteen

Back home, hours later, I slumped into the chair by my window. The thin tick of the alarm clock was a constant metronome against the mess in my head. My shoulders were tense, my knuckles white, my jaw aching. My skin felt raw. Exhausted, my eyes still stinging, I watched the river.

'A young woman died here.' That's what the garda said as she cleared us from the dressing room. 'Surely that's the most important thing?'

They'd tried, all of them, but the night was already lost. There was nothing like a bunch of burly cops descending on a nightclub to kill the buzz.

Robyn had stayed behind to help Mark. Del went to the station to help Merkin, to be seen to be there as much as to actually be there, he told us, so the detective knew that whatever he did he was being watched and would be accountable.

I was alone. Even the Liffey was quiet.

I read the letter from Patrick again. I thought about texting Stan, as if those were the only two actions my brain would allow me.

Merkin hadn't killed her niece. I didn't believe it. She certainly hadn't attacked her own shop with an unlit petrol bomb, but she was an easy fit and O'Hara was determined to make the pieces of the puzzle spell her name. And she'd do whatever she believed was the right thing to do, to protect her family.

Merkin obviously believed Niall had killed Francesca. She tried to contact him. She tried to cover for him. There was no reason at all that any of this made sense, but nothing any of us could say had changed her mind. She would admit to anything, she said. She was done fighting. She was tired.

Francesca had died with the note in her pocket, instructing her to meet someone at the club. Niall could easily have written that but O'Hara didn't want to look past Merkin to find anyone else.

O'Hara was like a child playing with block toys: he needed a square shape to fit in the square hole, and a star shape to fit in the star hole, but he'd found a triangle that they could squeeze through both and that was enough for him. Boxes ticked, numbers done; a Merkin-shaped murderer in a killer-shaped hole. He'd figure out the details later.

I yawned. I stared at the bridge without seeing it. The light flickered over the water. People crossed now and then, walking fast, getting out of the way of the late night. I pulled my camera to my knee but I was too tired to lift it.

I wanted to go to Merkin wherever she was and wrap my arms around her and fend off that rotten dog of a detective.

I didn't know what to say. HIV was out there, we all knew it, but she was the first person to tell me they had it. I'd googled $U = U$. I read until I understood: with medication, HIV is completely manageable and untransmittable. It wasn't like it used to be, like the scary adverts from the nineties.

To tell her I was sorry felt lame, and like I would be saying there was something to be sorry *for*, but even after reading all this stuff, I still felt like I should say *something*. I wanted to know more, and to talk to her. To ask a million new questions.

I ran my fingers through my hair, remembering how Robyn had brushed Merkin's. How each of the TRASH family had done what they could for their aging matriarch, however bitchy she was with everyone. None of them agreed with her actions but they loved her, so they supported her.

I pulled another cardigan around my shoulders. Without sleep I'd be ruined for work, but it didn't matter. Merkin would be stuck in that horrid interview room, or in a cell.

She was one of the strongest people I'd ever met, but however fond she was of Niall, if he had really killed Francesca, taking the blame for him didn't make sense to me. She gave us no reason. Why would he kill Merkin's niece? People didn't just throw other people off balconies.

But love makes us do screwy things. What would I do for my friends? For Robyn? For Del? What would I have done for my dad?

Merkin could fight with words and fists. She was the first to throw a shitstorm into the wind if her make-up was touched while she was onstage. She'd never been backward about coming forward. She was outspoken about the show and her drag and about dresses and fit – and in TRASH she would squeal and squawk about any number of tiny details, from the lighting to the curtains to the quality of the water in the dressing room.

But she didn't speak her mind or her heart about Real Life. Not ever. I didn't know what books she liked or what music she listened to, or what way she voted at the last election. I'd heard her grumbling about the lack of seating in the middle of Dublin once and the lack of outdoor space for young people, but I hadn't even known she had a niece – I only vaguely remembered she had a sister.

She'd told me she had HIV. She'd shared this really personal information with me, and I'd left it hanging in the room.

I started to text Del.

I frowned at the blinking phone screen for ages. Then out of the window. Then at the wall.

The world carried on, and no one cared if an old queen was in the gardaí station, and no one cared that Del hadn't slept again and would still have to go into work the next day and fight for other people's rights, or that Robyn was going with his ma to visit his sister at the prison that afternoon, or that Thora was trying to cope with her aunts, in any which way she could.

And so the river flowed . . .

Please would you tell Merkin thanks, I wrote. I didn't say the right thing but I wanted to. Give the big-nose detective a kick from me. I'm here if you need me. Always. xx

Del is typing . . .

The minutes went on and Del was still typing.

I got into bed. I left the window open, just a crack. The reply came as I was falling asleep. Two lines.

She says don't thank her, just get out there and find Niall, check he's OK. I say DON'T. Let the guards handle it. And don't do anything stupid, I have enough trouble with one of you here, not both. Love you. Always. xx

I closed my eyes, still listening to the sounds outside. I should have waited for Robyn to make sure he was OK getting back, but the last thing I remembered was hearing a man shout in the street that he was a knight, that he was a magician, and that he really needed a pee, before the world slipped away into darkness and sleep covered me like a thick blanket, closing me from the world.

◆ ◆ ◆

I walked through a dream world of grey. I pushed forward knowing only that I had to keep walking, not where or why. I could hear something pretty, a high sparkling, tinkling noise like a hundred thousand wind chimes, but I couldn't reach it. I drifted between pewter-coloured sheets trying to find the thing I wanted: Stan's kisses – the way Patrick looked at me – Stan's body – Patrick's hold – Stan's chuckle – sitting on the grass by the plane trees at Trinity alongside Patrick, with my hand in his, knowing how much I wanted to touch him all over and how much he wanted to touch me – sitting with Stan on a windowsill under the archway—

The paths kept changing.

Patrick became Stan, and then Stan became Annie . . .

And all the time, Niall Ash was laughing at me from a poster as it peeled from the wall, and Francesca's ghost pointed at me, turning the spotlight toward me, and telling everyone that I was falling over the truth and I was the one who couldn't figure anything out, who had no idea even what she wanted.

I woke with my stomach in knots. I grabbed for the alarm clock but it slipped from my fingers and fell to the floor. Its battery casing shattered and the battery skimmed over the rug. The tick stopped.

That was the problem with living interesting lives, Del often said. Only a year ago the most exciting thing that happened to any of us was watching the season finale of *Bake Off*. Now, after a murder and a mad bomber, none of us slept very well.

I rubbed my eyes. It was six in the morning and I'd been asleep less than an hour but I could hear something. A jingling. I fell out of bed and stumbled out of my room.

The back wall of our little sitting room was covered with a deep red throw that had been duct-taped to the ceiling. A stool had been placed in the middle. A table beside it was set with a spikey wooden structure that might once have been our clothes airer, now hung with twinkling fairy lights, and my lava lamp that usually lived on the sideboard. On the kitchen table stood a tower of books and a small Lego structure on top that looked for all the world like a picture frame.

I was clearly still dreaming.

'Fi?' Robyn stuck his head out of the kitchen, his face made up in full drag, his hair taped back from his forehead. 'Oh good, you're up,' he said. 'I didn't want to wake you.'

I pointed at the wall. 'What are y—?'

He stuck his phone in the Lego picture-frame thing and connected a lead to his laptop.

'Coffee?'

'It's really early.' I blinked as he put on another light.

'I know. I'm sorry, honey.'

He flicked on the kettle and reached for my mug. He was moving really quickly, still dabbing powder to his neck and chest.

Robyn was never up at six. Seven was fine, it was the time we usually aimed to get up before work – and mostly missed by another hour at least – but six was dark. It was sleepy time.

I went into the bathroom.

I was exhausted but if I went back to bed then all the things that had been running around inside my brain would stir up again and rampage around in my anxiety, being pointy and demanding. Sometimes, being awake was the gentler option.

So.

I brushed my teeth.

Pulling back the shower door I turned the water on hot, scalding my skin until I couldn't think.

The bathroom door inched open a tiny bit.

'You naked, sweetie?' Robyn called.

'I think so,' I said from behind the curtain. 'I usually am in the shower.'

'Any chance you could pause the shower for about twenty minutes? It's picking up on the mic. I'm really sorry.'

I wrapped my towel around my middle, still not understanding. He had his hands firmly over his eyes.

'I'm a terrible human,' he said. 'I'm really sorry.'

'Go, it's fine,' I said. 'All done.'

Robyn was rushing around the flat, his boa in one hand, his wig in another. His laptop now pointed at the throw, a round light behind it, a microphone taped to an old wooden hatstand he'd borrowed a while ago from the club. All around the little circle was every light we owned, including my bedside light, pointing to the space in front of the red backdrop.

It was still six in the morning. I closed my door behind me.

A mug of the good coffee and piece of cold buttered toast were waiting on my desk, along with a note: *Sorry xx.*

The music started. I peered into the main room.

There. Ready. Mae B was in the house.

Sitting on the round stool, she wore a mauve-and-pink striped foil dress with a boat neck, the shiny fabric clinging to her skinny frame and big boobs. She had bare feet and no tights, but her wig was enormous. Waves of red piled high, like flames. Her earrings were insane – clip-on dangly things dotted with rhinestones. Her make-up was slightly different to usual with a bigger lip and huge doe-shaped eyes. The dimple in her chin told me she was trying something new and exciting.

'Hello, hello, hello, Australia!' she said. 'It's Mae B here from Dublin!'

I smiled, happily. It's not every day I got to start the morning with a live drag performance in my own home.

'Everyone's favourite Dublin queen,' said a voice from his laptop with a gorgeous Australian accent.

The music started. ABBA.

I laughed, covering my mouth with my hand. Bloody ABBA! Mae B grinned, and low down, under where the camera would see, she flicked me a single-fingered gesture.

I watched the first two numbers. I usually agreed with Del that the only time for an ABBA song was at Pride, or when you were so drunk you could no longer remember that any other songs existed. Or preferably both. But this was way beyond taking anything seriously. This was hilarious. Deliberately.

Very different to Thora, Mae B used her hands more as the songs went on, almost vogueing as she lip-synched. I watched as she finished the chat with the host on the other end of the line.

The last song was a number by Tiffany that I vaguely remembered from an Eighties Hits CD we'd picked up from some thrift store. Mae B tossed her hair at the hook. With her feet, she nudged a fan I hadn't noticed under the table, clicking the button with her big toe, and her wig streamed back behind her. She was brilliant.

I utterly adored her.

She twisted her upper body, constantly using her hands and her face. After the host had applauded her with enthusiasm, the line disconnected and she flumped back against the wall, and I broke into very sincere applause, cheering my wonderful friend.

Mae B opened one eye.

'I'm really sorry I woke you,' she said. 'I don't even know how I thought I could do it without disturbing you. In fact, I'm not entirely sure why I thought I could do it at all.'

'Rubbish, you were so great,' I said. 'And . . . ABBA?'

She stood up, knocking the microphone, and I moved to help her dismantle the lights.

'Merkin's gig,' she said. 'Pre-arranged. It was fun. Although, it's been a while since I went the full ABBA. Ugh, I'm so tired. Del called at quarter to four when Merkin remembered. One hour to do this . . .' She ran her finger in front of her perfect face. 'Still, money in the bank, eh?'

'Oh, does it pay well?' I shifted a box of Diet Coke cans that had raised the laptop and helped her move the books.

She chuckled. 'See the empty box of lashes on the table there?'

'Yeah.'

'The fee almost covered the cost of them.' She peeled off her wig and turned so I could unzip her dress. 'But it's different. It may lead to more work,' she said. 'They seemed to like me.'

'You're hot in Oz?'

'Oz indeed,' she said, carrying her laptop back into her room. 'Without any disappointing wizards standing behind curtains.'

'I always thought it would be nice there.'

Mae B didn't say anything.

Dress and wig on the floor, Robyn was standing in the middle of the room, his phone in her hand.

'What?' I said.

He showed me the phone screen.

'This is weird,' he said. 'Annie just sent me a message. She says Niall texted her in the night. Look . . .'

The forwarded message struck out of the little screen.

Stop calling please, I'm fine, I'm staying with this guy I know, we're really happy, please respect that I no longer wish to see you. from Sparkle McCavity.

'It's like the other one. Is that Niall's usual tone? His emails were nothing like that.'

'I have no idea,' said Robyn.

'Weird,' I said.

He nodded. 'And that's coming from a man in full make-up before breakfast and a woman who can't sleep because she kissed a man who is also a woman but also a man, and she's in love with another man who isn't here and also kind of falling for the man who is actually a woman.'

I blinked. 'Helpful,' I told him. 'Thanks, honey.'

'I thought so. She's coming over now, actually,' he added. 'That's OK, isn't it? She sounds upset.'

'Can you ask her to get—?'

He grinned. 'She's already at Starbucks. She's just asked how you take it.' He lifted one eyebrow.

Chapter Seventeen

I mulled over Niall's text throughout the morning. By lunchtime, as I picked up Thora's shopping, I was certain the short message was the clue to figuring out this whole mess. Not that I had it totally figured out yet, but it felt like a key. It was a piece of the puzzle. A condiment jar.

The aunts' house was dark and gloomy behind its Victorian railings. The tall windows were dull, the grills mean against the peeling paint. Along the row, Del's building was lit from the basement to the attic, and next door, the nosy neighbour had all his lights on. The aunts' home was more like a dilapidated gothic mansion than a smart Dublin town house. It clung to its bleak, shabby age.

I wondered how Merkin had slept, or if she had slept at all, and where they were keeping her.

The front of the basement and the fourth-floor windows of the aunts' house were boarded. Three floors were enough, the aunts told anyone who asked. But Agnes would always glance up at the ceiling when she said so, and trace the sign of the cross over herself, while Flo would tell anyone who stood still for long enough about the spirits – the ghosts who haunted the upper floors of the old houses. The old, unhappy souls, trapped between the walls. The servants who lived and died there, who plagued her at night, calling and screaming and shouting through the veil, keeping her from her sleep.

As much as I tried to laugh it off, down in the kitchen with the gurgling pipes and the knocking walls, Flo's stories were starting to freak me out.

I was there three minutes before she started on about the spirits again.

'They're getting worse,' she whispered as I emptied the bins in her room. 'It used to be only now and then. It was terrible bad when the old lady next door was alive, God rest her soul. They cried through the night and it used to make me cry with them. But then it quietened, and I thought . . . Come here and I'll tell you.' She patted the chair beside her bed, reaching for me.

I took her hand. 'I can't really be too long today,' I said. 'I'm really sorry—'

'They are unhappy,' she said. Her watery eyes filled with tears and her cold fingers curled around mine. 'They don't approve of our Daniel, you know. I'm sure that's what it is. I don't know what to tell them. I don't know what we did to deserve him.'

'You got lucky, Aunty. And he's not doing anyone any harm,' I said. 'Lots of people really like drag. I do.'

'The spirits don't understand, though,' she said, genuinely upset. 'They never did understand all that . . . nonsense. I hear their cries, long and angry. They're from a different time, you see, dear, and . . .'

They were and she was, I thought. A different time and a different way. And the fact was that the aunts spent all their pensions on sweet sherry and dog treats, while Thora used her drag-earned money to keep them warm and out of an old people's home. And both aunties chose to ignore that it was Thora's TRASH friends who were coming over to help them every day. Including Del – the old ladies' favourite – who was the most fabulous and outrageous queen I've ever known.

But then as Edna said about Karen, it's always easier if it's someone else's child and not yours.

I ran a cloth over the table.

'Did you see the state of him today, though?' said Flo. 'That blouse was one of mine, you know. He says it isn't, but I know the collar. I had it made for me when I was courting with Frank Marshall from the Electrical Company. Daniel has no right to mock me so.'

I hid my smile at the thought that anything the tiny little old lady once wore would ever fit Thora's wide shoulders.

'Maybe it's a different shirt in similar fabric?' I suggested gently. 'Thora is—'

'Daniel,' Flo corrected me. 'His name is Daniel.'

Yes. And also, Thora.

'Sit with me, Fi,' said Flo.

'Just for a minute. I'm on lunch hour and I can't be late,' I said. 'Del is coming in later to do the vacuuming and Robyn is picking up a big shop for you tomorrow from Aldi if there's anything more you need that's not on the list.'

'But they want to tell us something,' said Flo. 'We have to listen or it'll get louder and louder.'

'Who does? Who are they?'

Flo scrubbed away my words with her stiff fingers. 'The spirits, dear,' she said.

'Do you still have the lesbian there?' Agnes shouted from the next room.

'It's me, actually,' I called back. 'I'll be with you in a minute . . .'

'We should get out the board,' said Flo. She lifted her chin and set her bottom lip in a thin line, no different to her nephew's trademark move. 'They won't stop until we do.'

'The board? Oh, I don't know . . .'

But I already knew that I didn't want to do it. The way her eyes darted to the ceiling again, the way she gripped my arm with her spare hand. She was freaking me out.

'The Ouija board,' she said.

'Ah.'

'Del promised he'd go up to the attic for it if you agreed and—'

'Why me?'

'You're a woman,' she said. 'They always liked a fertile woman to talk to.'

'Oh, well now, I don't think—'

But I wasn't paid to think. Actually, I wasn't paid at all, and Flo wasn't done talking.

'You're perfect for them,' she said. 'Don't you worry now. You have a hint of a young Aggie to you.'

'Don't talk shite,' said Agnes, clearly listening from just outside the door.

'It's not really my scene,' I told them yet again. 'That spooky stuff.'

'The dead are everyone's scene,' said Flo. 'I'll tell Daniel you said yes.'

I stood up, pulling gently away to pick up the tied bin bag. 'I'm not sure I believe in that kind of thing,' I said.

And more to the point, I had absolutely no intention of finding out.

'Fi?' said Flo.

But I backed away, smiling as I moved, trying to ignore the chill in my spine.

I finished up for Agnes and popped into the front room to say a quick hello to Thora, and then I was gone, grimacing at Del as he hurried past me on the way in with his arms full of clean laundry. He twisted his hips to the Duke Ellington music coming from next door.

'This way for today's unpaid housemaids, is it?' he said.

'Only for the brave,' I told him. 'Did you get any sleep?'

'Of course not. You?'

'Is that Del?' Agnes called over the banister. 'Flo says can you stop the lesbian? The spirits want her to do something.'

Waving as I moved, I hurtled back down the long street. Not that I minded helping out, but I drew the line at housekeeping for dead people as well as live ones.

I made it back to Jenkins and Holster with a minute spare. Glugging water from my flask, I left my bag and my coat in a heap and pushed my hair out of my eyes, fully aware I looked like a partially boiled hamster, but a hamster who was determined not to get fired.

I caught my breath, but when Mr Jenkins slipped out to make a visit to a supplier, I left my station for just long enough to make myself a latte and hide it back down under the till, sipping whenever I could, letting out tiny sighs as I felt the rich darkness fill my veins.

'You drink too much coffee,' Mickey sniped from behind his counter.

'Sure,' I said.

I'd have thought that much was obvious.

'He doesn't like it when you do that,' said Mickey. 'When you drink it from your till.'

I drained the tall cardboard mug and licked the foam that still hung around the rim. It was good coffee, even if I did have to pay for it. Not every job gave you good coffee. I should know. I was applying for everything I could.

Ignoring Mickey, I made another an hour later, and slowly the afternoon inched past and the clock made it to five. Stuck inside my head, I walked home through the busy streets, thinking about everything.

Merkin. Niall. Merkin. Sparkle. Merkin. Francesca.

Flash: Francesca, spiked on a lighting pole. Dead.

Flash: O'Hara's hands—

I shivered.

Everywhere I looked, Halloween decorations darkened my mood. At the corner shop, the doorway had a banner of plastic white ghosts with open-mouthed screams. At the shoe-fixing place there was a wailing hag that reminded me all too much of looking in the mirror.

I crossed the road.

Merkin was doing OK, Del said in a group message thread, cheerily titled, *DON'T PANIC*. They'd kept her at the station, but she was all right. He'd contacted a lawyer friend of his who was a hundred per cent meaner than Del was, and she was working to get Merkin to see sense and not to let her admit to anything she hadn't done.

I skipped past a lorry and my foot slipped into a puddle.

I just wished I could do something to help.

Find Niall, she'd said. But how?

I scrubbed my fingers through my hair as if it might help me think. I walked down the alleyway, under the archway—

The archway.

And then there was my own messy life.

Stan kissed like no one I'd ever kissed before. His lips were soft but strong – his moustache tickled me, but his hands . . .

Oh my.

But Stan was Annie. The man in the moustache who kissed me was also the woman who brought coffee to our apartment in her

192

leggings and running top, unmistakably a woman. He was she but she was he. It was both really confusing and yet also very simple. And incredibly sexy . . .

But then, there was Patrick.

I reached my front door no clearer.

I should call Annie. I needed to explain. And I needed to write to Patrick too. It was time enough to stop being pathetic. To woman up, and to at least be honest with myself. Just as soon as I figured out what it was that I felt.

I turned on our little heater and changed into my latest comfort fleece – a knee-length fluffy pink creation with ears on the hood and a tail at the back, a bargain from the fifty-cent basket in the charity shop on Aungier Street. I opened a can of soup and sat up on the counter by the hob, spooning the soup straight from the pan as it warmed.

I should do it right away, I decided. I'd call Stan and write to Patrick. Or maybe I should sleep on it. Do it the next morning. Soon, for definite.

And then I'd stop thinking about ghosts.

Mind you, if ghosts really existed (not that they did) then sure, couldn't Francesca tell us what she was doing at TRASH? Could Elvis pop in and sing us a little song with Judy Garland? Could da Vinci confirm if the Mona Lisa is himself there in drag? Could Shakespeare dictate me a post for my blog?

It was a farce.

And Flo talked about it like it was a shopping mall where all the spirits just hung around and anyone could come through on her Ouija board and call down to her. If that were the case, how would anyone know the dead were telling the truth? What if the spirit we got talking to was a real knob? If they'd lived their lives as a bit of an arse, then why would that be any different if they were dead?

Dumping the empty soup pan in the sink, I went to my room. I stood at the cold window, watching the river. I'd spent so many hours gazing at that one stretch of the water. The ghosts who walked the Liffey walls would have a song and a half to their names. For hundreds and hundreds of years, souls had lived and died alongside those muddy waters. Every one of their stories would be truly legendary.

Stories had a way of changing, over time. A man who fell to his death in a river, beaten by a bitter foe, might leave the silent shadow of his murder in his killer's blood for the rest of that life. Niall might have run away with a handsome prince. Or a celebrity. But if he had, then someone would have seen him. Someone would have responded to my blog, or the TRASH Facebook posts, or on Twitter, or on Instagram, or the posters of Sparkle's face all over the city with the club number on them, asking for information. Only evil is truly silent.

If Merkin was covering for Niall, why was she so sure he'd killed Francesca? And if he really had, for whatever reason, then surely she understood that he had to be locked away – that he had to pay for his crime?

Was O'Hara just gunning for Merkin because he was an awful human being or was it more sinister than that? Was he the killer – and if so, then what was his motive? Was Merkin frightened of him, or of Niall? None of it seemed to fit in my mind – murder, however messed up, had to have some kind of reason for the person killing someone else. If Francesca was pushed to her death on the lighting pole, then there had to be a reason the killer had pushed her.

And that was what I was missing: reason. It was too messy.

And someone did know something, because they were sending texts from Niall's phone. I didn't believe the text messages were from him any more than the others did.

Finally, a path started to appear through the confusion in my mind. My laptop keys were comfortable in my hands as I ran through my thoughts.

Maybe it was more about what I didn't see. I needed to ask the right questions, that was all. Go around the edges – wasn't that Columbo's method? Find another way into their heads. I had to get people talking, out loud; the dead and the living.

On my laptop, I played with a few photographs and chose an old one I'd taken years ago, a small child running over the bridge in a long dress. I cast out the colour and carefully, delicately, peeled away the layers until the child was so pale, she might not have been there at all. Her hair was wispy and her fingers were transparent, and by the time I was done I could nearly believe the lie under my own hand.

I started writing: *Is Sparkle contacting us from beyond the grave and if so, what would she tell us? DO YOU BELIEVE IN GHOSTS?*

I wondered how many readers would respond. After all, my blog wasn't much. It was an antiquated communication between the world and me – a series of bridge photos with meaningless words – and the only time it had ever mattered it still had not made a difference.

More importantly, I wondered how my friends would respond. Someone knew something, so who would speak?

I turned up the heater.

I didn't have to believe in ghosts. I didn't have to say Niall was dead. I just had to say something that might spark a light. Lower their boundaries. And if I got lucky, then the detective could stick his big nose into someone else's business, and maybe we'd find a clue as to where Niall was hiding, and who pushed Francesca. And who was pushing Merkin.

The first likes popped up. A fake picture was easy to believe, but guilt held its own shadow. All I had to do was find the shade.

People loved to argue when they knew they were right. If Niall were alive and well and guilty, then someone would know. Or if O'Hara had blood on his hands, then again, someone would know. Someone always knows, and everyone likes to be right. Even if only online.

It was foolish, but if all that was asked of me was to make a fool of myself then it was no different whether on a blog, or in the basement of a big old club. It was the very least I could do. And as Robyn would probably tell me, as far as being foolish went, I'd been practising all my life.

I flicked up Thora's number and pressed it. However insane my plan was, at least this time it wasn't criminal.

Chapter Eighteen

The date for the séance was set for the following Sunday, one week before Halloween. I walked slowly along the streets that had so often given me solace over the years. I dawdled. I bought coffee. I looked up at the bare trees.

I'd never believed in ghosts for one simple reason: my mother. She died when I was very young and if she could have come back to me, I had to know that she would. Not that I remembered her very well – not like I remembered my dad, with his laugh and his bright eyes and his quiet ways and the flowers in the garden. But every now and then, in the back of my mind, I almost thought I could hear her voice – and yet at the same time, I knew it could not have been hers. I heard a Disney mum or a Christmas advert. I heard what I thought was love.

I frowned as I walked along the pavement, and crossed to the square. I sat on the bench until I'd finished my coffee, and then finally crossed to number thirty-nine.

I stood on the step too long, my hand lifted to knock but still not moving. The séance was a sham, I knew that. I just needed someone to break.

Footsteps behind me woke me from my thoughts.

'Are we going in or running away?' said Del.

I barely recognised him. He wore a shapeless grey jumper and blue jeans, and his face was free of humour.

'I'm not honestly sure,' I said.

'It was your idea, honey.'

'I don't have a great record with ideas, though,' I said. 'I can list the not-stupid ideas I've had recently on one thumb, and—'

The front door opened. Robyn stood in the fancy hall. Excitement had brightened his eyes, but he looked wary too.

'Can I?' I said, lifting my camera.

He posed as I photographed him with the dark hall behind, the sparkling chandelier above and the light from the streetlamps casting his face into shadow.

'Shot number one,' I told him.

'How many are we taking?'

'Four or five. I want to rub their noses in it if I'm going to get them to argue that Niall is still alive.'

Del shuddered. 'This isn't fun,' he said.

'I hope we get Marilyn come through the board,' said Robyn. He dipped his knees and simpered in her voice. 'But if we get an evil spirit come forth and haunt us – or if I get possessed by some Tory English Spirit Monster – I'll never forgive you.'

'Can we at least get on?' said Del. 'I don't know why I'm here.'

'Because you're supporting Thora,' said Robyn. 'And I'm supporting Fi, and Annie is coming in case Fi kisses her again.'

'Shut up,' I told him. I caught Del's eye. He said nothing.

Robyn swept his hand through the air and bowed deep, playing to the floor. Del giggled, but I felt cold shivers run over my neck.

'It won't work,' said Del. 'I can see what you're doing, but no one is going to suddenly post on your blog that they are the killer.'

'Anything is worth a try at this stage,' I said. 'All I want is an argument.'

'I'll hold you to that if Ben appears,' Del mumbled. 'He always hated this jumper.'

We were to be in the dining room, Robyn told us. He'd already lit the fire. He opened the first door on our left. A long table filled the room with chairs for twelve, six either side. A sideboard stood against the back wall with a display of fancy silverware – two teapots, one coffee pot, a wide flowery bowl and a tall vase. The setting was spooky enough without the black lace hanging over the curtains, and just in case any of us were under the illusion that this was a joke, the aunts had Robyn put tall white candles all around the room, casting long rippling shadows over the waiting Ouija board.

'Well,' whispered Del. 'You were right, Fi.'

'I was?'

'Yeah,' said Robyn. 'Three for three. This was a shockingly bad idea.'

The aunts came slowly; Agnes holding on to the walls and Flo with her walker, the frame clicking as she worked her way down the long hall. Thora was the last of the family, her wigless face made-up for later, and, with her, Annie slunk in through the door, her expression unreadable, with Douglas running around her feet, wagging his tail.

'Mark has Gloria on stage again tonight,' she said. She scooped the little dog into her arms and buried her face in his fluffy neck. 'Just her and a couple of the baby queens doing Madonna again.'

'It's busy now but the numbers won't last with none of us on stage. Another week and we can call up TRASH on the Ouija board,' muttered Thora. 'It'll be as dead as the stuffed possum on the landing.'

Robyn winced. Del closed his eyes. Thora sat down and gathered her crutches, inching her foot underneath the table. She snapped a short word that the aunts pretended they couldn't hear.

I took more photographs of Robyn and the board.

'Who is on tomorrow?' I said.

'No talking about that filthy place,' said Flo. 'The spirits will be upset.'

'They're happy with the new television, though,' said Thora.

'Sin money,' said Flo. 'The old one was fine.'

'The old one was dead,' said Del. 'Why not give it a call now?'

Below us, something rattled. I jumped, grabbing for the back of a chair, but it was the same noises that could be heard all over the house – the walls, the creaking roof, the pipes, or, at worst, a rat.

I moved to put more wood on the fire, setting my hands to the heat and trying to make them stop shaking.

'Talking of spirits,' said Del. 'Special coffee for anyone? Shall I be mother?'

'It suits you, pet,' said Thora. 'Mine's a large.'

'Whoever said size doesn't matter wasn't holding the bottle,' said Del, but the delicate china coffee mugs rattled against one another as he poured. His eyes were red, his fingernails bitten. Too late, I realised that not everyone was quite as disbelieving of the spirits as me.

Thora cleared her throat.

'Ground rules,' she said. She waited until we were looking at the board. 'No moving the thingie,' she started.

'The planchette,' corrected Agnes.

'Isn't that the whole point?' I asked. 'To move it, I mean.'

'Fi, my nerves are shredded,' said Thora. 'If you're not going to take this seriously . . .'

'The spirits will move the planchette,' Flo explained. She took the chair on the opposite side of the table from her sister, and locked eyes with her. 'They never fail,' she told me. 'Especially now you're here. A woman, see,' she said in a loud stage whisper. 'They always liked a young woman.'

'Which isn't creepy at all,' muttered Annie.

Taking a small whisk, Del whipped the bowl of cream, his wrist flicking, then he poured it into the coffees. He picked up the whiskey.

'Sorry. To be clear. Does anyone here want to do this sober?' he said.

'Hell no,' I said.

Flo shot me a look.

'Count me in,' said Robyn.

'I'm not really sure I want to do this at all,' said Annie. 'But hey-ho, in for a Penny's special, girls . . .'

Del walked around the table, one by one to each of us. It was a performance in a way, I thought. Like gathering his notes when he was doing his lawyer things, or slipping into his heels before he went on stage.

A deep hush steadied the room. Flo put out both her hands over the wooden board. The alphabet was marked in a double line, the pattern like a sunrise, and above it, facing me, were the words *Yes* and *No*. On the lower part was what I first thought was a serial number or something but when Flo moved her hands, I saw it was all the numbers from zero to nine, and then underneath, just one word: *Goodbye*.

Blimey, I thought. It was a really good thing I didn't believe in this stuff, because it was starting to scare the pants off me.

Flo waited until Del took the chair beside her. I gulped a big sip of the coffee, slurping the cream by mistake, then avoided looking at Robyn or Annie in case I giggled again from sheer silly nerves. I took a picture of the fire instead, ignoring Flo's furious muttering about *taking our time*.

The candles flickered. The curtain moved without a breeze.

'Friends,' said Flo. Her voice was low and soft, her usual whine in check. 'Please place one finger on the planchette.'

Agnes cleared her throat. She reached out her papery, thin hand, setting her first finger on the triangle-shaped thing with a hole in it. The planchette. A great Columbo I was turning out to be, I thought. *Just one more thing . . .*

'The table is too big to reach,' said Thora.

'Then lean closer, man,' said Flo. 'God gave you long arms for a reason.'

Thora set one finger on the little triangle, beside Agnes. Annie did the same. Flo looked at me. I inched closer, pressing my finger on to the very edge of the wooden shape. With Del and Robyn connected to the scrap of wood, Flo swept the air with her free hand and took the last spot. Our fingers were touching.

Flo held court with the same fiery control Thora used at the club. She closed her eyes and tipped back her head, exposing a short, wrinkled neck and a string of pearls in a choker, over a high-collared black blouse with a lace frill. Neither she nor Agnes looked at Thora.

I wondered how Flo and Agnes would have coped with Stan in full drag and then I decided I really didn't care what they thought as long as they didn't upset him. They were sweet old ladies, but they knew full well that Thora's work was keeping the house. They'd had pronouns and names explained to them time and time again, patiently and kindly and yet they still refused to give way to any-one's preferences, choosing instead to label all Thora's friends as they saw fit. So I was the lesbian and Robyn was the thin one, and Del . . .

Well, I thought, Del was bloody good to them considering, and however decrepit the old ladies were, they could certainly choose to remember that.

Robyn kicked me under the table and I realised Flo was talking, using her soft and low voice to call in the spirits.

'Kindly souls,' she said. 'Kindly souls. Is anyone there?'

The planchette twitched. I was sure it was Flo moving it.

'Is anyone there?' she said again.

'Can we be more specific maybe?' I suggested.

'Hush, girl,' said Agnes.

'Sorry. Only it feels a bit like we're opening a front door and yelling into a street. Like, anyone could come in and . . .'

'Do shut up, girl. She's concentrating,' Agnes snapped.

Flo glared at me. I'd upset her now.

The planchette swept with one sharp tug up to the *YES*. Robyn snapped back his finger, his jaw clenched shut, no longer joking, and Flo smiled around the table like a small grey tabby cat. She guided the planchette back to the middle of the board.

'Are you a friend?' she said to the board.

YES.

'Are you here in peace?'

YES.

Well, they would say that, I thought. Like every bad guy who tells someone, 'Trust me,' and then shows themselves completely untrustworthy.

'We wish to ask the spirits what is upsetting them here,' said Flo. 'We wish—'

It was now or never.

'We wish to contact Francesca,' I said clearly. 'And Niall. Niall Ash.'

Annie jerked up as she stared at me.

'No,' said Flo. 'No, we wish—'

'We just want to know if he's OK,' I said, interrupting. 'If Niall is OK and if he's . . .'

The planchette juddered to the side.

'It's Sparkle,' I added, as if that helped. 'Niall's drag name is Sparkle.'

'None of that talk,' hissed Agnes.

Thora rolled her eyes. Douglas whined. Annie cuddled the dog a little closer on her knee, rubbing his ears with her free hand.

The planchette didn't move. Agnes scowled at me, clearly furious.

Flo was just about to start talking when the little marker twisted to the side.

B

E

A pause. Then our fingers were guided over the board.

The planchette moved without hesitation, jerking straight to each letter, one after the next after the next.

C

A

R

E

I knew where this was going, I thought. I glanced over to Robyn, who was mouthing the letters as they came. I lifted my eyebrow in question but he didn't move. I looked around to Del but he was also staring at the board in thick concentration.

BE CAREFUL.

At least the fake spirits could spell, I thought. I couldn't trust a spirit guide who couldn't spell.

But the planchette was still moving.

F

I

Everyone looked at me.

Be Careful Fi.

Great, I thought. *Bloody marvellous.*
So even the spirits were at me.

Chapter Nineteen

We left in dribs and drabs. No one even pretended it had been a good time. Robyn went first, as his head was pounding. Then Annie, muttering about popping into TRASH. Del helped get the aunts settled while I washed up in the old kitchen downstairs.

I made myself a coffee without the whiskey. In her bedroom Agnes drank the whiskey without the coffee.

Thora said goodnight, her ankle swollen as she hopped her way to the bathroom and back, still grumbling at me about my getting involved where I shouldn't and how she never asked Del to do the vacuuming twice a week anyway and how none of my blogs had ever come to anything and while Merkin was still clearly in trouble, I should bloody well stick to bridges if I couldn't actually help.

Del brought down the last tray of dishes and took over from me at the sink. Douglas ran in and out of the open back door, chasing moths. I sat up on the clean counter, draping the tea towel over my leg.

'Do you think that was for real?' I said, nodding to the ceiling.

Del shook his head. He stuck his hands deep in the suds, scrubbing at a tea-encrusted pot.

'The way I see it,' he said, 'it is, as you would say, complicated. It's neither truth nor lie and neither good nor bad. It's a piece of wood and a couple of bored old ladies.' He drained the water, setting off the sink's deep gurgle, and started cleaning the fridge door. 'What's bad is how people have used these things throughout history to con other people,' he said. 'But then, however adorable we lot are, there will always be wicked folks out there, doll. What difference is it if it's a ghost-con or an email-con, or a phone hack?'

'The aunts aren't trying to con us.'

'In their way, they may be, although they wouldn't see it like that. And there's you with your photos of not-ghosts on the blog, and the pictures tonight – and what is drag if it isn't a con? Oh shit, talking of which, can you call Robyn, please?' he said suddenly. 'Catch him before he goes to sleep in case his headache is getting worse. I need to ask him if he wants Merkin's bingo this week. I'm snowed under and Thora is ankled.'

I dialled as we chatted. There was no answer. I slid down off my perch, got out a frozen dinner for the next day and set it in the fridge to defrost. I called Robyn again as I went to get the dog from the garden but he still didn't pick up.

Silence hung over the frayed grass. It was nothing, I thought. I was just being edgy. He was watching something on his laptop probably. Captain Hastings, in one form or another. Not hearing his phone.

I let the dog sniff into all the corners but back inside, closing the door firmly with the top and bottom latches, I tried Robyn's number two more times and there was still no answer.

'He's probably in the shower,' said Del.

'It's been an hour since he left here, though,' I said.

I frowned. I gathered my stuff together and kissed Del, leaving him to say goodnight to the aunts. I waved to the neighbour at his window and I texted as I walked. I called again. I texted again.

All the messing with the Ouija board was making me paranoid. It had been a silly trick back when the girls at my school wanted to try it in the cemetery, and it was silly now. It was just an excuse for

Flo and Agnes to bully me. Still, I would post the blog and set the lame trap and put it out of my mind, and maybe someone would slip up, and tell me their truth.

I walked into town, darting around the night crowds. Just past the bank I tried Robyn again in case he'd been in the shower, but there was still no answer. I picked up my pace. I was probably worrying for no reason.

I ran up the stairs. The flat was empty. I opened each door again and again.

I phoned Annie.

'Hey, Fi?'

I took a breath. She would tell me that Robyn was at the club or that she'd caught up with him and he was now on his way home.

Only Annie didn't say that. She told me they hadn't seen Robyn at TRASH either. Gloria had thrown a hissy fit, and now Annie was pulling herself into speedy drag to finish the show.

No one had heard from him. Gavin had called her too, not being able to reach him, and Annie had just heard Mark yelling at Del on the phone for calling twice in ten minutes and how the guy had literally only been gone an hour and we were all freaking out like he was a toddler on the loose at Connolly Station.

I forced myself to breathe.

Not Robyn . . .

'He will show up,' said Annie. 'He knows how you worry,' she added.

But she wasn't there that summer, she didn't know what it was like to suddenly lose someone: to one minute see them standing by the railings and the next, dead. Gone. Robyn knew. So did I.

I tried Robyn's phone again and again, sending messages in every way I could think. I paced the floor. My skin felt itchy, like I wanted to shower off the darkness from the old aunts' house.

I turned on the stereo, then off. I picked up my laptop but I couldn't focus on the pictures from the night. There was nothing I wanted to watch and nothing I wanted to read. I went into the kitchen and threw the windows wide, feeling the bite of the cold autumn chill.

I looked into his room. His bed was covered with his new satin throw, the cream and bronze matching the curtains, the scatter cushions perfectly placed against the wooden bedhead. On the chair, his work clothes were folded for the morning, and on the back wall the three long rails of clothes hung neatly – two for drag, one for his boy clothes. All around the room he'd put up shelves, like it was a library rather than a bedroom, with books and DVDs and CDs, boxes of make-up, plastic tubs filled with earrings and hair accessories, flat caps and fancy hats, and in the centre the three wigs he liked the most: the big red wavy one he'd bought in replacement for his debut wig that Eve had the audacity to get murdered in, a blond Marilyn wig he was wearing when he met Gavin, and a cheap silver bob with sparkling lights on the tips that I gave him for his birthday.

It all looked normal, but I couldn't shift the fear in my bones.

My phone beeped.

Annie.

It's OK

I let out a long breath of relief. The doorbell rang. I looked out from my window.

Stan stood under the streetlamp, looking perfect in his drag in the soft light. I opened the window full and picked up my camera, waiting for permission before I took the shot.

It was OK, I thought. That was all I needed to know. I focussed my camera on Stan's handsome face.

It wasn't just the way he stood, it was something in his eyes – the strength, the absolute sureness of who he was, with the layer of Annie right there too. The mixture.

He was stunning, even in the quick drag.

I took three, four pictures, and then threw him down my keys, and I watched as he went to open my door.

But Stan came in with fear in his eyes, worry trenched deep in the shadows.

'Any news?' he said.

'But I thought . . .' I said. 'I thought *it's OK* meant . . .'

'Oh shit, sorry,' he said quickly. 'I just meant it's OK to answer the door. It's me, I mean . . . I figured it's late and with so much weirdness around, you wouldn't know who was ringing the bell. And I'm so sorry, Fi, I don't have any news. I don't know any more than you do. That's why I came over, I didn't want you to be alone.'

Tears pricked at my eyes. I went into the kitchen and closed the window, wiping the rain from the sill. It was late enough – not quite kick-out time for TRASH, but the crowds outside in the street were fading to the thin straggle that would keep up through the night, here and there, until the morning shift began.

I forced myself to breathe normally. In. Out. I didn't know what to do. What to say. I wished Stan wasn't there. And at the same second, I desperately wanted him to stay. He was right, I didn't want to be alone.

He talked about the club and about Gloria's tantrum, and he told me how he'd had to pull on his suit and 'tache and run down the stairs with still no idea what song he was doing until his feet hit the stage, just hoping his facial hair would stay on as he ran, and how Mark was getting really grumpy, and about how Gloria said the TRASH family were falling apart. And then I started saying that Robyn—

But I couldn't.

I called his phone again. I hit redial over and over again. I texted Del and Thora. Stan tried Robyn from his phone. We sat together in increasing panic, our limp phones in our hands.

I left more messages. By the time our coffee mugs were empty and we'd finished Robyn's stash of chocolate biscuits, Del called to say he and Gavin were also freaking out and maybe it was time to call someone in charge. Maybe we should call the idiot detective.

I paced over the same patch of useless carpet. I forced myself back up on to the counter.

Stan folded his frame into the little chair at the kitchen table. He leaned back, rubbing at his eyes and smudging a shadow. I shifted across the counter until I could reach the cupboard door. I opened it, then closed it again, seeing nothing I wanted inside. Then opened, then closed.

'Maybe he met someone?' said Stan. 'I mean . . .'

'No. He's in a relationship with Gavin.'

'But?' said Stan.

I shook my head. 'He's absolutely not like that.' I smiled, feeling nothing but sadness. 'And, umm, neither am I,' I said. 'Just . . . you know . . .'

'Me too, as it happens,' said Stan. 'I'm an old-fashioned, all-or-nothing kind of a guy.'

He flicked his phone in his hand.

I nodded, suddenly feeling the space between us in the tiny kitchen. I wanted him to hold me. To make it all go away. To take care of me. I was done dealing with this stuff on my own.

I wanted Robyn to be safe, to be alive, to be right there with us.

And I really wanted Stan to stay.

And then there was Patrick.

'I think—' I started.

My phone beeped. A text from Robyn's phone.

'It's him!'

I pressed my finger to the screen, so ready to hear something sensible, to know he was fine, to know I'd overreacted—

Please stop calling, Fi. I've met a friend and I'll be away a few days. I'm fine. Robin.

My heart thumped in panic.

'No,' I said. 'No. No. No.'

Stan crossed the tiny room to see. He set his hand over mine to steady the phone. He pointed at the spelling. 'No,' he said.

He held my fingers.

I pulled back.

'What?' he said.

Stan knew Niall and he knew Robyn, and he was forever getting grief from Merkin, and he could get the keys for TRASH, and—

I pushed my fingers through my hair, panic rising in my chest.

'What?' Stan said again.

I looked into his eyes. I was wrong. I was letting my anxiety rule me.

'Sorry,' I said. I put my hand over his, interlacing our fingers.

I called O'Hara, who didn't answer. Stan called Del.

I left messages at the gardaí station and the club, and Stan posted on all Robyn's social media, and then we sat on the counter together looking out at the rain in the street.

I started to say something else, to make yet another pointless and meaningless suggestion of where he might be, from the service station to the sauna to the twenty-four-hour gym he never visited in the daylight, never mind at night, but the words that came out instead were, 'I'm so tired.'

Stan opened his arms and I clung on, but when I looked up, I moved my head away.

212

'I can't,' I whispered. 'I can't kiss you again.'

'What's the worst that could happen?' he said.

I smiled. 'I'll fall in love with you.'

He laughed, but I didn't.

'First, I'll fall in love with you,' I said. 'And then obviously I'll mess it up because that's what I do. And then we will fall out, and you will ignore me, and I will cry for maybe eight to ten months, depending on how good the kiss was—'

'That's some kiss,' said Stan.

'Then I'll stop going to TRASH because my heart will be broken, and I won't be able to see you with all the attractive women on your arm—'

'Umm . . .'

'So then I'll fall out with Robyn because I never see him and he pretty much lives there now,' I went on.

'All from one kiss?' he said.

'I have form,' I said. 'And by then you will have met the love of your life and she won't say stupid things and I will die alone in a ramshackle cottage by the sea.'

'How ramshackle are we talking?'

'The plumbing works but the electric is dodgy.'

'You've really thought this through,' he said.

'And by then—'

'Fi?' he said.

'Yes?'

'Shut up,' said Stan.

He smiled. He touched his hand to my face, gently tucking my hair behind my ear.

'Go to bed,' he said. 'You need sleep. It's really late. I'll borrow Robyn's t-shirt and joggers. I need to take off this suit and binder – my back is killing me, and my boobs are done with being squashed flat under my armpits. Tomorrow we will start again.'

'But—'

'I'll stay a while,' he said. 'I'm here, Fi. I'm here as me, whichever me you need.'

I woke up alone. Not that I was expecting anything else. As Robyn regularly reminded me, we weren't the kind of people who hopped into bed with just anyone; we needed weeks and weeks of overthinking and panicking and analysing a relationship before we were ready to do that. And plenty of time to screw it up before we got jiggly.

Still, I thought, it had been nice to cuddle, even if it was just that. Trying not to think about Robyn or about anything, just falling asleep being held. Safe. Trying not to fall apart, and failing.

The flat was empty. I texted Robyn's phone again.

Hey babe. Call me OK? It's important. Love you. Always. Xx

I reread the weird text from the night before. They had misspelled his name. Robyn changed his i to a y at seven years old and anyone who knew him was aware of that.

I missed him like a second kidney; we'd always been close but since his sister had nearly killed us . . . well, that kind of changed things forever, the way I saw it.

My phone was hot in my hand. I texted with Del and Gavin and Annie, and then Thora and then Mark. No one had heard anything. And I had to go to work.

A memory burst through my fear. Time slipped away and I remembered standing in my dad's little hall and staring at our clunky old landline telephone, waiting for Robyn to ring me back. Three times and hang up, that meant we were home safe. Doing this twice, repeating, meant we were home safe, but we needed to talk, and the other person should shut the doors so neither side could be heard by sleeping parents, and we would call in ten minutes. Three times, though – we had only used that the once. Three times meant one thing. Danger. Call immediately. Help.

I called Robyn's phone and let it ring three times, then I hung up. Then again. Three times I did it, each time letting it ring only the three rings before hanging up.

But standing there alone in the apartment we'd shared for the past five years, I already knew he'd have called me back if he could.

Chapter Twenty

Robyn was gone.

Niall was gone.

Merkin had told the gardaí she'd killed Francesca. She wouldn't say why. And she refused to see Del.

As weeks went, it was right up there with my dad's funeral.

The guards took a cursory statement and glanced at Robyn's room. Edna was frantic, constantly going back to the them, making statements for RTÉ. Del sat beside her on camera, with Robyn's grandfather, Grandpa Joe, on the other side. Grandpa Joe held Edna's elbow in his frail, bony fingers, squeezing as her voice broke, bringing me to tears each time I watched the clip.

Gavin cried on the phone.

Every day lasted a thousand hours.

I worked at the shop, looking stranger each morning as I pulled clean outfits from the back of my wardrobe, but even Mickey didn't comment, and when Gavin came in to see me, all we did was hold each other, silently crying, until customers drifted away uncomfortably and Jenkins brought us to the stock room and made us strong, sweet tea from the staff kettle that no one used.

I grabbed clothes from the rail, from the floor, barely noticing what I'd put on, but by the following Thursday, I had nothing left to wear and no choice but to spend the evening sorting through the laundry. I stuffed the first load into the machine and set it going but as I pulled out Robyn's favourite third-date shirt, I broke.

Each day had ground to nothing. I couldn't think, I couldn't eat, I couldn't breathe. I didn't even want coffee.

My heart ached with grief. I crumpled to the floor. I shook. I gripped hold of the stupid shirt with the fancy buttons and the creases where he'd rolled up the sleeves and I held the cotton fabric so tightly in my hands that I tore the edge. Fear rolled through me, and with each sob my anxiety took over more and more as the tears fell from my eyes.

It was the not knowing, I told myself, trying to believe the lie.

My phone rang over and over. But it was Stan. Then Del. Then Gavin. Then Del again and again. I ignored each one as I let the world fall apart around me and I gave in to the sheer terror that my friend was hurt, was suffering.

Was dead.

People die all the time. My mum died when I was too young to remember her and my dad when I was old enough to know how much I needed him. I thought I'd done my grief. I thought I would have years until it would happen again. That was the natural order of things. Friends didn't die like this.

My breath caught and I gripped the shirt too hard, my knuckles white, my skin beading with cold sweat.

I was living my worst nightmare. All our nightmares.

I'd said I would call Edna again, but I had nothing to tell her. I'd told Gavin I'd call him. I'd said I'd help Merkin, but I had nothing. I wanted to go to Del, but I couldn't find the words to help him. I knew I should try to write to Patrick at the very least and tell him I had his letter and tell him how I'd read it over and over again, as I'd forgotten how it felt to be with him. And then tell him Robyn was missing and I was so frightened.

I should call Annie – Del – Gavin – Jenkins – O'Hara – Edna . . .

I should go into the gardaí station and demand to be seen, to be heard. Demand they find Robyn, like Edna and Gavin were demanding. I should be shouting and screaming and DOING something—

Nausea rippled through me as the crippling knowledge clamped around my chest that there was nothing I could do to make this right. No blog post would help here, no careful deduction of the circumstances. No beige mac. No talking to anyone.

I had nothing.

My phone bleeped.

Del.

I'm coming over.

I touched the screen. He'd see the dots if I tried to write. I couldn't see him. I'd failed them, all of them. No one had answered my Ouija board blog post with anything obvious. It was yet another stupid idea of mine.

Del is typing . . .

I know you're at home. I'm coming over.

I lay down in the pile of clothes. I couldn't do it. I had nothing to give to any of them. I was empty, afraid and lost. Del had been through so much and I didn't know how to comfort him, and I couldn't even get Thora her food now.

I heard the key in the lock a second before the door opened. For the tiniest moment I thought it was Robyn. I jerked up from the floor.

Del looked down at me with nothing but love.

'You gave me your spare key for emergencies,' he said.

I swiped the back of my hand over my eyes. 'An emergency is when I lock myself out, or when your house is on fire,' I told him.

'Not always.'

Dropping down he opened his arms and pulled me into a hug, and as I cried, he stroked the back of my head. We sat together on the floor in the middle of the pile of laundry, Del holding me, my face resting against his chest. He rocked me, ever so gently, and he brushed my hair away from my face with his hand.

'You OK there?' he said eventually.

'Sorry.'

'Don't be, Fi. Not ever.'

I uncurled myself and sat back beside him, tucking my hand into his, my fingers between his.

'Don't ever be sorry to need someone,' he said gently, kissing the top of my head.

'But I should be helping you.'

'Who says you're not?'

With a weak chuckle, I gestured at myself, at the laundry, at the mess.

He leaned over. 'Christ that shirt is ugly.'

'It's Robyn's.'

'Please tell me you're not going to try sniffing for him like a Labrador?'

I wiped my sleeve over my eyes.

'You want help doing this?' he said.

'Oh, um . . .' I started to move and dislodged a mountain of Robyn's laundry. 'No, no, thanks. Only I just need to—'

In the kitchen, the washing machine beeped its finale.

'It's enough,' said Del gently. 'Let's bag up this lot, and grab a very quick coffee – that's your job, I hate your kitchen. Nothing makes sense in there and I can't find the whiskey.'

'There is no whiskey in there.'

'Precisely.'

'Del?' I asked.

'That sounds expensive.'

I smiled, reached out and touched the tear on his cheek. 'You never talk about Ben now,' I said. 'The big stuff, I mean. I'm here. I want to be here. It's like all that . . . it's like it's behind a glass wall.'

He opened his mouth, then closed it.

'Some things are too much,' he said quietly. 'It's what you say all the time. I need to make sense of it. Nothing makes sense. That's what's doing my head in.'

I nodded.

'That's what's doing in everyone's heads,' he said. 'And this stuff . . . it makes *no sense* that Merkin is obviously covering for Niall, and *no sense* that he would have killed Fran, and it makes *no sense* now that Robyn is gone . . .'

I sat back on my heels, barely aware I was still holding Robyn's shirt. 'To borrow her name, I keep thinking that Mae B the way we are looking at it is all wrong.'

'What d'you mean?'

'It's us that isn't seeing things right,' I said. 'I keep thinking it. That's what's so frustrating. I've tried thinking upside down and I've even tried listening to Thora's aunts—'

'Both of whom are clearly one can short of a six pack.'

'Yes, but are they, Del?' I said. 'What if they're right?'

'That's enough,' he laughed. 'Come on, my little Hagatha Christie, up you get.' He pulled me with him. 'Let's get you down to where they sell alcohol and away from these dubious stains. Christ that shirt is really gruesome.'

'It's his favourite,' I said through a sob. Pulling myself together, I put on the coffee, my hands still shaking. 'Where are we going?'

'Can you handle TRASH?'

Honestly, I thought, *no.*

'Who's on stage tonight?' I asked.

'That depends who's dead before we get there. At this rate,' said Del, 'I'll be stuffing you inside one of Merkin's ballgowns and you can do the show with me!'

I looked around in a snap. 'You are joking, aren't you?' I said.

'About dressing you up? Yeah, you'd never get into her frocks – her waist is enviably tiny because she exists mainly on mint tea and tequila. About the dead bit? I really, really hope I'm joking.'

◆ ◆ ◆

Everything that could go wrong at the club, did go wrong. There just weren't enough of us. It started with the lights. Two bulbs were gone. I knocked over a stand on the side of the stage and Annie kicked in a third by mistake as she was trying to climb up and fix the one I'd just broken. Then Del appeared from the toilets with his hair soaking wet.

'Tell me no one flushed you,' said Annie.

Del grimaced. 'Worse,' he said. 'The plumber Mark called hasn't fixed the problem. It's raining in stall four again. And Google won't agree on how I should fix it. So I hit it with a shiny hammer.'

'Is it fixed?'

'Of course it isn't.'

Mark looked out of the dressing room, shook his head and went straight for the coatroom. As Annie started sewing the long rip in the stage curtain that had split when I knocked over the light, I ran down the stairs to help bring in the soft drinks.

'How late are we going to be to open?' Chris asked, taking three boxes in one load, their biceps strong as they moved. 'Who's on first?'

'Oh, um . . .' I hesitated over the big crate as I tried to remember. 'Stan has called another king. CK Dexter Shaven, I think?' I picked up two smaller boxes and winced at the weight. 'Gloria, of course – she wouldn't miss the demise of TRASH, as she put it – and Del is doing the second half, if he can get out of the leaking bathroom and into a frock. Ooof, that's heavy!'

I climbed the steps, carrying the boxes.

'They haven't sent the orange,' Chris said, already on their way back. 'I ordered it. I know I did. Can you tell Mark?'

I trudged back up the stairs. 'Mark, where's the orange?' I called.

'Orange what?'

He stuck his head up from behind the desk as, unawares, Del came around with a long metal pole and struck Mark square across the back of his head, sending him thudding to the floor.

I ran forward.

'Shit!' screamed Del. 'I killed Mark!'

From downstairs, the sound of the sewing machine stopped.

'Not quite,' said Mark, trying to sit up.

'Don't move,' said Annie, already running for the balcony.

'Are you OK?' I said.

'I don't think so,' Mark muttered, rubbing the back of his head. 'I'm not sure yet. Don't stop sewing. We're opening the door in twenty minutes.'

'False alarm,' said Del. 'Nice one not being dead, dude. Shit,' he cursed. 'I'm so sorry. Really.'

Mark's face was wracked with pain. 'If we find it's you and you're secretly killing us all off,' he said, 'you can chalk this one off to a fail.'

'It's not bleeding,' said Del. 'Or not, you know, very badly, anyway. I mean, it's not awful. Fi, pass me that cloth, would you?'

'Fi?' called Chris from below. 'Did you get it?'

'We're out of orange,' I told them. 'Shall I call an ambulance?'

'Londis is the closest.' Mark paled. 'Oh . . .' He looked up—

222

Del ran for the bucket from the bathroom, just in time as Mark retched.

'Mark, how many fingers?' I said.

'God, don't make me make a joke,' he mumbled from inside the bucket. 'And I can still see two of Fi. Can you please go away and—'

He leaned into the bucket, emptying his stomach.

'Fi?' called Chris, again.

I ran all the way to Londis and most of the way back in a hot mess, sweat rolling down my face, my trousers slipping down over my hips, one shoelace undone, my hair mostly escaped from the band. I set the cartons on the bar. In the foyer, Del stood half in his outfit, his wig in his hand, his mouth open in wide and silent terror. My heart stopped beating. The world tilted.

'You lot are such a cliché,' said Annie. She held up a card with an upside-down glass on the top.

'Don't you bring that thing down this way . . .' Del hissed.

'If you think I'm taking the spiral staircase with both hands on a glass containing a massive bloody spider, you're more daft than you look,' said Annie. 'And right now, sweetie, that's—'

'Any news?' said Gavin, at the door.

'Hold that door open, please?' said Annie.

'Are we open?' Chris called.

'Only to spiders,' I told them.

'It's going to be one of those nights,' said Del.

TRASH was still busy enough, whatever the drama going on backstage, but the crowd was listless. Stan was quiet, and his song choices were downbeat. Gloria was a professional under the lights but backstage she was a bloody nightmare. She worked through her pre-arranged numbers but by half-time even she was struggling, and CK Dexter Shaven had neither Stan's charm nor his sparkle. The sharp atmosphere between the performers seemed to rub off on the audience and way before eleven, Mark called a close to the show, letting the DJ take over.

I sat on the balcony, a glass of gin and tonic in each hand.

Del came out from the dressing room, dipping so his pink wig would fit through the gap. His make-up had been hurried earlier but he still looked fabulous: high silver brows with a deep grey shadow over the lines, then layers of pink and silver sweeping over his lids and four pairs of full lashes. On his ears, he wore big diamanté flowers and he had matching cuffs on both wrists, but every inch of his look was overshadowed by his bizarre outfit: a dress made from blue and cerise floral fabric, giant flower patterns ringed by ugly bottle-green leaves, like a sofa from a nineteen-seventies bedsit. As he reached me, he tugged on a cord on his left boob and the skirt pulled up over his knees, leaving the gold tassel dangling.

Despite the evening, despite my fear and my terror of losing Robyn, I giggled.

'If one of those drinks isn't for me, I'm pushing you over the railing to take your chances,' he said.

Stan grimaced as he came up the staircase.

'Too soon?' said Del.

'Only by about a decade,' said Stan.

'From Chris,' I said, passing out the drinks.

'Not from you then,' said Del. 'Good to know who to dip for.'

'Shut up and drink your gin,' I told him, grinning.

Stan took his and slid into the row behind us. He groaned as he sat down, and then leaned forward to talk to Del.

'Be warned, I think Gloria just stole CK's black eyeliner from the top box,' he said. 'It's some posh brand, with a red stem. It was definitely there the other week he says and it's not there now.'

'Merkin will fire her,' said Del.

'Merkin's not here though.'

'Has anyone talked to Merkin's family?' said Stan. 'It's ridiculous. She didn't do anything. I don't believe it. And I tried to go and visit her, but she still won't speak to anyone.'

'Does she have a family?' I asked.

'A late niece.' Del nodded to the floor below us, and Stan and I both winced. 'A sister, I think. Others, I imagine, who she would no longer associate herself with,' he added. 'Merkin is old, and all old people have history.'

'Surely they'll let her go soon,' said Stan. 'I mean, she can't keep saying she is guilty of something she didn't do—'

'She's stubborn,' I said.

'She's wrong.' Del shrugged. 'She's got herself twisted, thinking she's doing the right thing. She thinks Niall is guilty of murder, for whatever reason, and she thinks he'll come for us, for her drag family, if she doesn't stop him. She thinks she put him up to it, somehow. That she did something, unknowing. She's tried to find him, and that failed, so now she's doing the only thing she can to keep him from attacking anyone else.'

'But that's insane. Surely the police . . .' said Stan.

Yeah, I thought. The police . . .

'Right face, wrong time,' said Del. 'While she's sat there telling them all that she pushed her niece off the balcony and killed her, then they're not going to argue with her. I'm doing everything I can but she won't talk to me.'

'How can I help?' said Stan. 'Is there anything we can do?'

'Keep this place open,' he said with a shrug. 'TRASH is home for Merkin and Thora. They needed it, when Thora opened the club. It was different back then.' He took a long drink, wobbling his wig as he drank. 'They'll need it even more when this is done.'

Together, Del, Stan and I watched the dancers below, new couples matching up, friends chatting as they moved, the single woman who danced alone at the edge of the floor.

'I was thinking about going to visit Francesca's girlfriend,' I said.

'She won't see us. She doesn't want anything to do with TRASH.'

'She might see me though,' I said. 'I'm not TRASH.'

'Yeah, you are,' said Del fondly.

I blew him a kiss.

'I can come with you if you like?' he said.

I shook my head. I wriggled closer and hugged him, then stood. 'You're doing everything else,' I told him. 'You need to sleep.'

'You're going home?' said Stan. He stood up, moved closer. 'I can walk you?'

Del peered down at the dance floor, concentrating on the dancers as if they held his absolute attention. I opened my mouth to reply to Stan when a huge crash thundered from the dressing room, accompanied by a tirade of imaginative swearing in a thick Welsh accent. Del was on his feet even as I moved, Stan rushing forward.

A chair flew from the room into the doorway. I slipped back, catching the leg before it knocked into Del. A bag followed, then a glass, shattering against the wall, sending vodka and fizzy orange flying.

'You bitch!' cried Gloria.

'How bloody dare you!'

In the middle of the dressing room stood CK, the new drag king, his waistcoat hanging torn from his body, a long scratch bleeding down his face, and Gloria's wig in his fist.

'You get your filthy hands off my c—'

The next glass flew past my face, smashing on the wall behind Stan. Pushing past CK, I ran for Gloria, dodging a hairbrush and a bottle of water.

I grabbed hold of the first limb I could: Gloria's arm. Behind me, Stan reached CK as Del pushed him back, stepping between them. Gloria snatched a book from the table, sending it soaring, knocking Stan on his cheek.

'Hey!' I pulled her, tugging for the other hand.

'Get out of my face, girl,' Gloria snapped.

'Then stop throwing things at other people's faces!'

I caught her other arm and twisted it behind her. I held both her wrists. Gloria tried to kick forward, caught Del on his knee.

'What the hell?' said Del.

'She's stealing all my stuff!' shouted CK.

'What's here is my own things,' Gloria wailed. 'I've taken nothing. This is all my own. I left it here and now it's gone, and I see it there on your table and this is the second time this has happened, and—'

CK pushed his fingers through his hair, smudging grey over his temple. 'That's my bloody pencil,' he said. 'No one else uses that brand. That's the thanks I get for saving your bloody bacon tonight, you gobshite—'

'I've used this brand for nineteen years!'

'Take it down a peg,' said Stan.

'And you're OK with this?' yelled CK. 'She is nothing but a cheap wh—'

'Oh shut up!' I said.

Gloria kicked out at me, catching my ankle with her shoe. She was fast and slippery. Shooting out of my hold, she rushed forward, her nails already ripping the air as she got to CK. She threw a punch at Del who ducked. Gloria's fist clipped Stan's ear. Stan howled with rage, spinning back, slamming both his hands into Gloria's chest, pushing her against the wall.

Screaming and hollering, CK grabbed for a handful of Gloria's dress, pulling away one of her boobs in his hand.

Del turned, his face fixed with fury. He pulled back his hand and with one sharp punch he knocked CK from Gloria, sending the drag king slamming against the doorway, staggering as he went. I pulled Stan. Del grabbed Gloria and shoved her into a chair so hard the older queen's teeth shook as she opened her mouth to argue.

Mark stepped into the doorway, his eyes still haggard with pain.

'What the hell?' he barked. He looked down at the broken room: Gloria in her torn dress, with one boob left in place, her wig on the floor; CK panting wildly, one hand gripping the stolen tit and the other holding his jaw; Stan leaning against the far wall, his eyes closed; and Del, both fists still ready, his eyes flashing, his wild pink wig wobbling, and his feet completely sure in his high heels.

Mark said the kind of words that would have Edna in a soft faint, reaching for her rosary.

'Everything's fine,' said Del quietly.

CK rubbed his mouth, wincing. He shook Gloria's tit with disdain.

'I don't need this,' Mark sighed. 'I have Gavin in the office, in floods of tears. I don't care what happened here.'

'Then next time don't hire a kleptomaniac drag queen,' said CK.

'How dare y—'

Del put out both his hands. 'Darlings,' he said through gritted teeth, leaving no one unsure of how he felt about them. 'Shut up, all of you. Stan, take CK home. Gloria . . . Gloria, my pet . . .'

'She's no one's pet,' Stan snapped.

'And if she were, she'd be put down,' added CK.

I kept my mouth shut.

'Just another day at the farm,' muttered Del, as their voices disappeared. He turned back to Gloria and put both his hands on his hips. 'Did you have to upset one of the only seasoned performers we can get?' Del said wearily.

'You call that performing?' said Gloria.

I started picking up the things that had fallen – the chair, a book, a big chunk of broken glass.

'CK needs to grow a spine,' Gloria drawled. 'And balls,' she added meanly.

'And you need to shut up, bitch!' came the shout from the stairs.

◆ ◆ ◆

I missed Robyn so badly I couldn't think. Sweeping the last of the glass, I nodded to Mark as he walked past with the broken chair in his hands.

'So, just an average night then?' I said.

'At least without Merkin here, no one's actually dead this time.' He moved on without stopping.

'She didn't hurt anyone,' I said. 'Mark, wait! No, she didn't do it!'

But he didn't even lift his hand as he walked away.

He was wrong.

Merkin was difficult. She was rude and opinionated and moody and feisty, but she was a performer – that was her created character. She was artistic, as Robyn said. And look at her dresses, I wanted to add. Look at how she creates her art. She had tried to find Niall, not to hurt him, and she couldn't have done anything to Robyn anyway because she was in jail when he disappeared.

Niall had vanished. And now Robyn was gone. Was it Niall? Was it O'Hara?

Would we ever know? Were they both dead?

A leaden weight slipped down my spine. I grabbed the handrail.

The only thing I was sure about was that Merkin hadn't done it.

'Right face, wrong time,' said Del again, behind me.

Chapter Twenty-One

I slept on the sofa, dreams tossing me from one scenario to the next. I stood in an interview with the guards, and then an interview with Edna, with her and Joe and Gavin judging my ability to find Robyn.

I turned to fight but couldn't see who was coming.

Twisted pictures of all my worries ran through my dreams like the numbers on a fruit machine. Blink blink blink: flat broke. Blink blink blink: debt, cold. Blink blink blink – the worst – Robyn gone. Vanished.

As the sky slowly turned in my dream from dark grey to slightly lighter grey, I found myself standing in a long hall, the walls fuzzy like dreams could be. I walked down the middle to the desk at the end. Three people sat behind it, a board of directors.

I didn't know it would be a board of directors, I thought. I wasn't ready to be judged by directors.

I was already standing too close when I realised all three of the directors were completely naked, their elderly bodies brightly on display where they sat behind the long desk.

I stared at the first man's nipples.

I knew I shouldn't be able to see his nipples. That wasn't right.

'Fi McKinnery, is it?' he said. 'Come on, come on.' He beckoned me forward.

'No need to be nervous,' said the woman beside him, who looked a lot like the headmistress of my infants' school in Wolverhampton, apart from the fact that she was naked, and to my knowledge no headmistress I'd ever seen had been naked.

'Not to worry,' she told me. 'It's just an interview to see if you're worthy.'

I have never said I was worthy.

The third director chuckled. 'Everyone says it relaxes people to imagine an interview panel naked,' she said. 'So we thought we'd do it for you.'

I woke with a start, gulping at air.

Sleep was for the feeble, Del used to say. Now he said he rarely slept at all because bad things had a tendency to happen when he woke up.

I went back into my room and opened the window. Two drunk men were weaving their way along the river wall, somehow not falling.

God, it was endless. Niall was missing. Robyn was missing. Francesca was dead. Someone threw an unlit petrol bomb at Merkin's shop and now she was in jail telling everyone she was guilty, when she wasn't.

We were fighting an unseen enemy, a threat that made no sense.

I pulled up my laptop. More people had commented on my Ouija board post, but no one mentioned Sparkle McCavity.

You're a fool, said one. But they were probably right.

Looks like fun, said another.

I opened a letter I'd been writing to Patrick.

I started again, and this time I told myself I would simply say hello, and thank him for the letter, and tell him that I missed him.

My fingers froze over the keys, and all I could think about was Robyn saying the word *vagina*.

I flicked through Twitter and Instagram. I watched videos of Mae B on YouTube, but as the dark slowly faded into day I felt the night's cold fear in my chest cement into a stone-cold terror. This was all that was left. Empty videos on my laptop screen.

I knew my dreams didn't matter. Like it didn't matter if I was worthy or not. I pushed up from the bed, dressing quickly. I was not going to sit quietly and wait for someone to find Robyn's body floating down the river. I was done listening to a detective with even more ego than ear, and I was done letting terror take over my mind.

Edna was at the guards and Thora was on the phones and on the radio. The time to be quiet was over. It was time to make a scene.

Every hour inched away at the shop, but even there things were different. Mr Jenkins brought me coffee, the top spilling as his hands shook. He was practically Robyn's in-law, as he said, and Gavin was going crazy with worry.

It's the not knowing that was the worst, we all said, over and over. We were wrong, of course. Not knowing gave us hope.

I called O'Hara. He curtly replied there was nothing more he could do for me, and I begged him and I told him I could come over, and he told me he had no intention of flattering my tendencies for playing Miss Marple, never mind suffering my imaginative wailing any further.

I pleaded. Then I cried.

'Merkin didn't do anything,' I said to him. 'Please, Francesca was her niece. She had no reason to kill her. But what's more, she adored Niall. She was like his mum, see? And no one has seen him for weeks. And now Robyn is missing—'

'Not according to his text message.'

'Which he didn't send!'

'Fi,' the detective's voice had lowered. 'You need to let this go. Your friend is out somewhere doing his own thing. It's natural.'

'You don't have to like me,' I told him. 'You don't even have to hate me, but please, please believe me, there's no way that Robyn would go off somewhere like this. He just wouldn't disappear. He hasn't called his work. He hasn't called his mum. There's been no contact at all.'

'Didn't he do just that to you last June?' said O'Hara. I heard the sneer in his voice.

'Well, yes, but . . .'

There was nothing I could say to make him hear me. I tried again and again, explaining that what was going on just didn't add up and it just wasn't right.

'I hear you had a séance,' O'Hara laughed, not even trying to hide his ridicule. 'How did that turn out for you, Fi? Did the dead do a little song and dance routine? Did Cole Porter sing you ladies a wee song now?'

I hung up.

Git.

Something about O'Hara reminded me of being at school, the way some kids would laugh at me like that, or at Robyn. Some people were just born rotters.

Del was walking down the square, his quick strides covering the ground at twice the pace of mine. His smile was bright, but his eyes looked dull and tired, and as I got closer I could smell the whiskey on his breath.

'How's it going?' I said.

He spoke at length of a dull meeting at work, making me laugh as always, but as he took his key from his pocket, his hand shook, and his laughter was done before it met his eyes.

'Shall—' I started.

'Better hurry,' he said quickly. 'Tell Thora I'll be at TRASH later, will you?'

'Sure. But—'

'Another night of pretending everything is fine and lip-synching to the eighteen people in the crowd,' he added. 'At least Thora can say she was right – we're all failing together!'

I stared at the door long after it had closed behind him. A little later, I took Douglas out for a walk around the square. I looked up to see Del's light flick off. A taxi pulled up and he made a dash from the house, nearly running down the steps and into the car.

Douglas shivered and I picked him up. I was just heading back to the house when a young woman crossed the street toward me.

The woman was striking. Pale violet eyes in a round face, her full lips glistening under the light from the streetlamp. Her hair was short, and the cut framed her face in soft curls. The clothes she wore draped her body in soft layers.

She jerked her chin. 'Fi, right?'

'Yes?'

She hesitated, then spoke slowly. 'I'm Ingrid,' she said. 'Francesca was my girlfriend.'

'Oh, hi,' I said. 'I'm so sorry for your loss.'

'Thanks. I'm, umm . . .'

She was looking up and down the street. The aunts' neighbour watched from behind his curtains.

'Would you . . . come over?' she said. She took out a note from her pocket. 'That's my address. It's not far.'

'Of course,' I told her.

Bingo.

'I have to get Douglas home now and—'

'That's Thora Point's dog,' she said. A tear travelled down her cheek.

'I'll be over as soon as I can,' I said.

'It's just . . .'

The woman looked out, over the square. She thought, then nodded with a slow bob of her head.

The curtain flickered behind her in Milton's house. The woman glanced at him and gave me a strange look, then she smiled at Douglas, before walking away.

See, I thought. Everyone loves dogs. Dogs are the best. And nosy neighbours the worst.

I closed the aunts' front door behind us and scratched his damp little doggy head as I took off his lead.

'There,' I said. 'That's better.'

He wagged his tail as he scuttled down the stairs to the kitchen. I started after him when I heard something.

A voice.

A thin chill ran through me.

I could hear the old fridge below, whirring, and the freezer beside it. In the sitting room, one of the aunts was snoring, and somewhere upstairs it sounded like Thora was on the phone.

Down between the walls, the pipes knocked and whistled, the water running through the old buildings.

I shook my head.

The door at the end of the corridor opened and I heard the click, click of Agnes's walker.

'It's the lesbian here,' said Agnes. 'Wake up, Flo.'

'It's Fi,' I said. 'I'm not actually a . . . not that, you know, it would matter . . . but that is . . .'

'What is it, girl?' said Agnes. 'Are the spirits at you?'

Was that what I heard?

I felt the pain shift in my heart. Was Robyn calling to me from the other side? Cold shivers ran over my skin.

'Where's my Douglas?' said Agnes.

'Agnes, does anyone else live here except you, Flo and Thora?'

'Daniel,' she corrected me.

Not the time, not the time, not the time . . .

'Would it be all right to take a look around the house, please?' I asked.

'Why, do you want to move in too?'

Not if it was the last house standing in a world filled with zombies and axe murderers. Not if it was the only oasis in a wasteland built from Stephen King's story notes.

'It's a lovely house,' I said sweetly.

Agnes made the kind of harrumphing sound only made by a woman over the age of eighty.

'I dare say you'll manage the stairs better than the rest of us,' she said.

The old aunt slowly placed her walker into the hall. She turned away from me and worked her way, click by click, down to the bathroom.

'She didn't say no,' I muttered.

I walked up the stairs slowly, each step intentional as if I was entering another place. The carpet was worn in the middle and dark against the boards. The paintwork was chipped and old. Years of neglect had left the colours faded and the nails missing in places, generations of spiders taking over the small gaps between the wood.

Above me, the light seemed to move as I climbed. The chandeliers on the ground floor cast a bright stage compared to the slim single bulbs behind the red shades on the wall of the first landing.

Four doors, all closed, each one unmarked. I could hear Thora, now, the low rumble of her voice as she talked to the unknown caller. Her bedroom overlooked the square; two wide windows, both dressed in thick red velvet curtains, mottled with moth holes.

I padded on to the next door. A simply decorated bathroom with a big tub of products on a table, and a chair by the bath, set to enable someone getting in and out.

The third door led to a study. Books lined the walls, dust on the shelves. I found myself drawn forward, my head on a tilt to read the titles: Jackie Collins, Jilly Cooper. All hardbacks. I stroked the back of a Penny Vincenzi I remembered from the small collection of my mother's things that had stayed on the bedside table at my dad's house. The things that to me had become, to all intents and purposes, my mother. I closed my eyes for a moment.

I breathed in the stale air. Time had stood quiet here, rarely disturbed. The previous cleaner had vacuumed around the furniture, leaving a tide mark in the old carpet. The big wooden desk and chair were still in place from whoever last sat down. A half-empty pad of writing paper waited with two blue biros and a crumpled-looking envelope, but whoever wrote the last letter had been in no hurry to repeat their act.

Flash: Francesca.

Flash: Niall.

Flash: Robyn.

My heart ached so deeply I could feel the pain rippling through my chest. Was he dead? Was he lost? What was going on?

Be careful Fi.

I shivered, remembering the words, the silly game. I'd been wrong at every turn and nothing I did had helped to find Niall or to solve Francesca's death, or to ease Merkin's worries.

I looked back at the Penny Vincenzi novel, but my mum was no more there in the pages than she was in the ceramic frog and the old brass pill box with the silver chain inside. The few prize possessions that my dad said goodnight to every night until the end of his life. The representation of a woman I never knew.

I looked in the last room, a small space with a single bed, and nothing hidden in the old wooden wardrobe that stood at the chimneybreast.

The next floor of the house was bare. Five rooms this time, each one the cut slice copy of Del's apartment, all pretty much empty save for a few boxes and crates and some discarded furniture.

I stood at the window. The square looked different from here than from Del's, despite being only a few metres away. Del's rooms were open and elegant and well designed, and the ornaments were set just so, each one sparkling. His windows were painted immaculately, dressed with beautifully lush curtains, and the furniture had been placed to use the best light.

Something itched in my head. Posters at TRASH. The shop. The petrol.

I walked back through the aunts' house as if in a dream.

As his boy self, Niall was not just an assistant to Merkin. He was her support, her right-hand man. And he was where this whole thing had started. I had to force myself to start there and not to think about Robyn. I swallowed down the sheet-white fear that lodged in my throat every time I thought of my best friend gone.

I had to go back to the basics, to think about it in a different way. Most killing made sense, even if it was the kind of sense that only occurred to a rampant sociopathic homicidal maniac like Robyn's sister. People didn't often kill without reason, and they didn't disappear without reason, either.

Miss Merkin, although prone to theatrics, understood people. I didn't believe that someone she could take into her heart would be capable of that level of nonsensical killing, so it stood to reason that if Niall hadn't killed Francesca, and therefore something else happened to her, then something had also happened to him.

The fact that Niall's body had not shown up was a good thing. It meant that he was still possibly alive, at least until proven dead, and alive people were easier to keep hidden than dead ones. Patrick had told me that. Dead ones started to smell really quickly. Dead bodies were gruesome things.

It's the flies, he'd told me as we lay around in the long grass, talking about Robyn's favourite detective series. All these crime shows, and no one ever mentions the flies, Patrick had grumbled as Robyn screwed up his mouth in disgust. Flies, and poo, he added. You know the body leaks the things that are inside it, right? You can't just hack someone up and leave them there in the hall. The neighbours pretty much always complain about the smell. You'd be surprised how many we've had brought in after the pest control man had been called, he'd said.

I smiled, hearing his voice in my head, the way he saw life through the strangeness of his own square glasses.

He was a good man, was Patrick Midda. He was kind and careful, and yet he wasn't too careful of me. He didn't follow me like I was breakable, like Del and Robyn did sometimes.

And there was this fizzle that happened in my gut when I thought about him, and the way my head spun when he called, and the way I couldn't stop smiling those few months before it all went wrong.

I wished, more than anything in the world, that my dad were still alive, so he could have met Patrick. He'd have liked him, and he'd have liked Annie.

I shook myself. My dad would tell me the truth. Keep your head square, he'd have said. Eyes forward. I was looking for Robyn but I was avoiding seeing the one truth we had.

It all started with Niall Ash.

And Niall wasn't just Niall. He was Sparkle McCavity.

I did the washing up and I took tea to the aunts, both of whom were now asleep in their chairs. I turned down the fire just a notch – from tropical to just incredibly warm. I let myself out and, with barely a hesitation, I walked around the corner and down the road to Ingrid and Francesca's apartment and rang the top bell.

Chapter Twenty-Two

On the top floor of a modern apartment block, the young women's rooms were cluttered and untidy. Like a sepia image of Del's, the rooms were similarly set out, but these ones were furnished on the salary of two people who didn't inherit their basic furnishings from an elderly relative with exquisite taste.

Ingrid was twenty-two, maybe twenty-three, but as she led the way into the kitchen, she moved like an old man. She ran her hands through her hair, pushing it upright in a mess of thick waves, like a lawn left to its own devices. She wore skinny jeans and a baggy black jumper, holes in the cuffs with her thumbs pushed through, and she had cream woolly socks on her feet. By the door, boots and shoes were lined up in a long row, different styles, and I wondered if anyone had offered to help Ingrid with her late girlfriend's things or if they were still there because the idea of them not being there was just too painful.

'Can I get you a tea?' she said. 'We don't have coffee.'

'Tea's great, thanks,' I said. 'Look, can I just say I'm so sorry.'

'Yeah,' said Ingrid. 'Everyone is.'

We sat at the table. On the windowsill, two flowering pink plants grew without any bother to the room or the evident loss within it. We talked about nothing, about the weather and the cold.

The table wobbled, just a fraction, and I leaned on my corner to stop it moving in case it upset Ingrid any further.

'I wanted to talk to you,' said Ingrid suddenly. 'I've read your blogs.'

'Oh, um . . .'

I tried to remember what I'd written.

'We know Niall, of course,' she said. 'He's lovely – he's always been a great help to us, you know? We were at UL together, did he tell you?'

'Actually, I haven't ever talked to him,' I said.

'Oh right. Only you seem to be in with the drag family, so I thought.'

'No one has seen him,' I said. 'Not for weeks. And now Robyn is missing too.'

She knew that. The room fell quiet, the clock on the wall too loud.

I had so many questions, one after the other, each lining up inside my head, but my dad used to say that if you wanted someone to tell you something then the only way was to shut up and listen.

'I did think I should tell someone,' she said. 'I waited for you to go to her house, there, on the square. I figured you'd come here actually. To talk. They call you Hagatha.'

'They call me many things,' I said.

'I know we shouldn't have been in the club.' She picked at her cuffs. 'Thing is, you see – and I was going to tell Thora Point, and I was going to tell that detective, only I didn't want to go asking for trouble . . .' She stopped. Frowned. 'We were rehearsing this piece, this play I wrote, and I applied to the Arts Council for a grant but sure it never came through and rehearsal space is expensive, and we don't have a fancy place just for us like that . . .'

She stopped. I gulped at the tea, spilling a little on my jumper.

Ingrid focussed on the nothing-space in the middle of the room.

'We weren't doing anyone any harm,' she said. 'If anything, really, we were doing some good, I figured. I mean, you know, the arts are important, like, and I was only using TRASH right when no one else was there, we were in and out of the club no bother. We never went in before four, we made sure the bar staff and the cleaners were all done and that, and we were gone by eight in the morning. And we never disturbed anything. We might have had a drink, but never much. And we moved a few things so we could set the stage like we wanted but . . .'

'You moved the light?' I said.

Ingrid brushed her hand over her face.

'I figured Thora Point would never know so it didn't matter,' she said. 'What difference did it make to them? I was taking these pictures, you see, to send off our application to the festivals for next summer, and it was Francesca who said the light looked good next to the staircase.'

'But how did you get in?' I asked her. 'The place is alarmed.'

'Niall. He works at Miss M's, and since Thora isn't even running TRASH at the moment and everyone figured it would just close . . . and, I mean, we weren't doing anyone any harm. It was just this one time, we told him. He wrote Fran a note to meet him there, the first time. He copied the key for us from Miss M's keyring, and he wrote down the code. He made us promise we'd give it back, only he's not been there, and I could hardly walk up to Thora Point and give it back to her. And we weren't doing anything wrong. And it was meant to be this one time but the space was awesome for rehearsing. The energy was so good, and when Niall never asked for the key back and no one changed the alarm code . . . I figured maybe he wasn't worried and—'

'Not bothered about breaking and entering?' I asked.

Ahem . . .

'We had a key, though,' said Ingrid. 'So it wasn't really illegal.'

Right. So.

'When it happened, Fran had gone back to get the other bag,' she said. 'We had to take our stuff there and back every time, you see – we didn't want to risk anyone finding it and figuring out what we were doing. Thora Point would never have let us, and Miss M was all about following the rules. And I said to Fran . . . Anyway, it was going so well and I was really happy with what we'd got, I forgot to check we had everything. I left the bag there and I think we left a couple of glasses on the bar too – we only took a bit, like, they'd never notice it was gone, sure half of them drink like fishes – and we always cleaned up after . . .'

She spoke into her mug.

'I figured there's no point in saying, you know? Not now it's all over. I mean, that detective, he'd only want to arrest me for going in there, even though I didn't do anything, but I'd like to get the bag back . . .'

'Breaking and entering isn't exactly applauded.'

Note to self.

'But we were only borrowing the space,' she said. 'I'm not like you, Fi. I don't make friends with people who can help me.'

'That's not exactly how my life works.'

'Please don't put this in your blog,' she said. 'Miss M has always been so good to us. She pays our rent here, did she tell you? We'd been looking for ages and when this place came up . . . she said it sounded just what we needed. Since Fran's mum lives in England, you know, and it's not like . . .'

Yeah, I thought. Not like you had someone else to pick up your mess for you, and not like you could get a job, or two jobs, and live in one room for years and work and save like Robyn and I had done before we got our different-rooms-apartment.

But self-righteous anger, as Del said, should be left only for marches and hairdressers.

'I'm so sorry,' I said. I touched her wrist. 'It must have been awful. Really, it was a terrible accident.'

'Oh, it was no accident,' said Ingrid. She looked up at me clearly for the first time, her eyes wet with tears, her mouth set in a line. 'Fran hated heights. She didn't fall . . . and she didn't do it on purpose, either, no way. I was making an omelette for her. I mean, she was just going back to get the bag, that was all, and to move the glasses, like. It wasn't even the middle of the night, it was seven or eight in the morning, you know? We were having breakfast. She was coming right back when she got the stuff . . .'

I set down my tea. 'So what do you think happened then?' I said.

Ingrid shrugged. 'It's obvious, isn't it? Someone killed her. Someone else was there, and they didn't want her to see them. And I'll tell you this, Fi,' she said, pointing her finger at me. 'We weren't the only ones getting in and out of there. I'm sure of it. But it wasn't Miss M, not in a million years. That old bitch raised Fran since she was a baby. She loved Fran more than anyone in the world. It was this other queen. I saw her one of the nights. Big blond wig. Really bad make-up. Shiny stuff on her.'

'Which queen was it?'

'I don't know, they all look the same, don't they?'

I took a breath, keeping my expression friendly, reminding myself that Ingrid was grieving – and if she ever came into the shop I'd double her idiot-tax. 'Well, no, not at all the same,' I said. 'Was she tall? Short?'

'I dunno. I didn't really see her face, anyway,' said Ingrid. 'So, can I have my bag? It's OK,' she said. 'I mean, I won't make any trouble.'

I turned the mug in my hands.

'She's all right, you know,' said Ingrid. 'Miss M, that is. She gave Niall that job at the shop even though he had no experience and she paid the rent here . . . Of course, that'll stop now, I reckon. Now they have her in jail. And it's not like I have my own auntie. I don't know what I'm going to do.'

'I imagine Merkin feels very much the same,' I said. 'You know she told the guards she killed Francesca, right?'

'She didn't do it,' said Ingrid with a shrug. 'They have to let her go.'

'Yes, but they don't seem to be doing so,' I told her. 'Look, if I call the guards now and you can tell them what you told me here and—'

'Oh no,' said Ingrid quickly. 'No, I'm not doing that. I told you. I have enough to deal with trying to find somewhere to live.'

'OK, but I think Merkin needs you. And maybe you have friends you could stay with, or—'

'Yeah, but who wants to share a place with their friends?' said Ingrid. 'I mean, it's not like we're still at college, you know?'

I stomped back to the square, kicking at rocks and sticks and anything in my way. At Thora's I stopped. I stood on the step. I pulled out my phone and dialled the detective's number. Unsurprisingly, the call went to voicemail.

'Hey, it's Fi,' I said. I spoke up. I spoke strong. 'I'm just on my way to see you at the station. Look, I know it's weird between us and a lot of that is my fault, but I think I've figured out what happened with Francesca. I'm on my way now.'

I'd have a quick word with Thora and then head over to the station. And on the way home, I'd get a takeaway. I really had to eat. If I had to spend the evening with the skin-crawlingly creepy detective, then I could at least get noodles after.

I could hear banging. The same banging we had heard from the kitchen.

Wall pipes didn't bang from outside a building. And they didn't bang in threes.

Bang bang bang. Stop. Bang bang bang. Stop. Bang bang bang.

'Hello?' I said. 'Hello? Is someone there?'

'Fi?'

It was Robyn's voice – it was definitely Robyn's voice! The words were muffled and so quiet, but the voice was clear. It was him, I was sure. I'd known him since we were eleven.

The banging was coming from next door. It was down by the basement. I could see a light now. I could hear voices calling. Not just Robyn's voice but—

I walked slowly down the steps. I never even heard the door opening behind me.

Chapter Twenty-Three

I woke in a dark, damp place, pain splitting my head, lights throbbing behind my eyes. Sickness rolled through me, and I gulped, the taste of petrol cloying in my mouth. A cloth was pressed to my face and on my tongue. I tried to bring up my hand to touch my neck, but my hand wouldn't move. I was stuck. Tied.

The scream balled in my throat.

'It's OK,' said a voice. 'Fi, it's OK.'

I fought to make sense of what was happening, panic rising with every second. There were more words muttered beside me, but I could not hear them – the sounds were screaming together, the dark was inside me, my body was constricted. I was half lying down, half sitting up, leaning against something solid, my ankles tied together, my knees the same. My hands were stuck behind my back, hurting so badly. There was a weight on my hip and when I tried to move, I felt a pull around my middle.

I cried out again, but once more the noise was strangled behind the thick, oily fabric in my mouth. My breath came too fast, my heartbeat was racing.

I couldn't see.

'Fi,' said another voice. 'Fi, isn't it? Fi? Listen to my voice, Fi. You need to breathe. Breathe slowly.'

The voice was too far away. I couldn't breathe slowly. I couldn't breathe at all.

'She's not listening,' said the first voice.

Robyn.

It was Robyn. 'It's OK,' he said again. 'It's OK, honey.'

The tears I had held back now filled my eyes. This was not OK, it really wasn't. OK was about as far away from—

But that had been Robyn's voice.

'Shhh,' he whispered. He was close to me. 'Stay quiet. Stay still,' he breathed.

There were noises. Another voice, a long way away across the room. The darkness came and went, black and grey and black and grey, and then there were footsteps going away – going up – and the darkness changed, softer, more complete, and I knew that the footsteps were on the stairs, up and up—

A door closed. A lock turned.

Silence. Long, long silence.

'Fi?' said Robyn.

I felt hands on my side; my body was rocked. I shied back. Something heavy was beside me, moving me, pushing against my arms. Terror roared in my head.

Then, the fabric moved from my face, falling from my mouth, from my eyes.

The room was dark but there was a glimmer in the top corner of one wall, a gridded light. A window. I tried to move—

I was stuck. Ropes tied around me. Thick ropes. Mean ropes.

Movement to my side rustled and brushed against me. I pulled away. I struggled to see, to make sense of the shapes.

'Hey, it's me,' said Robyn. 'Breathe slowly, take a minute, honey. Breathe in through your nose, out through your mouth. Come on, babe. Please. Come back to me, Fi.'

I squeezed my eyes closed, cutting away even the thin streams of light. I focussed on my breath, on his voice. *IN. OUT.* It was Robyn. Robyn was here. We were OK. Wherever I was – and by now I had some fair idea coming back to me – Robyn was here too. He wasn't dead.

I caught a sob in my throat.

'Get a grip, girl,' he said softly. 'If Milton hears you, he'll be d-down.'

I tried to move toward Robyn's voice, but a tight band squeezed my chest. The ropes.

I couldn't see him but I felt him beside me. I felt his hand, his fingers on mine, just the tips, and I stretched back toward him until my fingers were laced with his.

Slowly, I caught my breath. He didn't speak for a while. He just squeezed my fingers over and over again.

'Hey,' I whispered.

My voice was gravelly and strange. I stuck out my tongue and ran it under my teeth. The inside of my mouth was thick with the taste of oil, or whatever had been on that fabric.

I took a couple of long breaths, filling my lungs.

Slowly, my eyes made sense of the shapes and the room came into focus. I let go of Robyn's hands and shuffled around.

'I-i-if you lean against the wall it helps,' he said. 'T-takes the pressure off the middle.'

I followed his guidance, pulling myself back bit by bit. I was lodged between a wall and a wooden crate. Underneath me were clammy, stinking blankets; my jeans were cold and wet, my knees throbbing. I shivered, the chill suddenly in my nerves. I forced myself around, pulling on the ropes until I was sitting up, my hands against the wall behind me, my shoulders back.

'Well,' I said. 'This is fun.'

'I win,' muttered the low voice from the far corner.

The outline of the speaker was small, the shape grey.

'He said your first word would be cursing,' said the man in a thin whisper. 'I told him it would take a while before the cursing started. Even Robyn here took an hour or two, once he'd stopped crying, that was.'

'I didn't cry,' said Robyn.

'I bloody did,' said the other man. 'Still am. No shame.'

'Niall?' I said.

'Yeah. I'm Niall, and neither of you are dying on me tonight, thank you. I'm so sorry, Fi,' he said. 'I'm so sorry about all of this.'

'It's not your fault,' said Robyn, his whisper louder.

'Hush!' said Niall.

Above us, a floorboard creaked. They both fell silent. My heart hammered in my chest and I wished I had Robyn still holding my hand.

In the silence, I started to piece together what happened. I was on the step at Thora's. I heard the banging. Three and then wait. Three and then wait. Three and then wait. The code. Then a voice, and then pain – sheer agony of pain in my head as something struck me—

And then nothing.

Milton, Robyn had said. The neighbour.

I looked up at the window. The light was definitely a street-light, so it was dark outside as well as in.

Unless I was wrong, I was in the basement right next door to Thora's aunts'. More importantly, so was Robyn, and so was Niall. They were both alive.

'You OK?' Robyn whispered, barely loud enough for me to hear.

'Define OK,' I said. 'I'm fairly sure I'm alive. Probably?'

He huffed a short laugh with no humour. 'Hang on t-to that thought,' he said dryly.

'Shh,' warned Niall again.

I twisted some more, ever so slowly, until I could look into Robyn's eyes. His face was swollen, his lip cut, and stuck on his head was some kind of bandage crudely covering bleeding.

He shrugged. 'It's not as bad as it looks,' he said.

It was a thousand times worse.

I stared at my friend, beaten and bruised, there in the dark. It was only hours later as I fell in and out of some kind of sleep that I wondered if I looked the same.

◆ ◆ ◆

The sunrise brought fresh cold. Again, we could hear movement upstairs. Both Niall and Robyn followed the steps with their eyes. The front door opened and closed and then the air changed, just a tiny bit, as if sucked from under the door at the top of the stairs.

The room was big, the ceiling high, but the stark walls and the bare, aging pieces of furniture that stood around were all just out of reach and did nothing to soften the space.

As the daylight streamed through the tiny gaps in the window grille, I could make out posters all around the walls. Often the same one repeated five, six times; the corners torn, the edges ruffled and creased. Sparkle McCavity's face beaming down at us in stark comparison to the thin boy on the other side of the room.

I hurt all over. My shoulders were agony. My hands were twisted behind me. My legs were bruised, and one knee was bloodied, the stain seeping through my jeans. I adjusted my position over and over again but nothing I did relieved the pain. And worse – even worse – I really needed to pee.

Robyn and Niall were waiting for something. Niall gestured with his eyes to the ceiling, to the window, and I heard the heavy front door close again and footsteps outside, down the steps. They waited ten, twenty seconds, and then I heard them both breathe out long sighs.

'Shit, shit, shit, shit,' said Niall.

'OK, we have about t-ten minutes,' said Robyn, talking at a normal volume. 'Maybe fifteen. Are you hurt, girl?'

'Ten minutes until what?' I said.

'He comes back,' said Niall, through his teeth. 'Milton Doyle,' he said. 'Age around thirty something, I think. Used to have a mother here . . .'

'The one next to the aunts?' Without thinking, I went to move my hand to scratch my head, but my hands were tied.

'Batshit crazy,' Robyn added. 'Got me when I left the aunts. I didn't know Niall was here. I dropped my keys down the bloody steps and went down to get them. Cue psycho bloke. The next thing I knew I got a knock on the back of my head and I woke up here.'

'God, I'm so, so sorry guys,' said Niall.

'Not your fault,' Robyn told him. 'Fi, we can talk later when he takes his walk, and Niall can knock the pipe there. Milton heads out to get the milk or paper, we think . . .'

'I've got to pee,' I said quietly.

'He'll take us, one by one,' said Niall. 'We're allowed to the toilet over there.'

'Be careful, he's armed, though,' said Robyn. 'He looks small but he has this blaster thingie – it shocks you and it really hurts. He's slap happy with it too. Don't try anything.'

'But—'

'Not yet,' said Robyn. 'He got you three times last night while you were barely conscious, even after he'd dragged you down the stairs.'

He shook his head and winced. 'We'll have time to talk later, this evening. He goes out every evening and we shout. Niall bangs the pipes and—'

'Someone will hear the pipes,' said Niall. 'Next door . . . you heard, right? Robyn said how you heard us. He said to do the threes.'

I nodded, dislodging the pain in my head like a billiard ball, sending it rattling from inside my skull, behind my eyes.

'Shit,' I hissed. I felt sick. I was going to throw up.

'As situations go, I'll give you, it's not ideal,' said Robyn. 'We're OK though. Keep telling yourself that, we're OK.'

Despite myself, I grinned. 'We've lived in worse places,' I said.

'Really? My corner has a cockroach the size of Douglas.'

'That's nice. You've always wanted a pet.'

'You two are weird,' said Niall.

'Yeah.' I looked over to Robyn. His body was cramped and twisted, tied like mine with thick rope, his hands behind his back, his legs bent under him. The cords ran to the wall, heavy knots tied, the sides scratched. I wondered how long he'd picked and scratched with his nails.

He shrugged. 'Take it slowly when you get up for the bathroom,' he said. 'You'll feel like you want to throw up.'

'With you there, mate,' I told him.

'There's a sink by the toilet too,' said Niall. 'Get him to undo your hands if you can. The water from the sink is safe to drink but he won't want you to do so, so be quick.'

'Don't eat the food,' said Robyn. 'It's drugged.'

'Same as the water he brings you.'

'All the fun of the fair,' I grumbled.

'Yeah, he's a real charmer, this one,' said Niall. 'A real catch.'

'Like syphilis.'

We fell quiet again. Outside, the footsteps were back. Robyn suddenly jerked his head toward me.

'The gag!' he said.

The soggy oily rag was hanging around my neck.

'Sorry?'

'He mustn't know I can reach you!'

There was no ignoring the terror in his voice. Shifting my chin down, I caught the fabric with my teeth and pulled, gagging and retching, nudging with my shoulder and shifting against the wall until it moved. By the time the inside door opened and an electric light blinked on above us, I had the wad of fabric stuffed over my mouth, the folds caught between my teeth, at least while I kept it pressed against the wall.

The man who stood in the doorway was exactly like I remembered from the doorstep. He looked down, assessing us. I tried to look back, but the light made everything swim and the stubborn pain in my head shifted my sight until the stairs doubled and bowed, the walls breathing.

The man was looking at Niall.

So, I thought. *This is it. This is why.*

'Hey, sweetie,' said Niall.

Milton walked slowly down the steps, one at a time, placing his feet on each board as if judging the exact place to do so. In his right hand he held a truncheon-type thing – a thick black pole about the size of my forearm. It was the stick that Robyn and Niall were watching, not the man. Not his eyes – pale thin eyes – and not his mouth, the way he smiled as if he knew something that we didn't. And not his feet as they brought him closer, one precise step after the next.

Then he turned to me. My blood chilled.

'Fi, isn't it?' the man said. 'Fi McKinnery?'

Step. Step. Closer. Closer.

From his back pocket he pulled out a phone – my phone, the same scratches on the top corner, the sticker on the back.

'Your friend Del seems ever so upset you're not picking up,' said Milton. 'And Stan, too . . . Or is it Annie? I'm never quite sure, but then reading your messages it seems . . . neither are you?'

I felt the flush of anger rush over my body, the heat in my chest and my neck and my face. I wished I'd locked my phone. I wished I had turned away from the step. I wished . . . I wished so damn hard that I'd told someone where I was going. We had been so careful. Every time we went anywhere since the summer, we'd told someone. It was a symptom of the experience when someone tries to kill you, Del used to joke. We'd text first, and then we'd talk when we got there. Every time. Leave no misfit behind, that was what we said. Make sure none of us were ever alone.

'*Hey, doll* . . . that's from Del,' said Milton. '*Hey, Fi* . . . that's next. Then after a while he stops saying *Hey*. Funny that, isn't it? They all stop, after a while. He sent you twenty-five messages last night. He said he was coming over too. I might head back to your place today, see if he comes round . . .'

He waggled the strange weapon in his hand. I jerked forward, my eyes wide, my begging cries muffled by the rag in my mouth.

'Don't hurt him,' I tried to beg.

But the words came out stifled.

And there it was. I'd lost.

I saw it in his face, the moment of triumph.

'I might, I might not. There's nothing you can do to stop me,' he said. He brushed his fringe from his eyes. 'You won't care, by then. You'll be dead.'

Chapter Twenty-Four

He took Robyn first. He stood behind him, holding that strange weapon-stick an inch from my best friend's shoulder blades. He pushed with his feet, kicking Robyn around the stairs. Robyn swayed as he stood but he held up his head. As the man unlocked his hands, Robyn almost bit back the cry on his lips. He rolled his shoulder forward.

'Go on with you,' said Milton. 'I don't have all day.'

I wondered what it was that this man did for a job, for a living. What it was that kept him behind those closed doors all day? I wanted to ask him.

But more, I wanted to hurt him.

The bathroom was at the back of the cellar space. I peered around to see, but Niall shook his head. I tried to hold his gaze but the guilt and the horror and the fear in his eyes was too much.

I'd never truly wanted to hurt anyone as far as I could remember. But this man standing there behind Robyn? I wanted to hurt him.

Desperation ran through me like hot oil in my veins, filling me with strength.

I wanted to beat him raw. I dug my fingernails into my palms. I wanted to pull him away from Robyn and—

'Can I wash my face?' Robyn asked.

'Why? You planning on looking pretty?' said Milton. He chuckled.

'I'd like t—' Robyn started. 'Please.'

'Be quick,' Milton said. 'You're not meant to be here – neither of you are meant to be here!'

Robyn drank quickly from the water. For a moment I thought he was managing to hide it, but then the man reached out with his foot and kicked, hard and sharp to my head—

The room flickered. I was in the club, holding Gloria. I was there, on the floor. I was at school, my own legs bearing the brunt of some kid I'd just pulled off Robyn.

'Get down,' Milton said to Robyn. 'You do that, she hurts. You get it?'

Robyn moved back to his ropes, his entire stance looking defeated. His hands were still wet. Water dripped from his face. Slowly, he wiped his hands on his shirt. He knelt down and tried to set his arms behind him again. He tried twice but they wouldn't move that way. The pain was clearly too much.

'Please,' he said. 'It's my fault. I must have slept on them funny. May I please keep my hands like N— Like Sparkle?'

'Sparkle McCavity needs to do her face,' said Milton. Again, he brushed his fringe from his eyes. 'Sparkle McCavity needs to be pretty.'

'But Robyn could be pretty too?' said Niall. 'If you want, that is. You'd have us both here for y—'

At first it looked like the man might agree, but then he yanked Robyn's hands back behind him.

Milton set the weapon down on the floor so he could grab both of Robyn's hands and clip on the handcuffs. Robyn looked at me, but I couldn't reach. As Robyn fell forward, he let his shoulder take the roll. He opened his eyes, just a little – just enough – and I got it, I understood what he was saying. I nodded, barely moving.

Milton needed both hands to tie us.

He would put down his stick when he brought me back from the toilet. Robyn wasn't strong enough to fight. He would have been normally – he was a great deal fitter than me – but he was covered in cuts and bruises and goodness knew what else, and his body was bent from pain.

But I was going to be next.

I hated pain. I knew from the way the man looked at me that he would hurt me. It was a look that made even a beautiful face age-old ugly, and there was nothing about Milton that spoke of beauty.

'Turn,' he said. 'Stupid bitch.'

The man probably didn't like women, I figured. He had issues.

He pushed me until my head hit the wall, and then kept the stick poking at my neck while he waved me to walk.

He was left-handed, so. I moved up slowly. My shoulders were agony, but I let myself feel the pain, to show him I was weak to his hand. I played my card – I was nothing, I wasn't a threat, my body language told him. The pain ran up and down my body – worse than anything I'd ever known. Worse than my appendix pain. Worse than when I broke my arm.

He pulled me around but he didn't really want to touch me. He'd rather use his stick.

Milton's breath smelled of something sweet like candyfloss. Like plastic clouds. His eyes watered. If I'd photographed him, I'd have put him against a plain white wall. Preferably with numbers across his chest. His hair was a dirty blond, the long fringe constantly irritating his eyes. He wore a cream checked shirt under a brown V-neck jumper and his jeans were straight cut, loose. He moved his hands constantly, clenching and unclenching, gripping his weapon stick. It was his security, his happy place: causing pain.

I tried to smile but there was no point. Milton hated me, for whatever reason. There was nothing I could do to soften his cruel loathing.

I edged toward the bathroom, but he laughed, pulling me back toward the stairs. His grin was like a grimace, a leer of power. I suddenly really, really didn't want to go up the stairs.

'Please,' said Robyn. 'Please, Milton. Take me instead. D-don't hurt her. She hasn't done anything. She's nothing. She's nothing to any of us. L-let her go, please, and she won't tell anyone . . .'

Milton laughed. 'Oh, you think?' he said. 'You want me to believe that this Fi McKinnery of the blog – the foolish bridge blog – won't tell anyone?'

Without warning, Milton spun around and jammed the baton at Robyn, pressing it into his arm. The stun gun crackled, a blue light at its head. Robyn fell back. Milton lifted the weapon again, and this time brought it down like a truncheon on the back of Robyn's head in a crack.

I cried out. I lurched toward Milton but he lifted the stick again, over Robyn's head.

'Stay there, Fi,' said Niall.

Milton smiled slowly, a slick cat smile, as he turned back to the other man.

'Wise words, my love,' he said. 'Now, Fi . . .'

I tried to speak. I lodged both feet on the floor, trying to make words through the gag. Milton pulled off my gag. His hands smelled of something nasty and something wrong.

'Please,' I begged. 'I just need to pee.'

'Oh no,' he said. 'No, I don't think we need to worry about that. You and I are going to take a little drive.'

I didn't need Robyn's whimper.

'A drive?' I turned, just a little. His left-hand side was the strong one. I pulled back my arm, inch by inch. 'Where to?' I asked him.

'Does it matter?'

'Well, if I don't know where we're going, how do I know what to wear?' I said. I laughed, as if it was funny. Over by the wall, Niall laughed with me.

'Can I come?' he said. Behind Milton's gaze he nodded to me, to the bathroom. 'A family day trip.'

'I'm sorry,' I said. 'But I really, really do need to pee.'

'She'll only end up peeing in the car, if you don't let her,' said Niall.

'Why?' said Milton.

'Oh, you know girls,' said Niall.

'Oh, yes,' I said. 'Yeah, we're really bad at that.'

In truth, I could go twice as long as Robyn and still hold it until we made it home. We're amazing, women. We have to be. We go for hours, some of us, and that's even considering how much coffee I drink.

'Women are dreadful,' I said. 'Ghastly.'

'Are you a Brit?' he said.

'Me? No.'

I was half English and half Irish, but . . .

'No,' I said, letting my vowels expand. 'Oh no, to be sure . . .'

Too far, Fi.

Milton frowned but he seemed worried about his car. He undid my hands and nudged me forward to the bathroom. Slowly easing my arms forward, I staggered as I imagined burying my fist in his face. I'd never actually punched anyone before. I tried to remember what Del had told me about hitting, if you had to. Was it thumb over fingers or thumb inside fingers? And what if my thumb was the strongest bit of my hand? Did I aim for the nose like they did on cartoons or for the jaw like they did in the movies? But then in the movies, they were only aiming for the cheek because the punch was slid. It was fake. It didn't connect.

261

The toilet reeked of pee. It didn't have a seat. I fumbled with my trousers. I needed to go so badly that my mouth was salivating, and my bladder hurt with the sheer effort of holding it.

I sat on the edge of the rim and tried not to think about the dirt, or about the spiders in their webs over my head. I was taking too long – I could feel the irritation throbbing in Milton but now I was there, I just couldn't stop peeing. Even if he blasted me with his pointy stick I knew I would not stop.

As I finally finished, I took a scrap of paper from the roll, the tiniest bit. I cleaned and then reached to the sink to wash my hands.

'What are you doing?' he said.

'I got pee on my hands,' I lied. 'I don't want to get it on your car.'

My mouth was so dry I was desperate for a drink. I washed my hands quickly and cupped the water but as I started to bend down my head there was a knock upstairs. A heavy doorbell rang.

'Move!' Milton grabbed my shoulder. I scrabbled as I lurched toward him, my hands flailing.

The blast hit me on my neck. The pain ran through me as the electricity flooded my body. I saw him lift the weapon stick. I saw it coming down.

◆ ◆ ◆

'You've really got to stop fainting,' said Robyn dryly.

I blinked as the light blared into my eyes. The walls were swaying, breathing in and out, but at least this time I didn't have the rag inside my mouth, only over the top. I groaned. Inch by inch I worked my way back to Robyn, and after feeling him fumble at the back of my neck, the gag slipped down to my throat.

I swore, repeatedly, each word whispered in a bite of rage until I had used every curse I knew. We were tied up, we'd been hurt and threatened and humiliated. But as the room came back into focus I was done being frightened – I was absolutely bloody furious.

'See, that's my girl,' Robyn whispered.

'Well, this is shit,' I said, as we worked around until our backs were to the wall. 'Now, who wants to tell me what's actually going on in this hellhole?'

'Sparkle?' said Robyn. 'You want to take this?'

'Christ, don't call me that,' said Niall. 'I'm done with drag. Never again. I swear, if this is ever over, if I ever see another wig . . .'

'Oh, I don't know,' Robyn said. 'I'd say your look the other night was spectacular.'

'That's because you have terrible taste in clothes and make-up and wigs and shoes . . . Oh, and music too,' said Niall.

Robyn giggled, but there was nothing to laugh at. A tear rolled down Niall's cheek. He caught his breath.

'He was just another geeky, weird, quiet little fan,' he said. 'We get them now and then. The weird ones. And usually I love them . . .'

I glanced at Robyn.

'He used to bring us gifts,' said Niall. 'He had flowers sent to where I was going to be, and to the shop. Like, loads of flowers. I didn't think anything of it at first. He never put his name to them, but I knew they were from him. I wasn't playing dirty with his feelings. I never encouraged it . . .'

Robyn and I were quiet.

'Sometimes I wondered if the flowers were from Miss M. Merkin is kind of in love with me,' he said, in the end. 'I mean, everyone knows, right? She never said so to my face, but she didn't need to. Jesus, I worked hard for her, but she was never creepy.

She was sweet. She taught me to stand up for myself, to believe in myself, and—'

He sounded angry.

'It's OK,' I said.

'Yeah, but it's not OK, Fi,' he told me. 'I let it happen. All of it. I started to believe I was someone. And then the flowers came from Milton, and the gifts came, and I didn't stop him. I let him send them, because it was flattering, you know? It was a bloody ego boost. I had a fan! Milton showed up to all my gigs. He was always there, and I'd say hi. I'd kiss his cheek, you know?' Niall looked sick. 'And I'd see the smile on his face and in my head . . . God forgive me.' His voice broke. 'I'd laugh. And I never even thought about him until I woke up here.'

Robyn leaned toward me.

'We think Milton mostly lives on the upper floors,' he said. 'He's pretty set in his routine. We should have a g-good hour or so now but keep your voice low and be careful when he comes down. Don't get hit by that thing he carries.'

'This would be more a do-what-I-say-and-not-what-I-do-type situation?' I said.

'That stun gun is his favourite toy,' said Niall. 'Apart from yours truly,' he added. 'From what I can tell, from what it did to Robyn the first night he joined me here in my own personal hell, it's much stronger than a normal stun gun.'

'Also he likes hitting people, but he isn't any good at it,' Robyn added. 'His arm gets tired.'

'Thank the gods for small mercies,' I said. 'Our latest psychopathic lunatic is a wuss.'

Upstairs, someone walked past the window. I opened my mouth to shout, but Niall held up his hands.

'No,' he said. 'Save your strength, they're too far away. They can't properly hear us unless they are right outside the window there like you were. We can try later. I've been banging on the pipes and shouting every time he goes out.'

'Someone came over earlier,' said Robyn. 'That knock on the d-door. When he had to tie you up again. Our little Hitler was furious to be interrupted from dragging you away to kill you.'

'Was it one of us? Del?'

Had Milton hurt him?

'Could have been anyone. The walls are thick, the window the same,' said Niall. 'I'm telling you, the only way out of here is to somehow get that stick off him – and before you think it's that easy, then we'd have to figure out how to get through that door.' He nodded to the stairs. 'It's a foot thick and he's got a security code on the lock. He changes the code every day. And he only unlocks us once a day to pee.'

'He's kind of obsessive.' Robyn nodded to the posters on the wall.

'You don't say.'

Niall growled. 'So even if you get past him, you can't get out,' he said. 'He will never give up the code willingly. I've watched his fingers, it's eight digits.'

Great, I thought. *Bloody great.* So we were stuck. The best we could manage was to get free of our ropes and then we'd still be stuck in this pit.

'Is he really going to try to kill me?' I said. The words sounded ridiculous out loud.

'Try? Yes, probably,' said Niall.

'But we won't let him,' said Robyn.

'We have no chance of stopping him,' Niall told him. 'You're on your own, Fi. I'm sorry, girl. Do everything you can – there's no fairy godmother with a bunch of talking mice.'

Upstairs, the front door opened and closed with a bang. Floorboards creaked and groaned, the staircase aching under his slight steps. The sounds grew fainter and then music started, the same old songs I'd heard from the aunts' house next door.

'This is really weird,' I hissed.

'Oh, he's all kinds of messed up,' said Niall. 'It's put me right off jazz.'

'It's ruined Rick O'Shea on a Sunday morning for me,' Robyn muttered. 'From now on, the only thing we're playing is disco and nineties rave stuff.'

'I might just stay here,' I muttered.

'So, what's the plan?' he said.

'The plan?'

'You always have a plan.'

'In case you didn't notice, I was busy being unconscious,' I said. 'What part of that do you think gave me time to make a plan?'

'But you have, haven't you?' he said. 'You have s-something?'

The pain in the back of my head bounced against my eyes.

'She always has a plan,' Robyn said to Niall. 'And don't worry if they sound stupid at first . . .'

'Oh, thanks!'

'That's only because they usually *are* stupid plans,' said Robyn.

'You can go off some people,' I told him.

Upstairs, the floor squeaked, the footsteps in time to the music.

'I reckon he dances,' said Niall quietly. 'He misses his mamma. She brought him up in this house, you know. He used to talk about her, when it was just him and me . . . Oh God . . .'

'Did she also tie people up in the basement and feed them tranquillisers in their food?' said Robyn.

'It's sad, really,' said Niall.

'Remind me to revisit that thought after we get out of here,' I told him.

'See?' said Robyn. 'Fi has a plan. I knew it.'

I rubbed my forehead against the wall. 'I have something,' I said. 'But it's not smart.'

'I'm in,' said Robyn.

Upstairs the song ended, and another started. A Vera Lynn number.

'I'm so, so in,' said Niall.

Chapter Twenty-Five

Milton was thirty-five, I reckoned, with the musical taste of a man who did not move on from his favourite five songs. He played the same tracks every night, Niall said, and I imagined Milton sliding out old records from dusty cardboard sleeves, from their thin paper linings, and setting them on a gramophone that his mother had used when she was young, and her mother before that.

He wore loose slacks and checked shirts and sleeveless sweater vests, changing his entire outfit every day, Robyn told me. He never varied the fashion. I pictured him as someone who drank milky Horlicks at night. When he was done mentally torturing the drag queens trapped in his basement. He would eat the same breakfast every day, when he had finished checking on his prisoners. I wondered who he would have been if he hadn't been quite so barking mad.

He was clearly obsessed with Sparkle McCavity but he didn't care about Niall at all. True, every morning, he took the guys to use the bathroom. But I assumed this was more to save himself from cleaning up mess than to ease their discomfort. I logged this thought. If he didn't like mess, then the chances were he wouldn't murder any of us here, in the house. Which was something. Not a lot, admittedly, while he had the three of us chained to a wall and that evil stun gun in his hand, but it was something. Even if I got out of the house there was the walk to his car . . .

I refused to panic. If nothing else, I was determined to keep my mind. At least my gag was off.

The daytime was quiet over the square. No one knew we were there. Milton was a perfectly normal man, by all accounts. If I had thought of him at all after our brief meeting on the step, I would have remembered him as quiet, maybe a bit dull. Nervous. The aunts had liked him well enough, and they spoke about how good he was to his mother.

I gathered all the knowledge we had in my head.

I could do this.

'Education beats fear,' I whispered to myself. I had to know everything I could about him, and that way he would be a human being, and not a monster. I could take on a human being. After all, monsters were only what we made them. Only the stories we told.

As Robyn whispered to me, going over everything he could remember about Milton, he winced. I could see how much even the act of talking was hurting him with the bruising on his face. When he smiled, one of his teeth was cracked. I could have taken up that baton and beaten Milton for it there and then, for the money and care Robyn had spent on his damn teeth, the endless orthodontist appointments Edna had taken him to when he was in school. For the pain.

I breathed slowly, fighting the aching in my shoulders and my back. The rest I could live with – my hips were bruised, my legs scraped and battered, but my arms pinned behind me meant I had no let-up from the constant hurt, and Robyn looked a thousand times worse.

That bastard would pay, I promised myself. He'd go to jail. His name would be in the papers, and on the news. And people would know him for what he was. He'd be shut away from light in a prison, like he'd shut us away. Only he'd be shut away alone from all the nice things in life, like friendship and cushions and chocolate cake and freshly made real coffee with the milk perfectly frothed on top, brought by a best friend who only wanted to help, even if he kept saying *vagina*.

My head swam; I had to focus.

Left hand. Pointy stick. Likes things clean. Doesn't understand women.

I had to move like Del had tried to teach me, to twist from low down and to disarm him. But then if he wouldn't let us out of there, then what?

I looked up at the window.

The space between the bars was just about large enough to get through if I knocked a hole through the toughened glass.

I looked around the room. Milton had obviously planned to keep Niall for a while, I figured, but Robyn and me, we were a panic move. He must have had the basement ready for ages. Months, even. The Sellotape holding up the posters was dry and cracked, the walls were dusty, and the blankets smelled damp. It wasn't a room where anyone lived, it was storage space. One old fridge, a bunch of cardboard boxes, a few throws.

I pictured him hiding down there from his mother, with his posters and his sequins.

Great.

Time dragged. After a while, even my sarcasm deserted me.

'Fi?' Robyn whispered.

'Yeah, honey?'

'If I die, will you tell Gavin that I . . .' He didn't finish the sentence.

'Sure,' I said. 'But you're not going to die.'

'I miss him. I feel like everything is fading.'

'That's because you're hungry,' I said. 'You need a big dinner of noodles and—'

'No,' he said, so quietly I could barely hear. 'The room is b-black and white, girl. I can't . . . I can't see right.'

I tried to speak; my throat was tight with fear. Hot tears burned at my eyes.

'Hang in there,' said Niall. 'You hear me, Robyn? You hang in there. I'll call him down. I'll have him give you water.'

'No, not if he puts drugs in it,' I said. 'Robyn needs medical help. If we have a chance to beat him, Milton has to think nothing has changed. That he's strong and we are weak. If he feels like he's in charge when he comes down, then he won't suspect anything. He can't be ready for something new. Robyn? Can you keep going?'

My breath stuttered. Was I risking my best friend on a hunch?

'Maybe it won't work anyway,' I said. 'Maybe we should yell, or shout, or . . .'

'Fi will do it,' said Robyn, dreamily. 'She's great, you know. Even when there was a bomb . . . everyone else was running away. And she could have run away too, but she ran straight to it.'

'That's more of an example as to how my plans err on the stupid side,' I said. 'Del is the smart one, not me. And you were there with the bomb. You're stronger than anyone I know.'

Robyn smiled. His eyes were dry. 'Nah,' he said. 'It's who you are, love. You take on the dragon. You always have.'

'With you beside me I can do anything,' I told him. 'So no dying, OK?'

'OK.'

'I need you right here,' I said. 'You die and I'll fall apart, Robyn. I can't do it.' My voice broke.

'I think he's coming,' Niall hissed. 'That's my number.'

The music had changed. Footsteps worked over and back.

'Stay asleep,' said Niall. 'Trust me.'

'I need to pee,' Robyn whimpered.

'You listen to me,' said Niall. As he sat up, I saw the strength in his face, in his body. 'You can't take another beating, mate. You're better off peeing in your shorts than dying. You stay with us, OK? Fi is going to get you out of here.'

'Fi?'

'I'm here,' I told him.

'I trust you,' he said quietly.

So, now I couldn't fail. Niall was crippled. Robyn desperately needed help. I didn't have time to fail again.

The plan was simple.

Get up. Disarm crazy person. Tie up crazy person. Free friends. Escape.

It would work because it had to work. Because we were out of options.

I rolled forward to look like I was asleep. The door opened.

Niall kept him talking. He told Milton we were asleep, and I let myself slump into the pain in my back. I closed my eyes but kept them fluttering, just a slit, and I watched as Milton sat on the stairs.

Niall had a wig on his blanket. He clipped huge sparkling earrings to his ears, fumbling them at first, struggling to reach up his hands. He painted his eyes with the few colours on the floor beside him, and he drew thick lines of grey and black where his eyebrows were – eye liner with a red stem, I remembered CK or Gloria losing. He painted his lips in a bright candy pink. He looked weird. More like an aging Bette Davis than a young Marilyn.

I watched him arrange the shawl around his shoulders, struggling with his hands still tied together.

He was still Niall. He had the make-up done – of sorts – and the wig, and the shiny earrings. But the queen was dead, and he was a man in a dress. A doll in a horror movie. Far from shining and glittering, he was scared and damaged.

'You're so beautiful,' said Milton. 'I always wanted a best friend. I knew the first time we met that it was you.'

I looked at Milton's face under the naked light. His eyes were eager, his mouth open, his lips wet. He never once looked behind him. Not that he was at any risk from us, halfway up the stairs, but he was at a show. His eyes shone with magic, and he was as excited as the young ones who lined up at Thora's performances, and who followed Mae B around with their phones and their giggles, screaming when Del pointed them out in the crowd. Milton was a truly obsessive fan. By far the most intense I'd ever seen. And that was saying something.

I glanced at Robyn. He was asleep, or pretending to be asleep, but he was still breathing. That was good. Breathing was good, I told myself. Alive was a start. A low bar, but a start.

Milton pressed a remote control and a small stereo I hadn't noticed woke in the back of the room. Flickering blue lights rolled along the little screen. The speakers were stacked one on top of the other.

Speakers with speaker wire.

I watched the show.

Niall couldn't stand. He tried, more than once, but in the end, he had to stay on his knees. It was excruciating watching him move his arms with his hands still tied, turning his head. His lips framed each word automatically, but his eyes held only fear, and still there was Milton sitting on the stairs, lapping up every second of his private show.

Milton didn't want a friend. He wanted a bird in a cage. Sparkle McCavity wasn't Niall Ash. She wasn't even a fictional being, an act or a show, anymore. She was his, now. Kept for only him to see, there in the dark, damp basement.

Milton didn't realise Niall was weak with hunger, sick and exhausted and in pain, any more than he noticed Robyn's suffering;

he saw only the ruffles of the stupid shawl and the curls of the dirty wig that wasn't quite straight, and the shine of the earrings clipped to Niall's red ear lobes.

Niall did five tracks for Milton, a mix tape of messed-up drag. Milton watched, transfixed. He wiped a hand over his eyes. He was crying.

By the end of the show, Robyn had slumped deeper to the wall, his arms twisted around to the lock on the wall. Milton was deep in his own world, his mouth turned in a sweet smile as tears rolled down his face, his eyes glazed and lost.

It was the middle of the night. The key to Robyn's handcuffs was on Milton's belt. It might never work, we might both be dead by morning one way or another, but by the look of his face and the flickering of his closed eyes, I had to try.

I waited until Milton's tears had slowed and his breathing was calm.

'Excuse me, sir?' I said. I spoke clearly but in absolute submission. 'I'm really sorry to bother you, but . . .'

Milton looked confused, staring at me as if he'd forgotten I was even there.

'I was wondering if I may use the bathroom, please?' I said.

'But you've already been,' he said.

I looked at Niall. He sat curled into the wall, his knees up in front of him, his arms tight around them.

'Women need to go more often,' I said.

'No, I don't think so.' Milton started back up the stairs. His eyes were a little glazed as he turned to me.

'It's a girl thing,' I said. 'You see, I know you have plans, but even if you kill me . . . Well, my boyfriend used to be a pathologist, see – or rather, he still is but he isn't my boyfriend anymore – and anyway, he said how bodies tend to empty when they die – they leak and that, so even if you were to, you know, then I might make a mess of your car and . . .'

I smiled, ever so sweetly; the words *I hate you I hate you I hate you* ran in a tickertape through my brain.

Milton shook his head as he went for the door. I thought I was done but then Niall called out.

'Could you just take her?' he said.

'I'm really sorry,' I said. *I hate you I hate you I hate you.* 'I'll be quick, I promise.'

'I can't cope with her whining,' said Niall. 'Or, um, making a mess.'

Milton faltered a little on the stairs, then slowly, each step lasting a hundred years, came toward me. I kept my head low as he bent to free my hands from the wall. Then he was right over me. Right on top of me, his shoulder on the wall to balance.

One.

Two.

Three—

I moved quickly, slamming the back of my head into his face. I spun on my knee and shifted up. I nutted him with my forehead, right in the middle of his nose, knocking him over on to the floor. Turning, I grabbed for the weapon. I couldn't feel it behind me.

'Left!' said Niall.

I felt the bar in my fingers. I wrenched my hands as far around as I could until the front end was pointing toward him and I pressed the button on the side. Once, twice I blasted him until his body stopped shaking.

I unclipped the key from his belt and backed up to Niall for him to unlock me. I was shaking but Milton hadn't moved. As Niall freed my hands, I ran back, flipping Milton on to his belly and tying his own hands behind his back with the cuffs, fastening him to the bar that had held me.

His gaunt face stared, unseeing, at Robyn. His nose was broken, blood streaming over his lip, and his lip was cut open, and the side of his head was grazed where he'd fallen; he was unconscious, but he was alive.

'Well, Fi,' said Robyn. 'That's what I call using your head.'

Chapter Twenty-Six

Running first to Robyn and then to Niall, I undid them. I stuck my hand into Milton's pocket and found a small key, unlocked the chain on Niall's ankle, but although Niall really, really tried, neither of them could stand. With a sickened grimace I searched Milton's pockets, but he didn't have a phone on him, only a used cotton handkerchief that I folded into a square and pressed on his forehead to stem the blood on his cut.

'What the hell, Fi?' said Niall. 'Let me at him!'

'I know,' I said. 'What I want more than anything else is to kick him, but I'm not going to lie awake every night from now until I'm eighty-seven feeling guilty for killing or hurting this arsehole.'

'Let me,' said Robyn weakly. 'I can do it.'

'You can barely sit up,' I told him.

I lifted Robyn, and with his arm around my shoulders, helped him to the bathroom. His wrists were cut and bruised, and his body was ruined. But even as I led him back to the stairs, I knew it was the right thing to do, keeping the crazy lunatic kidnapper alive.

'What if he dies of natural causes?' said Robyn, reading my mind.

'He's going to jail,' I said. 'They can do what they like with him there.'

I climbed the stairs and tried the door. The lock held. I tried the keypad a few times. 99999999 and 12121212, and then just punching numbers at random over and over again.

I kicked the door, hurting my toe.

'Very helpful,' said Robyn. 'I'm fairly sure kicking things works.'

'What's your birthday?' I said to Niall.

'Huh?'

'A date he might have known. A date he might think he shared with you.'

We tried any number of dates – Niall's birthday, his gigs from the posters. Anything we could think.

'I don't—' said Niall. Again he tried to stand. 'Fi, sorry, I'm not feeling so good. Can you?'

I helped him to the toilet and waited with him while he threw up.

'I'm so gonna kill him,' Robyn muttered.

'Kill him later,' I said. 'We'll get ourselves out first, and then you can kill him. OK?'

I left them both on the stairs. Robyn held the evil nerve-gun-wand-thing in his hands, glaring at Milton, but Niall looked anywhere else rather than the unconscious man in the corner of the room.

'I need to get up to that window,' I said.

'OK,' said Robyn. He started to try to stand up, holding the banister, but his legs buckled, the weapon slipping.

'Keep that pointed at the bad guy,' I told him. 'It's OK.'

It wasn't even remotely OK. It was terrifyingly far from OK. It was weird and wrong and sad and smelly, and I was absolutely aware of how shallow and weak Robyn's breathing was – how he had spots of blood on his hand when he coughed – and how broken and beaten Niall was.

I put both my hands on the wall, hoping for a hook or something that I could pull myself up with. There was nothing. The window was at least nine feet from the floor, made from that tough glass that I was fairly sure was unbreakable, never mind the bars across it, but I'd think about all that once I got up there.

'What's here?' I muttered. 'What do we have?'

There's no shame in trying, my dad used to tell me. You only look foolish if you never try. *Well, if the spirits really can see us,* I thought, *then please, Dad, please tell me what I'm meant to do now . . .*

I walked back around the room. Lipstick, eye pencils, weird shiny drag that smelled of lavender and cold cream. An old plate. I held it in one hand then set it down. Blankets, throws . . . the chain . . .

I unlocked the long chain that had held Niall and swung it up, but the lock only clunked against the glass.

I looked back at the fridge.

Moving more like a sick sea turtle, limping and lurching, I pulled the fridge to the window. I balanced the stereo on top. Climbing up, I was so nearly there, the sill only inches from my reach.

'Fi?' said Robyn.

I spun around, barely stopping myself from falling off the fridge. He held up the stun gun.

Milton stirred.

I took the torture weapon, held it in my hand. I could hurt him. I could do it, I thought. It would be easy. I could press the little button and I could watch him suffer like he had watched Robyn – I could make him cry like he did Niall. I could kill him.

Only I couldn't, and neither could Robyn, not really, and unlike the crazy man in the corner, I never wanted to be someone who could do that stuff. I was quite happy being the quiet, slightly weird someone who tried to stop people getting hurt.

I took a breath.

'Robyn?' said Niall. 'Fi? Quick!'

Robyn had slumped against Niall.

'Shit,' I cried. I was out of time.

I climbed back up at the glass. I didn't think, I didn't even try the button, I just swung the heavy bar at the window, shattering the glass. I smashed and smashed and smashed. Outside there was noise . . .

'Hey!' I shouted. 'Help! We're in here!'

I bashed out the rest of the glass and jumped up, lifting myself, squeezing through the gap. My head went through, my neck, my shoulders . . .

I swore.

My boobs were stuck, the pointy edges of the glass sticking through my jacket.

'Need a hand there?' said a low voice from outside.

'Help!' I screamed.

'Is that Fi?' Someone was running. 'Where is she?'

A bang, and then another, and the front door crashed open.

My head was twisted. I couldn't see them – I could hear them but I couldn't stretch out. The fridge was getting wobbly, the glass digging into me . . .

'Get an ambulance,' I shouted. 'Robyn O'Neil and Niall Ash, both inside, extremely bad injuries. Get an—'

Behind me a crash shook the room. I tried to move forward but my boobs wouldn't shrink, and I tried to slip back but the glass cut me even more. My feet were slipping on the stereo.

'Careful! Don't move,' said a voice below me.

'Hang in there,' said another. A voice I knew so well. A low voice, a sweet, sweet voice. I was dying, I had to be. I was hallucinating. Hearing voices in my final moments . . .

Someone took hold of my legs. There were more and more people.

'It's OK, Fi, it's OK.' 'We're here now, it's OK,' said the voices.

'Get Robyn,' I told them. 'I'm fine. Take Robyn . . .'

I heard a siren coming. The glass was really cutting into me now, really hurting my boobs. I closed my eyes, pressing my face down to the wooden sill. I could hang on through the pain. It didn't matter. It only mattered that they saved Robyn.

'Hey,' said Del. He put his hand on my thigh. 'I'm here, Fi. I've got you. I'm going to get you back in now.'

I felt his hands around my waist. They were working together, breaking the glass, and lifting me up. Slowly, careful hands eased me back through the broken window.

Strong arms lowered me.

'Hey,' said Patrick. 'Fancy seeing you here.'

Together, Del and Patrick helped me down until I was sitting on the fridge. Del took off his shirt and folded it, pressing it to my chest. The door hung open, split, an axe leaning against it. On the stairs, three guards surrounded Robyn.

'Is he OK?' I said. 'Tell me . . .'

'Never better,' said Robyn, as they lifted him on to a stretcher. 'Fi . . .'

A uniformed guard came forward toward me. Moving like a ferocious mama bear, Del planted himself between us.

'Back off,' he hissed, his hands on his hips.

'I'm OK,' I told them.

'Fi, you're bleeding,' said Patrick.

I stared at him, blinking. It really was him. It was Patrick. 'But you're in South America,' I said.

'Oh, that was the other thing I was m-meant to tell you,' Robyn said weakly. 'I might have accidentally called Patrick's boss at the

281

dead place and left a message, the other week . . . told him . . . emergency . . . how you m-miss him, and . . .'

'I came as quickly as I could,' said Patrick. 'I see now, not quickly enough.'

'If you'll come with us,' the uniformed guard snapped at me.

'It was him,' said Niall. He pointed at Milton. 'He's the one that did this,' said Niall. 'Not Fi. Look at her: she was trying to escape. She was trying to save us.'

'I was totally saving us,' I said.

'Until your boobs got stuck,' said Del. 'Which isn't funny at all . . .'

The voices merged as Niall shouted and Del ranted, but when the guard freed Milton's hands, no one could deny the fear, the agony in Niall's face.

Milton tried it on all right. He pointed at me, claimed I was the kidnapper. Even said how he'd never met the other two. But his declarations were met with a tirade of protests from Niall and Robyn. And seeing as it was his own basement we were in and the walls were covered in posters of Sparkle, even the detective with the least couldn't miss that one.

'Milton Doyle, you're under arrest,' said O'Hara. He strode down the stairs, picking a scrap of wood from the broken door.

'I didn't mean to kill her,' Milton whimpered. 'I'm so sorry. I never meant to hurt her—'

'You chained this lot up to the bloody wall . . .' said the officer holding him.

'No,' said Milton, turning his dull face to the officer. 'The girl at the club. I pushed her. I didn't think she'd fall. I was just bringing Sparkle's clothes home, that's all. Her wigs and her favourite earrings, a few bits and pieces so she could do her face the way she likes. I knew that was where Francesca and Ingrid went. Sparkle went to meet them. I followed. They'd been going there loads and they never reset the alarm when they were inside. I saw her that morning. I followed her in. I wanted to see the queens' clothes, and touch them, pick the best for my girl here. I was only thinking of her, I wanted her to look pretty, and if Francesca hadn't seen me then it would never have happened. I never meant to hurt her at all, but she figured it out, you see, she was going to call you. She was going to stop me and Sparkle being together.'

'You pushed Francesca from the balcony at TRASH?' said Del.

Milton nodded, snivelling. 'But it was all such a big mistake. We've been so happy here, see, and I'd never do anything to hurt her . . . Only I can't have anyone stand between me and her, you see? It's real, what we have. But people don't see that. Like the old hag at that fancy bride shop, poking her nose in all the time. She wouldn't just let us be. She was trying to keep Sparkle and me apart, because she wanted Sparkle for herself. I just wanted her to leave us alone, that's all. Why can't people leave us alone? I told her, if she didn't leave me alone then I'd take away what she loved. I'd burn down her shop!'

He brushed his fringe from his face.

'So, I put on Sparkle's face. I took ages getting it right, I did all the make-up like she does and I wore her wig and her earrings, and I made sure the old bat saw me with the Molotov . . . I just wanted her to back off, that was all, but I never meant to kill the girl . . .'

'For the record,' Del told the officer, 'the suspect admits full guilt in the matters of the harassment of Miss M and of murdering Francesca M—'

'That's my job, thank you,' said Detective O'Hara, interrupting.

'Then maybe you should bloody do it for once,' Del snapped. 'Do your bloody job rather than picking on the first easy bloody target you can find and trying to make a case to fit. *Detective!*'

'But you'll tell them for me?' Milton stretched his hand to Del. 'You can get me off, right? You can tell them how we're friends.

You're a lawyer, I know you are – I've seen you on stage, and Sparkle has told me all about all her friends. And I can pay you . . .'

Del looked down on Milton Doyle. Then he turned away.

'Please?' said Milton.

'Let's go, Fi,' said Del. 'You're bleeding on my shirt and there's another ambulance on its way.'

Patrick carried me up the stairs. I blinked. It really was him. I closed my eyes for longer and then opened them again, but it was still Patrick. He was really there.

'You're staring at me,' he said.

'You're here?'

'You needed me. I came.'

'I was totally rescuing myself,' I whispered.

'Atta girl,' said Annie as she came down the hall, a baseball bat in her hands, with Thora right behind her, holding an antique bed warmer in one hand and her crutch in the other.

'I *was* rescuing myself,' I muttered.

'Of course you were, darling,' said Del, tucking in my leg as Patrick carried me through the broken front door. 'This way, Fi, honey, let's get your breasts sewn up. I tell you, it's a lot easier having removable boobies. Robyn . . . hang in there, love?' He raised his voice as Robyn was lifted into the first ambulance. 'One more victim and one crazy evil bad guy in the basement, people.' He directed the next team of guards as they hurried past us, then turned to the crowd forming in the square. 'Now, everyone standing around out here attracted to the blue flashing lights like moths to a flame, I see you pointing your cameras, and if I see a single photo of Fi's bare boobies or of my double chin from that low angle, I'll be coming after each and every one of you with a legal suit.'

I closed my eyes and leaned against Patrick. They were all there. My friends. My family.

Chapter Twenty-Seven

The day grew old. I slept through as much of it as I could but by the late afternoon I knew I had to go out, and there was something I needed to say.

Annie and I walked slowly through the crowded Dublin streets. At my nod, we wandered through the big Trinity door, squeezing past a family of French tourists who were pointing at the notice-board, at one of our HAVE YOU SEEN THIS QUEEN? posters with Sparkle's face.

'We don't have to talk about this now,' she said.

But we did. I did.

'The thing is,' I said, as I picked my way through the jumble of feelings in my head, 'I've never been that good at dealing with things that didn't make sense. As it turned out, thinking I was going to die was a really handy way to get things sorted in my mind. Nothing like that to work out how you feel about stuff, eh?' I headed for one of the buildings. 'I think I fell in love a bit with Stan,' I said.

I took off my coat, spread it on the step and settled. Annie hesitated. I patted the space beside me. As she sat our legs touched.

'He is the best of me,' she said.

'No.' I nudged her, my shoulder to hers, and smiled. 'No, he isn't. He's you and you're you, and I get that. It's just . . .'

She nodded.

'It's just that you're straight?' she said.

'Oh, I wouldn't go that far.' I blushed, the colour rising from my chest, staining my neck and my face deep red. 'Actually, I don't know,' I said truthfully. 'But I really like you – as Annie and as Stan – and I don't want to mess that up in an experiment to find out.'

We sat together, sipping the Jenkins and Holster coffee, watching the tourists milling about with their phones in their hands.

'It's the moustache, isn't it?' she said.

She was teasing but as I thought about it, I thought she probably wasn't wrong. It wasn't just the moustache of course, but it was the act – the costume. It was the way Stan moved when he was in drag with such confidence and swagger, and how his charm was so addictive. He could hold my gaze like no other but when we were there, when we were just Annie and me, two people sitting side by side, the magic wasn't about sex. It was love, for sure, and I really hoped it was forever, but it was a friendship.

'Sexuality is weird,' I said.

'You're telling me?' she laughed. 'I dress up as a man and I perform for men who fancy men, which I'm not, and for women who fancy women, which I am, but not on stage.'

'You're a bisexual's dream,' I told her.

'Well, I'd like to think so,' she said with a wide grin.

'I'd rather have you as my friend, if you'll take me, than lose you as my girlfriend,' I said. 'And also,' I added. 'You don't love me, either. Not really.'

'I could?' she said.

'Because I'm so lovable? I'm such a catch?' I gestured to my bandaged body, my bruised face.

She laughed. 'Moot point, I think,' she teased. 'Come on, the man who actually is in love with you, and whom you love, is waiting.'

'He can wait a bit longer,' I said. 'I'm with my friend.'

I turned my face up to the sun. It wasn't a bad day, as it went. It was cold, sure, but it was the end of October so it was bound to be cold.

Her words suddenly settled in my brain.

'Do you really think he's in love with me?' I asked her.

'He flew back overnight, on a series of tiny, crappy little planes, and then a really big and expensive plane – for you,' she said. 'Not because you were stuck in some basement – he only got through to Del when he landed at Dublin airport. From what I can gather, he flew back because Robyn left a message for him via his boss, that you were kissing someone else, and that if he wasn't careful, you were falling for them too.'

'Oh.'

'It seems Stan has a lot to answer for,' she chuckled.

In my pocket, my phone pinged. Robyn. Then Del.

Are you ok?

Hey, girl – just checking you haven't been re-kidnapped.

I tipped the screen to Annie.

'They're bound to be more clingy,' she said. 'And you're just as bad. How many texts did you send Del this morning?'

I scrunched up my face. 'Maybe five?'

'It's healthy for now,' she told me. 'Just maybe, you know, allow yourselves a week or so of obsessive behaviour, and then . . .'

'Chill out a bit?'

The clock bonged, and her phone pinged.

The moment was over.

'Thank you,' I said.

'What for?'

'For being a bloody good human,' I told her.

She reached over and gently took my chin. She moved slowly and when her lips met mine the kiss was soft and sweet. She pulled back on the strength I knew was there, and she touched her hand to the side of my head, just lightly, a butterfly touch.

It was lovely.

But it wasn't magic. It was real, and it was beautiful, but it wasn't my fictional crush. I wasn't kissing Stan.

'Can't blame a girl for trying,' she said. She stood up. Grinned.

I pulled on my coat.

'Are you at TRASH tonight?' I said.

'Of course,' she told me. 'It's Halloween.'

'Oh and, umm . . .' I chewed on my lip. 'There's—'

'Just one more thing?' she teased me.

'The séance. Was it you, pushing the wood thingy on the Ouija board?'

Be careful Fi.

'Not me,' she said. 'Maybe the aunts were telling the truth?'

The club was pumping. No one in the crowd knew how Del was feeling as he walked the stage in his pink-and-white spotted leotard and matching ruffle skirt, with his trademark outrageous make-up and Robyn's curly wig. No one also knew how he was drafting a case against the guards for their treatment of Merkin, and how he'd arranged for her to stay at his place just for a few days and for one of her shop girls to look after her. And as the crowd whooped and cheered when Stan and Del did 'Baby It's Cold Outside' together, no one would possibly have guessed how Del had collapsed on the hospital floor and cried in relief that morning, once we were told Robyn was stable.

The spirits weren't wrong, I thought, even though the voices the aunts heard were coming from next door and not from the other side of the veil. Halloween was the time that the wall between the dead and the living was thinned, but I was done with Ouija boards and I was done with mysteries.

For now, at least.

I watched the queens perform, filling myself up with the shine and the glitter and the incredible dance moves – and most of all the quick comedy, the laughter. The light. I stayed until nearly the end of the show and then I took out my phone.

I waited on the bridge. Patrick walked quickly until he saw me, then he stopped and smiled.

We turned together and strolled down the pavement, alongside the Liffey wall.

'So, Robyn got a message to you?' I said.

Patrick nodded. 'The message said – and I think you can quote me – that if I wanted you to go ahead and fall in love with someone else then that was fine, I was to stay out in the wilds of South America trying to solve some pathology riddle a million miles away, and that the chap kissing you was absolutely lovely and fully deserving of you.' He stopped, breathed. 'He said he thought you'd be really happy. But that neither you nor I were very good at knowing the end of a story. And not knowing the end of our story, he said, would only leave three people unhappy in the end.'

We walked a little further along the riverbank. Our feet found the same rhythm. Tucking under his arm, I leaned against him, resting my head just a little on his shoulder. I'd talk about it all again in the morning, but for now I watched our shoes – his dusty runners and my tall black boots casting shade from the bright streetlight, and I reached out and put my hand in his.

ACKNOWLEDGEMENTS

My heartfelt thanks and admiration to all the drag artists who bring life and sparkle to Dublin's bars and clubs. From live shows to podcasts to bingo to Pride, Dublin's drag queens and kings are the very best and they're in no way represented by my messy little troupe at TRASH. Love and thanks especially to Phil T Gorgeous who generously gave up their time to chat with me about kings. Stan owes more than a little of his charm to Phil's charismatic stage presence and fabulous drag shows.

My thanks to Adrian at Lighthouse Theatre, who told me all about Fresnel lights and didn't flinch when I explained what I wanted to (fictionally) do with one.

Huge, huge thanks to Ed Wilson at Johnson and Alcock, to Russel McLean, and to Leodora Darlington and everyone at Thomas & Mercer.

I'm extremely grateful to Jane Flynn, Jane Warden, Anne Jewell, Susan Gerritsen, and Jacqui Grima for beta-reading.

Friendship is a big part of my TRASH stories. From walking around and around St Stephen's Green with me, drinking coffee and talking about my fictional drag family's shenanigans, to reading early drafts of everything, Amanda Singh has been there for Fi, and for me. Her friendship means the world.

Lastly and always, my thanks and love go to my husband, Roger Gale, and to our dog, Rupert, who likes to have the last word.

ABOUT THE AUTHOR

Kitty lives with her husband, Roger, on the very westerly edge of Co. Clare, Ireland. She adores drag in all its forms and crime fiction in all its chilling splendour. Kitty is bi/queer. From a well-spent youth divided equally between the library and the LGBTQ+ scene, it was only a matter of time until both worlds collided in a flurry of fictional sequins. Follow Kitty on Instagram @kitty_murphy_writes.